THE CULT OF
THE SOULS

DESCENT INTO MADNESS
BOOK 3

Jeffrey Donner

Table of Contents

Part I 1

Preface 13

Chapter I 21

Chapter II 25

Chapter III 39

Chapter IV 41

Chapter V 45

Chapter VI 47

Chapter VII 51

Chapter VIII 53

Chapter IX 57

Chapter X 63

Chapter XI 67

Chapter XII 69

Chapter XIII 77

Chapter XIV 79

Chapter XV 85

Chapter XVI 91

Chapter XVII 93

Chapter XVIII 97

Chapter XIX 101

Chapter XX 107

Chapter XXI 111

Chapter XXII 117

Chapter XXIII 121

Chapter XXIV 125

Chapter XXV 129

Chapter XXVI 137

Chapter XXVII 141

Chapter XXVIII..147

Chapter XXIX 155

Chapter XXX...161

Part II **165**

Chapter XXXI 165

Chapter XXXII...171

Chapter XXXIII...175

Chapter XXXIV...179

Chapter XXXV 183

Chapter XXXVI...185

Chapter XXXVII 193

Part III..**197**

Chapter XXXVIII 197

Chapter XXXIX...201

Chapter XL 209

Epilogue..213

Author's Note 215

Other Books by Dr. Donner (All Available on Amazon).....................217

Part I

She awoke with a start. Although it was not unusual for her to wake at this time, it seemed as if something was horribly wrong. She felt a fear and was feeling panic. It was almost 3 a.m. and the room was pitch black. Something had aroused her from a deep sleep, was it a noise or a dream? She opened her eyes and to her astonishment, there was a figure sitting on the end of her bed. She knew immediately it was not a real person, and she also knew that she was not sleeping or imagining this. The woman who sat there was not facing her, but was looking toward the wall. She had no solid body. She was like a mist or a ghost like figure. The apparition was thin, wearing a velvety dress. She was lovely and appeared to be staring out into space, completely ignoring her. Her hair was flowing upward as if caught in the wind. But there was no wind, only stillness.

She was not afraid of this apparition. She could not understand why fear was not flowing through her body. She should be shaking and feeling frozen with terror, but she was not. There was something about this apparition that was not alarming, but was actually soothing in an odd way. She quickly wondered whether this was her time to die. Was this a spirit summoned to take her to the afterlife? A chill ran down her spine with that thought. She knew that when she could not explain something her mind always wandered to the negative. If this was death's call, she was ready to accept this fate. She had thought about it many times, even considered it a few times, but if this was her time, she was not ready.

Life had certainly not met her expectations. If this were the end of her rocky journey then she would have to accept fate. But why now?

The woman just sat with her hair seeming to blow in a breeze, but there was no breeze. In fact, the air was still. The apparition stared at the wall, as Franclynne focused on her, trying to clear her eyes from the remnants of sleep. She was still not 100% convinced this was not a dream, or worse, a hallucination. Another thought quickly filled her mind. Was she having a nervous breakdown?

Franclynne stared at the apparition. She tried to focus on her features. They were not familiar. There were no memories of this person.

She was young, but not a child. Her mind became hyperactive, dancing between fear and confusion. Finally, after a time that felt like days, but was actually only about 30 seconds, with Franclynne frozen, half in fear and half in wonder, the woman turned her head to meet her astonished gaze. The apparition stared deeply into her eyes, almost as if evaluating something. Shudders ran down Franclynne's back, and for the first time in this experience, she felt bone chilling fear.

Franclynne sat up stunned. Many disparate thoughts and emotions flooded her consciousness. Did this really happen, or did she finally wake from a dream? "Be prepared?" "Be prepared", for what? She would not sleep again this night. She arose from her bed and, surprisingly for her, did not feel panicky. She did not feel happy either, she felt... normal. That, in and of itself, was an unusual feeling for her. Franclynne Longaire had not felt "normal" in many years. However, on reflection, she had never felt normal.

She quickly thought back over her childhood. People always complimented her about how pretty and smart she was, but she never really felt closeness to anybody. Her mother was a distant woman who would isolate herself in her bedroom. Her excuse was that she was praying. Franclynne always felt this was just an excuse to be alone. Her father was an alcoholic. He was an angry man, and Franclynne feared his return home every evening.

Franclynne arrived at the jail. She had received a call from Captain O'Brian that they needed her assistance. However, when she arrived, another officer met her at the entrance.

Franclynne followed the officer downstairs, and then stood in utmost shock when she saw the odd woman to whom the officer alluded. Franclynne let out a little cry,

Finally, the embrace ended and the two women began staring at each other.

That small admission, not much to most people, was enough to open the emotional floodgates and Beth almost fell out of her chair. With her hands over her eyes, she sobbed. After a few seconds, Beth did roll out of the chair and onto her knees, continuing the uncontrolled crying. Franclynne, left her chair and joined Beth on the floor.

Beth stood and paced around the room. Franclynne knew that she had something still heavily weighing her down. She tried talking a few times, but could not get the words out. Then she sat, took a deep breath, and began sobbing. Finally, she lifted her head and said,

Angelique loved coffee. She decided to call in sick from work and spend the day thinking about her life and her therapy appointment. She found a secluded, out of the way outdoor restaurant in a town about forty miles from her home. She did not want to be noticed or bothered by anybody. She felt guilty about calling in sick, but she always felt guilty about one thing or the other. She used to joke that the only thing her mother taught her in life was how to feel guilty. Therefore, the feeling was not that unusual for her, it was like a family friend.

After her coffee and muffin were delivered, Angelique put her mind to the problem at hand. Angelique was tired of being abused. That word 'abused' was new for her. It had not been in her vocabulary until it was said by Franclynne during her session. It took her aback when it was spoken, because she had never considered herself as someone who would stand for abuse. But in retrospect, she had to accept the fact that she was engaged in an abusive relationship. What else in her life had she been avoiding, or worse, denying? That was a truly scary thought. Somebody she knew had called it an 'Aha moment, when you see things that you had been blind to. Very scary, for it brought up many other possibilities.

Angelique knew it would take time for her to ingest this insight. Then something else seemed drifted to the surface. It had been buried for many years, but it hit Angelique like a ton of bricks. She remembered now that when she was seven, she had been raped by a male babysitter. She had pushed it so far into her subconscious that only now did it begin to emerge into conscious thought. Her hands began to shake at the realization, and the coffee began to spill on the table. When she realized this, she grabbed a napkin and began wiping up the liquid. This seemed steady her. The realization was frightening. The images seemed to cascade back into her consciousness without filter.

As she sat at the cafe, she wondered if this was this part of the reason she allowed herself to be so controlled. Was this the real reason she felt like chopped liver? She really didn't know, but it seemed to make sense to her. She would have to ask Franclynne the next time they met.

But here she sat, drinking her hot brew and considering her life and how it had deteriorated. She really did not want to be caught in the past, she wanted to solve the present. What did she really get out of her relationship? When looked at, her boyfriend was more childlike than manlike. He was demanding and more of a burden for her than a help. He was nice at the beginning, complimenting her and calling her his 'soul mate'. She put her head down when she realized how quickly she bought into what he was selling, an emotional snake oil salesman.

Now the task was to figure a way out. She knew her boyfriend could be dangerous so she had to think about her strategy, not just make an impulsive move. She was the major money earner. He could not afford to stay in their apartment if she left, but she knew he would not leave on his own. Maybe she should just pack a bag and go to a girlfriend's house. Her friends had been unanimous in their dislike of the boyfriend, so Angelique was sure they would welcome her. She knew this would not be pretty but she knew she had no choice. When you are trapped, you must escape. She was a prisoner of an emotional war and had to find a way out.

Surprisingly, Angelique felt a major weight lifted from her shoulders when she finally accepted that she was going to go through with her exiting strategy. Just the realization that she was developing a plan seemed to lift her. She felt like she could breathe again. Every journey begins with a first step. She had heard that somewhere. She needed to save herself and not let him intimidate her. No matter what the consequences, she had to move, not looking back and move. This would be like pulling tape off your skin. There would be an immediate sharp pain, which would lessen over time. But like a bandage, underneath the covering were quite a few emotional scars, and they would take longer to heal.

When Beth arrived at Franclynne's' office, the next day, her face was gray. Franclynne had been taking off time to go with her to her chemo sessions. Nevertheless, something else was needed. She offered, in a very assertive fashion, that Beth and the children needed to move in with her and La. That would allow Beth to rest, and give the children a full-time nanny. Beth was hesitant. It wasn't that she did not trust Franclynne or La, it was just a step back away from freedom and a move toward dependency. It was a recognition of the inevitable. She was fighting that in her mind. Recognizing the inevitable. But which inevitable held the most pain, the acknowledgment of her own death, or the awareness of what would happen to her two lovely children?

When Franclynne and Beth were gone, La was in charge of Beth's two children. La also spent time with the children at other times, and was growing steadily closer to both Ellie and young Theodore. La was a very protective babysitter. She was amazed at the beauty she saw in these children's eyes. It changed the way that she viewed people. In many ways, they were like her pet rats, innocent and special. It was also surprising to her how easily she seemed to relate to them. She did not have to worry about the deception that plagued her life, for these two young people were up front with their feelings. There was no veil over their emotions as there was with adults. When they hugged, they meant it. She could feel it through her clothes. There was power of the hugs from these little bodies. It was for La, a transcendent experience. It actually gave her strength, and with every hug, the bond became stronger.

The court proceedings had not been going well. There had been two preliminary hearings, and it was obvious that the judge was leaning to allowing the children to have unsupervised visitation. Previously, the judge had put restrictions on visitation for Sean because of his recent history of aggression. He ordered that Sean take an anger management course and engage in psychotherapy. Two letters were presented to the judge during their most recent appearance before him. The first was from the social worker that ran the group about anger. She wrote, "Sean was an excellent patient, and participated in the discussion. He clearly has done his homework, as well." His therapist was also positive in his reporting of Sean as a patient. He wrote, "Sean has opened up about his aggressive thoughts and actions. He has begun using strategies to curb his reactions." Both Beth and Franclynne were stunned as they sat and listened in the courtroom.

That night, when Franclynne got home, she was clearly upset. La also became upset when she read the concern on Franclynne's face. She listened carefully to the legal dilemma. La did not really understand the subtleties of the argument, but she listened. La was not the most perceptive of people, but she could see fear. And what she saw in Franclynne's face was terror, and defeat.

The act of telling her mother how much she cared was truly exhilarating for Jillian. Afterwards, she realized how much it had been weighing on her. Now came an even harder task for her. What would she tell Bobby? Actually, she did not even know if he wanted to speak to her at all. She gathered her courage and decided to show up at his brownstone with the rose that was left on her doorstep. She really had not decided what to do or say, but she knew she had to go and confront the situation.

As she was walking toward the brownstone, her thoughts drifted back to her childhood. Her mother, especially, was a nice person. She had manipulated her at every opportunity, lying and only telling half-truths. She certainly did not deserve to have a daughter like her. She thought about the pain she must have caused, every time her mother realized she had had lied to her. Jillian felt horrible. She stopped walking, went over to a nearby tree, and threw up on its base. She was ashamed of herself, and the only way to atone for her past was to change her future. Begin to treat people differently.

As she approached the building, she noticed his car parked outside. He was probably at home. As before, Jillian became very unsteady as she ascended the stairs. The fear she had the last time she was at this place returned. The bravery that she felt when she made this decision to go, quickly evaporated, like mist in the morning sun. Was she such a weak person? Just walking up to the brownstone created such a strong effect on her? What was wrong with her? Was she too broken to be fixed? Her internal beating subsided when she felt warmth on her arm.

She noticed that the sun was out. He thought it funny that when she had Bobby on her mind other things seemed to disappear. It was warm, the sun felt good on her skin. Was it a sign that something good was about to happen? She also noticed clouds in the sky. They were quite beautiful. She rarely looked up, she was always too self-consumed. This was new. She vowed to practice it more, to see things, rather than just looking and to notice her surroundings.

A strange look came over his face, followed by a pause.

Jillian stood frozen. She had pictured many outcomes, but this was not one of them. It took a few minutes for her to move. She looked down and was still holding the rose. Anger brewed up within her and she ripped the flower apart, throwing it against the door. She was not quite sure what she was angry at. She just felt furious.

Tears filled her eyes as she walked away from the brownstone. In truth, she knew that she deserved this outcome, but she was still unsure what she had really wanted. Later, in reflection, she realized that what she wanted was for him to see her and respond by telling her how much he missed her and wanted her back. However, Jillian knew in her heart that she deserved this rejection. She had done it many times to others, and her sins in relationships had finally caught up to her. You reap what you sow, she thought.

The office was not extravagant. In fact, it was plain. The seats in the waiting room were not fancy, nor new. In fact, they looked old. One of the chairs had a ripped seat. There were some plants, but two looked closer to death than healthy blooms. There was no fancy artwork to decorate the walls. Even the magazines that were left out for people to read were old. The secretary sat quietly behind a desk. She also was a plain woman who did not display much emotion. She sat stoically, keeping busy with some kind of work. La had been sitting for over twenty minutes and the phone had rung almost one time in each of those minutes. The secretary did not say much on the calls, just commented, "Yes, yes, I know", or, "I'll make sure he gets the message." La could not read anything into the conversations, although she listened carefully. She was not quite sure why she listened, but for some reason it seemed important to her. Besides, she had nothing else to do.

Therefore, here she sat. She had been here for almost an hour, and she was intent on staying all night, if need be. Franclynne did not know she had gone to this office, and La was not sure what she was going to say when she was let into the inner sanctum. La had searched for almost two days before she actually found the office.

It took another ten minutes and then the door to the inner office opened and JJ Aaron emerged. When his eyes met La's, a big smile emerged on his face and he hurried towards her.

La sat down in a large, plush armchair. Except for the plush chair and books dispersed all over, the office was plain and unassuming.

JJ Aaron waited a few heartbeats and La sat silently.

La dropped her head. It was that giving a clear explanation was a difficult task for her. She knew what she wanted, but abstracting it was difficult.

La nodded her head in affirmation.

Sean sat down in the leather chair. He was spending a large amount of money on this attorney. It did not matter that the money he was paying he had embezzled from his firm. He was still spending the money that he wanted for other things. He looked sternly at the attorney. He was clearly ill at ease.

The attorney flinched, but held his tongue. Although it was not direct, the attorney accepted the criticism with a hard swallow. He had achieved much success in his professional life, and he did not need to be treated in this manner, especially from an individual he considered a sniveling, arrogant, man. As he sat opposite him, the thought of just throwing him out of the office passed through his mind. For some reason, that he did not truly understand himself, he said nothing.

Sean seemed amazed that Markus was talking back to him. He sat stunned for a few seconds, and then began to speak again.

Sean sat quietly. His gaze was on the floor, and he glanced every occasionally toward the envelope that sat only a few inches from him. He did not seem to be intimidated, but he realized he was at risk of losing his representation. He would have to be more careful, control himself. He tried very hard to sound regretful.

Irritated, and now feeling like he was being backed into a corner, Sean rose from the chair and slowly walked over to the window. He believed that the confidentiality stuff was bullshit. Nobody keeps secrets, especially not attorneys! He glanced back at Markus. He would betray me in an instant if I told him about my past, or what the truth really is. He doesn't give a shit. He wants to help me, my ass! Crap, he wants to know so he can fuck me. But, as he thought, he also knew that he needed Markus if he were to get what he wanted. He also knew that his time was running short. It would not be long until his business finally figured out what he was doing and where the money went.

The apparition's face grew larger, and her eyes seemed to pull Franclynne towards her. It was an addictive stare. She wanted to avert her eyes, but was transfixed to her face. She began to worry that this mist, this specter, would encompass her, dissolve her body. And yet, even though worried, she was not panicky. The air was still, time ceased to exist. Finally, the apparition's gaze changed into a smile. Amid this, Franclynne dropped all internal barriers, opening her soul to this apparition. There was no choice. Some force she could not understand compelled her. She wondered again whether death was visiting her, but she sensed a compassion about this vapor. Should she reach out and touch this mist? She wanted to, but somehow knew she could not. Finally, the woman smiled and said, without any emotion, "*Be prepared*", and no other words. The apparition smiled again and disintegrated into the night, like a cloud that was there one minute and gone the next.

Prelude

The old brownstone was situated in the middle of this block. It was a regal building, laid in dark brick with black wood surrounding the windows. Steps led to a platform, which then led to eight steps to the front door. The black iron railing contrasted the dark gray of the stone on the entrance. She had been here before, but under dissimilar circumstance. It now felt different, strange. Her emotions had changed the venue, altered the experience. Her mouth was dry and her legs not as steady as they usually were. It was an unusual change. This was a place that one relished being at, but all of a sudden became a place of anxiety and tension.

She grudgingly walked the final eight steps arriving at the large wooden front door. The wood was also stained dark, giving it an imperial look. She had not noticed the contrasts before. Why was she becoming more observant this time, why did it matter? There was no doorbell on this brownstone, only a doorknocker made of heavy metal. It was old and looked of an Italian design. She was not sure why, it just seemed Italian. However, more than that, it now seemed imposing. She had noticed the knocker before and it had always intrigued her. Now it was definably imposing. It almost looked twice as large as she had remembered it.

She carried a red rose in her hand. It was their thing, but in truth, its actuality his thing. Every time they met; he had given her a red rose. She could never have believed only a few months ago that such a blossom could mean so much to her. Nevertheless, here she stood, with this flower held tightly in her hand. She had never paid too much attention to flowers. They were beautiful, but she never really stopped to smell them. But now the flower that she held had a significant symbolic implication. She reached the front door and hesitated. She did not anticipate this, as the fear rose through her veins. All of a sudden, her hand seemed to turn to stone, and she could not imagine herself reaching up to use the knocker.

What was she doing here, what was the point? She was not quite sure whether she should be here. This action was taking an emotional risk, something she rarely did. She had never let herself care enough to be hurt. She thought of emotions as playthings, not to be taken seriously. She believed she was immune to emotional hurt, but here she stood in pain. She was always the one to make others suffer when relationships ended. In fact, in this situation, she had acted according to her actions of past relationship. She had broken off the bond against his protests. Well, he really did not protest, although she wanted him to. She wanted him to beg, profess his desire, and need for her. It disappointed her that he didn't argue the fact, just accepted it in a matter-of-fact fashion. She wanted tears, promises of change, but none followed her declaration. She realized, after the fact, how important this declaration of loss would have been to her own feelings. She would have felt better if they argued, protesting their undying love for her. Maybe it was a control or power issue. She really did not know the underlying reason. She just knew it felt good.

She knew he was not that kind of man. He was direct. Everything was ordered and planned. Although he displayed emotions, he seemed to be able to turn them on and off at will, like one manipulated a faucet, making the water hotter or cooler. He certainly controlled himself and his reactions, just the opposite of her. She was spontaneous, over reactive, and some would say, a little hyperactive. He seemed to turn inward, while she was always out there. They made a perfect couple- Yin and Yang. They did have dissimilar interests, but in sexuality and passion, their styles fed off each other. In bed, they were like wild horses, intensive, exhaustive, and hedonistic. Then, after only a month, she seemed to lose a little interest. This was a pattern for her, somewhat self-destructive and she was aware of it.

It was a fleeting thought that came to her early one morning. The sky was gray and beginning to thunder, and she began to believe that this relationship was more like a lightning bolt, burning hot but disappearing into the ground, never to be seen again. She suffered with these images. They would seem to intrude in her mind, altering the course of her life with regularity. On that day, as part of her disparaging side, she did not want to see him, although every other day she had anticipated her sexual urges upon his arrival at her place of work.

She was not educated, although she had her opportunities, most of which she seemed to burn without regard. She knew she was not stupid, but she just did not care. She could never wrap her energy around anything for any length of time. She would always claim to be bored of things. Something always seemed to intervene and divert her effort. She was considered the black sheep of her family, and she played the role well. It became a self-fulfilling prophesy, and she embraced the role and played it out in dramatic and flamboyant fashion.

In the past, she fashioned many explosive events, which would lead to others turning their backs on her and shaking their heads in disgust. She was not like most others and played her emotional hand specifically to point that out. She could be brutally honest in her criticism and others claimed that they could see flames arising from her eyes when she angered.

Over the years, she had many jobs, none of which could be considered a profession, mostly minimum wage, transitional type things. She never really lasted long at any one position, nor within a relationship. She often considered whether this was a pattern for her. She spent many hours dwelling on this relational design of hers. She rationalized and intellectualized it in many ways, trying to explain to herself why she was so impetuous and imprudent. Was she not caring? A 'butterfly woman' she would joke with herself. One of her exes gave her that moniker. She took the name as a compliment, but maybe it was not. It had always seemed to be a strength, at least that is what her defensive mechanisms led her to believe. But now, as she stood frozen in front of this door, maybe she needed to reevaluate her usual excuses. As she aged, at some point she became aware that being a 'butterfly woman' was becoming more of an emotional hindrance than an asset. She was no longer a young adult who could justify her hurricane-like changing emotions. She had a flirtatious pattern and she did not seem able or motivated to break it. She danced around the flames, which was more of a rush for her than the actual conquest. If it was not emotionally dangerous, it might appear too dull for her tastes. If nothing else, it was exciting and gave her a sense of purpose. She would sometimes go to a bar, specifically to see if she could get two men to fight over her. It was a rush, and somehow it gave her a stronger sense of self.

At night when the world was quiet, she had self-queries of why she ran from things. She adamantly denied to herself that it was fear. However, in quiet moments, she grudgingly considered her vulnerability. The significant other in a previous relationship had called her an 'avoider, someone who ran from responsibility, circumventing all accountability.

She did have many friends, well more acquaintances than real friends. These were people who said hello with a smile, but were really not close. Her bubbly personality and her seductive body made her attractive to others. She was not model material for she was too small, but she never had a problem finding bedroom partners, either male or female. They each had their advantages, but she would tire easily of both, usually before the other person would. She was not quite sure why. Was it fear, or just stupidity? Whatever, she would just stop showing up. Years ago, she had decided to stop trying to figure it out, for she reasoned it did not really matter. This is who she was and she accepted that.

So here she stood, rose in hand, facing this large, imposing wooden door. She began playing with her long hair, a sign of her anxiety. She could not swallow; her mouth was so dry. It took courage to come here in the first place, but she was not sure she had the intestinal fortitude to knock on the door. After all, she was breaking her pattern, reaching out to someone to continue a relationship, not to end one. She knew, at some level, that her past behavior of always running away showed lack of courage. It took no daring to run away. It took courage to stay. Yes, she took chances, but always with a way out, always with a parachute, always with an escape pod. When she got too close, she ran. That vulnerability frightened her. She was an emotional coward, and she rationalized it any way she could.

This large, ornate, wooden wall stood before her like a demonstrative obstruction, blocking her ascendance. Yet, even with her hesitations, she stood admiring the intricacies of the design. However, the longer she stood, the more her nerve faded. It was like a mist leaving her body. Her courage began to take its familiar route. She wanted to run.

Preface

It was a pleasant afternoon and La was going on her daily walk. Staying inside always created anxiety for her. She was antsy when four walls surrounded her. Outside she felt free, not constrained. La had grown up abandoned, forced to live on the street. Because of this, she had gotten into the habit of taking daily walks. She had no destination, no specific path for her walks. It was not scripted, but she would go whichever way her spirit would take her. She relished this time; for it would allow her part of the freedom she found when she was homeless and living under the bridge.

The bridge was always in her thoughts. When people would say, "there's no place like home", La thought of the bridge. It was dirty and trashy, but it was her home. The house that she lived in was just a place. It was not a home.

However, today was different; there was a different air about the streets. They were the same boulevards that she passed every day. The houses did not change, she even recognized many of the cars that she passed, often parked in the same places. She had them committed to memory. Nevertheless, today there was a qualitative difference. She finally concluded that the variance was not in the outside area; it was something within her. She was now convinced of that. Her emotions were bordering on despondency. Her mood had been deteriorating for some time now. She was becoming more and more depressed, and there was no apparent reason for this. La was not a deep thinker, but she attributed this downturn in her spirit to two things.

La had been living under a bridge when she first gained notoriety. Her favorite rat, Fromage, had died and her therapist, Dr. DeJarden, joined her under the bridge for the funeral service. Local media covered the incident and it actually made some national outlets. The video of the two hugging and crying went viral. La was committed to her rats. She found them intelligent, loving, and much more trustworthy than humans. She was dubbed, 'The Rat Lady.' When she would walk the streets, people would point at her and she could hear them say, *"That's the Rat Lady."*

This current feeling was much more intense and mood altering. She had once mourned the death of a pet rat, but this was different. Whereas the loss of her pet broke her heart, this loss, the death of her friend, Dr. DeJarden, had damaged her soul. The grief was a corrosive element, eating her from the inside, and bent on destroying her very being. She was reactive, and her emotions lay clearly on her face and her sleeve. It had already been a number of months and the pain still felt as though it had just happened. Nothing she did seemed to alter the intrusive thoughts and feelings. She still cried on a regular basis as the images of Dr. DeJarden continue to plague her memories. Although it was not romantic, La knew she had loved Helen DeJarden.

La had gained international notoriety by brutally murdering a psychopath who had kidnapped, tortured, and eventually killed her friend. Actually, Dr. DeJarden was not a friend, although La considered her as much. Truly, La thought of her more like a deity than as a friend. She had quickly become dependent on this therapist, and felt her own moods sway to the rhythms of her friends. Dr. DeJarden was La's therapist. However, to La, she was more than that. La was symbiotically tied to Helen DeJarden.

When she had met DeJarden, La had been homeless, living under the bridge with only her pet rats for company. La loved her rats more than any person, until she met DeJarden. It was at that moment that life changed for her. She had never known or felt the unconditional love of another person until having that relationship. She had never loved another person. Her experience had taught her that other people were only interested in using her for whatever purpose they desired. But when she met Helen DeJarden, her world had changed. Her life, up until that meeting, had been shaped by deceit and pain. Other people, especially men, had used and mistreated her. La carried around a large amount of emotional scar tissue, dragging her fear and pain wherever she went.

La had lived in many places in her life, none of which was hers. She finally decided that the bridge was preferable to living in a man's hell. Essentially, it was more than home. It represented freedom for her, freedom from abuse, freedom from pain and freedom from men. She still could feel the presence of the bridge. It was a pull, she felt as if she belonged there. It was the pull that a salmon must feel when it was time to return to the stream of their birth. It was magnetic, like gravity pulling her back. La knew that she did not fit in the house. She was a round peg in a square hole. From her first step into it, she knew it did not fit her. It was like a tight shoe that scraped your toes until they bled. No matter how pretty they were, they were not for you.

The act of murder had vaulted La into a media spotlight. The media scared her, for she was a woman more content with aloneness than with the spotlight on her. The media were pushy. They wanted to benefit from her destructive act, use her for their purposes. They were bloodsuckers. La reacted with anger as they shoved microphones in her face. At one point, she was on all the channels as "The rat woman who tried to save her friend". She hated that statement, for it contained the word "tried". "Tried' to her, meant that she had failed.

La received many invitations for interviews after the incident. People wanted to buy her clothes and other essentials. She turned them all down. Because she was homeless, the county had given her a new house, free of charge to live in. That, in and of itself, confused La, as she believed she had committed the greatest sin imaginable, and people were treating her like a hero for it. She had killed a priest, a messenger of the invisible God. La had no choice; the man was torturing the only person alive that she loved. It was not heroic in her eyes, it was necessary. It sat on her mind liked burnt toast. She could smell it, she could taste it, and it made her nauseous. La just did not understand the society in which she lived. She was an alien in her own world. Nothing seemed to make any sense to her. There were no rules. All the rules would change depending on the particular circumstance. To La, that there were no real truths. Life was dependent upon the situation and what other people wanted at the time. It confused her to the point that her head would hurt whenever she thought about it.

Her friend, Helen DeJarden, died from the assault, which left La inconsolable. She held her as she died. La could still feel the life leaving her body. She blamed herself for the death. She had known her friend was upset and she followed her to the priest's house. She believed she waited too long to intervene. If she had acted earlier, her friend would still be here to give her hugs. She ached for the hugs, missed the human contact. She had lost her pet rats, she had lost her bridge, and she had lost the only person she loved.

Reluctantly, La moved into the house that was given to her. It was not an easy transition, as the city had demanded that she could no longer reside under the bridge. However, the house, although beautiful, was many miles away from the area with which she was familiar. This house seemed like a different country to her, a different planet. She now felt more lost then she had ever felt when living under the bridge with her pet rats. Every bone in her body was crying for her to return to the place she loved, not this gilded palace, which she really did not deserve, nor want.

Religion was also something La did not understand. This house was given to her because she sinned against the invisible god. She committed a sin, and yet she was rewarded for it. It made no sense to her. She had failed to save her friend, and this house, this place, only reminded her of that failure, and her loss. Even though it was considered a sin, if given the same circumstance, La knew she would murder the man again.

The sun shone brightly on her as she walked the streets. La was more comfortable outside than when she was restrained by artificial walls. The sky was cloudless, a beautiful shade of blue. People passed her and, in her assessment, their eyes looked blank, like empty vacuums. When she was living under the bridge, even if she was in pain, she felt more alive than she felt in these pristine surroundings with all these superficial zombies. On some level, this did not make sense to her, but it was how she felt. With pain you felt alive, with this she just felt empty.

The person she loved the most was dead, by her account, because of her negligence. She tried replacing this pain in her heart with spirituality, but that really did not work well. The invisible god had betrayed her as well. She had not yet accepted the death of her friend, Helen DeJarden. She hated the man who killed her. If she could have, she would have killed him many times. He not only killed her friend; he destroyed her life. Killing was wrong, but she would have committed this sin many times over, to save her friend. Nevertheless, for all the tears that she cried, for all the tears she spent, nothing could change what happened, and La could not accept this. The thoughts of her friend, and what had happened, were never far from her consciousness. They sat with her like a skin disease, continually itching at her soul.

Her thoughts often drifted as she walked. As her mind wandered, retracing things she had done, La failed to notice the man who was approaching her.

"Excuse Me".

The words shocked her, dragging her out of her reverie. La stared at the man. He was an old man with a long beard. His black beard had many streaks of gray running through it. The man's face was lined with wrinkles, the sign of years of hardship. His brown clothes were tattered and his eyes were pleading as he stared at her. However, he read her surprise and said, *"I'm sorry, I didn't mean to scare you"*.

La stared not saying anything, still trying to understand what was happening. Instinctively she took a step backward, although there was nothing about the man that suggested she should be fearful. The man hesitated for a moment, and then asked, *"Do you have any loose change you can spare? I would like a cup of coffee."*

La now refocused on him, her emotions settling She immediately recalled the days when she had not eaten at all and felt frantic for some sustenance. She remembered the taste of stale bread when she was hungry. She could recall how delicious it tasted when she was desperate. La looked the man in the eye and, without change of expression, said, *"Follow me"*.

There was no discussion as the two walked the three blocks back to her residence. La led him to her house, invited him in, and made him breakfast. The man did not eat as if he was starving. His movements were controlled. La noticed his subdued reactions; it was unusual for her to notice such things. It also confused her, because he really did not seem like a homeless man. There was something about his look, that made him appear different. But La shrugged it off.

"Thank you very much; you have been very nice to me. May I ask why?"

"That is a stupid question", La thought to herself. However, she just looked at the man and shrugged.

"Finish your breakfast; I'll be back in a few minutes."

La returned with a large black garbage bag filled with things. She looked at the man sitting at the table and without hesitation, or emotion said, *"This house is yours. I give it to you."*

"What?"

The old man said in shock.

"Did you not hear me? I said this house is yours."

And with that, La threw down a piece of paper on the table in front of him and turned to leave. The man rose from his chair and called to her as she was leaving.

"My name is JJ. Aaron. Remember it. You will hear it again!"

Prelude

She could not just stand here. She felt stupid. She had worn her sexiest dress to come here. It was red silk, matching the color of the rose, and it really turned him on (or at least it used to). He had purchased it for her for she did not have the means for such a garment. Actually, he did not purchase it; he had given her a credit card and sent her alone into the store. She never had a credit card of her own, in her life. It would be too dangerous, as her impulsive urges would put her in debt, quickly. Why did she wear this dress? Did she want to reignite their relationship? She did miss him. But did she really miss him emotionally, or only between her legs? She really did not understand her fluctuating emotional states. It was riding a wild, untamed horse. She was becoming more confusing to herself by the day.

She worked in a high class, organic food store. She knew and liked most of the clients. She would discuss erudite subjects with them and it made her feel more accomplished than she actually was. She loved the flirting with both the men and woman. It stroked her self-esteem, and she would review some of her interchanges late at night, smiling to herself about a witty comment she had made. She could use language well. Sometimes people would laugh and she really did not understand why, but it did not matter. The important thing was the attention she received for her witty comments. Some people actually commented that they would specifically go to her checkout line to be able to talk (flirt) with her. It really did not matter to her if they were old or young, good looking or not. In fact, one of her favorite customers was a grumpy old goat who seemed to smile when she spoke with her. She actually looked forward to this older woman shopping. It made her day.

Her flirtatious attitude was interrupted one day when she saw him in line. She was on the cash register chattering away in her usual manner, when she noticed him standing five people behind the current customer. She felt her body shiver and she began inexplicitly stuttering. She lost her focus and forgot about what she was talking. The woman she was speaking with actually asked her if she was all right. She had to consciously divert her stare away from him, for she worried she would start drooling, and her fixation would become apparent. She looked at the woman she was talking with, *"I'm sorry, my mind just wandered away to something I've been worrying about."*

As he came closer on the line, she could feel sweat on her thighs. Sweat on her thighs? This had never happened before. She smiled at customers, pretending not to notice him, but she paid attention to every little movement of his body as he stood and proceeded toward her. She noticed his stance, his hair, and the way he held his arms. She could see every wrinkle in his face, and it all attracted her. What was happening? This was highly unusual for her. She was usually laughing and giggling, but now she was serious and hyper-focused. She was having trouble talking to the customer in front of her, as her gaze and her thoughts were being pulled back to him on line. What was happening?

Chapter I

Sean Whitford lay still on the gurney. He could feel his arms and legs shaking from the anxiety that was flowing through his veins. While being prepped for this 'day surgery' procedure, one of the nurses kept him busy with idle talk, while the others prepared his body. Sean had just had his 55th birthday, and now he wondered if he would see his 56th. He was scared and anxious. His doctor had told him that this procedure was not dangerous, but Sean was terrified nonetheless.

Over the past two years, he had developed heart fibrillations. They had become so serious that he had lost consciousness a number of times. The severe nature of his condition has forced his physician to take away his driver's license, and it had become increasingly debilitating for him. This horror story began one day after dinner when his heart began racing and he felt a little faint. After a thousand tests, it was determined that Sean had been having these events for some time, but the severity and intensity were increasing. The trouble had been interfering with his daily functioning. He was becoming conscious of the feeling of his heart racing, and it was distracting him from other more pleasant activities and even work. He had fainted twice. The doctors had given him medications to control the events, but they all seemed to have only short-term effects. They made him tired, but did not stop the events. There were discussions about placing a defibrillator in his chest in order to shock his heart back to normal beating if it stopped. The procedure he was waiting for was an ablation. If this did not work, then the defibrillator would be implanted.

Although a day surgery procedure, an ablation is no easy event. You must lay still in the electrophysiology room for up to five hours. The doctors go up through the groin with a special catheter into your heart to ablate/burn the portion of the heart or artery that is creating the electrical malfunction. Through a catheter, energy is sent to scar the unhealthy heart tissue and deflect the energy into a more proper pattern. Sean understood that fibrillations were like a seizure event of the heart. In the electrophysiology lab, the doctors try to find the heart areas that are creating the difficulty and ablate that area, hoping that the energy will lead to a more normal rhythmic pattern. Most of the time the procedure works, and individuals are relieved from the fibrillations, but some people have had to have numerous ablations until the exact problem area is found.

Dr. Levine walked into his cubicle preceding the day surgery. He was a very pleasant young man, and Sean and his wife both had faith in his ability. Levine smiled as he entered the space. *"How are you doing, Sean?"* Trying to smile, Sean said, *"Fine. Today is a good day for this procedure."* *I'm sure it's going to go well,"* said Levine. *"Why?"* Sean responded. Levine smiled and lifted his leg up to the gurney on which Sean laid. *"You see, I have new shoes."* Levine smiled again and put his leg back on the floor. He smiled and patted Sean on the shoulder. *"Don't worry, Sean. Everything will be fine."* Levine then turned and walked off.

The entire situation had disturbed Sean, as he had developed a 'why me?' type attitude. He had been married to his lovely wife for seven years, and his problem was seriously beginning to interfere with their relationship. Sean was scared and worried. He and his wife Beth had two young children, Ellie and Theodore. He thought of them and what would happen to them if he died and left them alone.

Sean was hoping for this 'miracle' cure. But when he arrived at the hospital, he was distressed to learn that during the procedure, his hands would be tied. This was necessary because he could not move because that might disrupt the delicate procedure. Although a nurse sat by his side, Sean could not see the doctors during the procedure, for they remained behind him on their computers, watching monitors of his heart functioning and the catheter that was now inside of his artery.

Sean felt numb, as he lay on the table, completely helpless. The mixing of the feelings of fear and hope was an unusual combination of emotions. During the procedure, his mind continued to drift, even though he could feel the burning of the catheter inside his chest. When the electric pulse was sent, the pain was intense, but luckily only lasted a second or two. He wondered about his wife and his children as he continued to attempt to distract himself away from the procedure. He tried thinking of other things, but none of them stuck.

All of a sudden, almost two hours into the procedure, the doctor appeared on his right side. He looked down at Sean and said, "Mr. Whitford, I'm afraid that we are having trouble locating the exact place on your heart that is causing the problem. Because of this, I will have to give you a drug that will speed up your heart to artificially create the fibrillations we are looking for. "The doctor hesitated, but then continued. "Mr. Whitford, this procedure is not pleasant. Your heart will race and you will probably lose consciousness."

Sean agreed with the procedure, feeling that he had no choice. Of course, it ranked up his anxiety fairly dramatically. Sean nodded his head and steeled himself for the upcoming event. The nurse took a syringe and emptied it into his veins. Although he was not able to see the doctors, he could watch a monitor that showed his heart rate rising. It quickly reached 200 beats per minute, and Sean began having difficulty staying conscious. His chest felt as if it was going to explode. The pain was rising exponentially. As he turned to the nurse sitting next to him, he said, *"I'm going to lose consciousness"*.

And then, immediately, his mind went blank.

Chapter II

She walked up the steps to the courthouse. Her legs were wobbly and she traversed the few steps with some difficulty. Franclynne had not slept much the night before. She often had problems sleeping. In fact, she could not remember the last time that she slept throughout the night. Last night, she had finally fallen asleep at midnight but woke up in a body full of sweat at three in the morning. Although she usually suffered with sleep disturbance, this night was different. She had been subpoenaed to court. She had been subpoenaed before, but this time she could not recall the names, or the purpose of the people who were on the court document.

Franclynne Longaire had only recently, within the past year, become licensed as a psychologist, and this was going to be her the first time she was appearing as in that capacity. She had testified in court before, and it was not a positive experience for her. In fact, there was nothing about the experience that did not terrorize her. She called the district attorney's office to get more information so she could at least prepare herself with some knowledge of the situation. However, a young, obnoxious attorney met her call:

"Hello, sir. My name is Dr. Longaire. You have subpoenaed me court to testify in a case I know nothing about.

"I'm sorry doctor. I cannot tell you anything about the situation."

"So, I need to go in blind?"

"That's the way it is."

His voice rang out with a dismissive attitude.

"What is your name?"

"Halstead, Doctor."

"Attorney Halstead, you know giving me only two days' notice is really unfair. I have a busy practice and I have to cancel many clients to attend a proceeding I know nothing about." The busy part was an exaggeration, but she used it as a possible way to gain information.

"I'm sorry, Doctor, but my subpoena trumps your schedule, and for that matter, anything else you have to do." His attitude seemed to get more repugnant the more he spoke. *"Self-righteous bastard,"* she thought.

"What? Why are you taking an attitude with me?"

"Look doctor, make sure to be there when you're supposed to, or I will send a U.S. Marshall to get you."

Franclynne now felt a combination of fear and anger. She was not the one to confront someone else. She would move mountains to avoid such a confrontation. Her throat immediately dried up, and she could feel her arms shaking. However, she steadied herself and said, *"Who is your supervisor?"*

He did not give her a name, but just said:

"I will see you in court, Doctor."

Immediately, and with little dispatch, the attorney hung up the phone. The situation completely threw her emotional compass off. She felt like a criminal without the knowledge of anything that she had done wrong. Besides being fearful, she felt like she was being strong-armed. She did not know this attorney and there was no reason for the 'Godzilla' approach. There were many times in her life that Franclynne could remember being bullied by others.

Prior to her occupation as a psychologist, Franclynne had been a teacher. The school in which she worked was a very toxic environment, run by a group of women that were called, 'the coven.' If the coven did not like you, if they considered you an outsider, they made your life hell. Moreover, they did not like Franclynne. Franclynne was a quiet young woman, not wanting to get involved with any in school politics. She wanted to do her work and be left alone. This did not meet the guidelines of the coven. Awful rumors circulated about her, and although she was beautiful and statuesque, Franclynne's ego was quite brittle. This experience destroyed her joy of teaching.

She was also reaching the point where she was becoming conscious of her growing hatred for men, as it was often them that initiated the intimidation. Well maybe it had not yet reached a generalized hatred, but it certainly was hovering around mistrust and dread.

Franclynne had a horribly traumatic past, which continued to plague her daily. It was an act of will that she had only been hospitalized for short periods of time. Of all the situations she could recall in her past, men were always at the center of the hurt. This situation felt horribly familiar. This bullying from the attorney created a physiological and psychological cascade of feelings, which always left Franclynne cowering in a very dark place. The past trauma was always just under the surface. It always lingered in her subconscious, past, but always present. When a situation like this arose, the past quickly re-emerged, and old feelings of fear, vulnerability and helplessness, began flooding her thoughts. She always thought of it like a closet door she was trying to keep closed. She always needed to exert pressure or else the door would swing open letting out the horror of her past experiences to plague her present and future. The problem was that circumstances would make her lose her focus on the door, and the past would begin dripping out like a leaky faucet. Once it began to open, she would have difficulty closing it again.

Tonight, she was losing the battle of the door. Her mind raced from the moment she woke awake at 3 a.m., until when she finally began dressing at five. That time between three and five always terrified her. There was no purpose for it, only fear. It seemed to bring out all of her memories, without her ability to stop her intrusive thoughts. She was a psychologist who couldn't control her own intrusive thoughts. Ironic, she would think.

The trouble was that the past would intrude on the present. Her mind would race between worries until they all merged into an emotional conglomerate. When she could not solve a current problem, her mind would revert to the trauma, and it would engulf her. She would often think that it was happening again. In this state, she would, for reasons unknown to her, go into the bathroom and lay on the floor. She would bring her pillows, blanket with her, and close the door. She would wedge her legs on the closed door so nobody on the outside could push it open. Sometimes the memories became so vivid that it felt like a knife cutting through her. Although she rarely told others, when the situation reached this level of breaking point she would dissociate from the emotional agony. In her mind, she would retreat to her grandmother's kitchen. It took years for her to realize that it was the wonderful aromas that made it such a protective place. Time would stand still for her when she was in these dissociative states, and she would see her grandmother cooking her homemade bread. She could smell the delightful aroma of the dough rising and being beaten back down. Her grandmother would allow her to help beating the mixture down and kneading the dough. For Franclynne it was a place of wonder, and most importantly, a place of safety.

Once she came out of this reverie, her problems would reemerge into her consciousness. In this situation, she was immediately brought back to the court appearance. She had dissociated for at least an hour, and happily, she still had some time before she had to rise and get dressed.

"Why are they calling me? Who are these people behind the subpoena? Did I do something wrong?" This was like a cruel joke, blindly walking into an unknown situation. It somehow reminded her of deceit.

Her thoughts perseverated on these unanswered questions. To make matters worse, such anxiety immediately transferred into her digestive system. From 4 o'clock a.m. to 5 a.m., Franclynne spent much of the time throwing up in the toilet. By 5 a.m., she was drained, exhausted, and terribly scared. She sat on the bathroom floor crying into her hands, and to make matters worse, she did not actually know of what she was afraid! Was it the court, or the horrible rape and physical abuse she had sustained in the past?

At five a.m., she began reviewing the last two years of her life. She racked her brain trying to identify the names on the subpoena but to no avail. Her memory was blank, only the fear of the unknown remained. Of course, in the darkness and quiet of her bedroom, her mind exaggerated everything. She experienced all the symptoms of anxiety and panic. At one point, muscles in her chest began to shake and it took all of her effort to calm it. Her arms and shoulders also shook as the anxiety raced through her body. Her thoughts also regressed to the trauma she had lived through. She had to block it, for she could not return to the kitchen and the dissociative state. It was too late; she had to start preparing for court.

The dissociation also frightened her. It was almost as if she had disappeared within her body, backed away from reality, and separated herself from where she was. Franclynne never quite knew how long she would stay in this state before her consciousness returned. It seemed that sometimes it lasted a few minutes and sometimes hours. This time, when she 'returned' from her grandmother's kitchen, she was on the bathroom floor with a towel over her, lying in the fetal position. Afterward she concluded it had only been an hour of 'lost time'.

Immediately following her prior trauma, when she returned from the hospital, she recalled an incident where she was out walking. It had been raining and she was waiting at a corner to cross the street. A car raced by and splashed her with mud. Franclynne remembers jumping back and feeling the watery mess and dirt on her blouse. The next thing she recalled was being in her living room and looking down at a new pair of shoes she was wearing. She did not recall where she got the shoes, and for that matter, how she got home. She remembered nothing of the entire afternoon. It was as if she was drugged. The incident had scared her for days. It was one of the first times she recalled an episode of dissociation, but by no means would it be her last.

Two years prior Franclynne had passed the licensing exam and was now finally a licensed psychologist. The journey had not been an easy one for Franclynne, as her long-term memory was weak, especially for facts. Moreover, teachers required the regurgitation of facts, especially graduate school professors. She was much stronger on process, not so strong about facts. Therefore, having to make a court appearance in which she was going to be asked about a case she could not remember was a terrifying event for this young woman. *"And god, what happens if I dissociate while on the stand!!?"*

The trauma that Franclynne had experienced was that she had been kidnapped and tortured by an Eastern priest. Her therapist, Dr. Helen DeJarden, was also kidnapped and eventually beaten to death by the priest. She was saved only by the intervention of a strange woman, whom she came to know as the "the rat lady ''. Franclynne tried to stay in touch with her, but that did not happen. Her life had become very busy, and she knew that sometimes people lost contact. Friends would come and go.

Nobody in her graduate program could match Franclynne's diagnostic clinical skills, but remembering facts-who did what, when, and where, was not her natural talent. Nor did she care about fact. She cared about emotions. Facts, she felt, were memories from the eye of the beholder. Different eyes see and remember different facts. Facts were always distorted and manipulated for whatever purpose for which they were being used. She felt the same way about statistics. She operated under the assumption that there are lies, damn lies, and statistics. She barely passed the graduate course in statistics. She believed that the professor had a thing for her. Although nothing happened between the two, she frequently caught him staring at her. It made her quite uneasy, but she passed the class.

Moreover, this court thing scared her to the bone. Authority figures in general threatened her. She did not have a positive history with people who made decisions, especially those who had some control over her. She found many people in authority to be duplicitous and self-righteous, and a courtroom was the ultimate place of helplessness. She had been a teacher before becoming a psychologist and never really meshed with the faculty. Besides her pupils, she had only one friend in the school in which she worked.

Franclynne hatred to be judged and was very self-conscious when she thought people were watching her. Actually, her feelings were closer to paranoia. Her traumatic past usually came back at inconvenient times to haunt her. It was like a personal terrorist waiting to see a weakness to strike. This was another problem that raised its ugly head in graduate school. Having her conclusions about cases ripped apart before others frequently brought her to tears, leading to many nights of crying and insomnia. She was called before a group of professors to question whether psychology was the best profession for her. They questioned whether she had the internal fortitude to continue, and argued that her emotional lability would not serve her well in evaluating and helping others steady their own emotions.

Franclynne ignored the skeptics. Her mentor, therapist, and best friend, Helen DeJarden, had set her on this path and she would not deviate. She felt she owed it to her. Anyway, she argued to herself, why she should change because of the conclusions of people who really did not know her. Nevertheless, eventually she had passed every test and answered every question, many just by the skin of her teeth. She got the impression that some of the professors just liked her and cut her some slack. It did not really matter now, she was licensed, and, barring any unforeseen circumstance, it could not be taken from her. However, was this court appearance an unforeseen danger? Sitting in a court, in front of confrontational attorneys and a judge was terrifying for a self-conscious person like Franclynne.

Loss was a very big issue in Franclynne's life. She had experienced more than most would consider fair, and she rarely dealt with it well. She felt every loss as if a piece of her body was being ripped away from her soul. She had lost her mentor to a psychopathic killer in a situation that almost took her life as well. She had lost many years of her life when this same psychopath had torn part of her memory from her. The woman who had saved her life had not been heard from in almost two years. Her name was La, but most of the word knew her as 'the rat lady '. She missed this eccentric, unusual woman. The only thing she had left from her past was a little dog named Skittles.

Franclynne sometimes believed that Skittles was her soul mate. When she had to stay up into the night and cram for exams, the animal stayed by her side. It always welcomed her when she returned home with many kisses. Franclynne explained all of psychology to her, and the animal appeared to understand every word. When she would wake, sweating and scared, Skittles would snuggle next to her, and the closeness of the warm body relieved some of the tension. Besides a few friends, this animal was all she had.

It was difficult not to like Franclynne Longaire. Even so, she only let a select few get to know her. Some considered her very attractive, but in fact, this was just an underestimation of her true grace and beauty. She was quiet and demure. She created no controversy, but she was more actually more detached from others than she was social. Most people only see a person's outside, looks. She knew that most people were quite superficial in their evaluation of others, focusing on looks or clothes, and she took advantage of this weakness. It was ironic, but Franclynne saw clothes as a costume that people wore, nothing more, nothing less.

Franclynne herself had an unusual rhythm to her. It was hard for others to describe. People would say the way she held herself, her walk, were unique. When she spoke to someone, she looked the person right in the eye, and such contact, from such a beautiful woman, unhinged some, even other woman. When she entered a room, there was a presence felt, the air and the atmosphere seemed to alter. Reality shifted.

Franclynne Longaire had a secret. Her friends called her the 'Sherlock of Psychology', because of her ability to read people. However, her skill had nothing to do with deductive reasoning, the skill that made the famous, fictional detective so successful. In actuality, her deductive skills were not feeble, but they were not the origin of her success. Franclynne was a synesthesiac.

Synesthesia is a rare neurological condition. The sensory systems are wired differently than almost everyone else. Franclynne could smell emotions. When she was a child, she was tested for this aberration. It was found that her sense of smell was almost fifty to seventy-five times more sensitive than that of others. When she entered a room, Franclynne knew what everybody felt by the variance in their scents. Nobody could hide from her passive scrutiny. There are only two situations that confused her - one, if somebody wore a large amount of perfume or aftershave, and second, if a woman had a large discharge during her period. Even if somebody had not showered for days, Franclynne could sense things through the sour smell. Her abilities ran much deeper than just picking up emotional aromas. If given the time, Franclynne could detect an individual's immune system. She could tell if they were sick, had pneumonia, or a sinus infection. All the smells were slightly different. She could also detect lung disease, liver problems, and kidney disease. One of her specialties was detecting the rotting stench of Parkinson's disease, and she could often predict whether a person had a traumatic brain injury. Another ability that her sensitive nose possessed was the ability to track a smell. If she could concentrate enough, which she usually could not do, she could tell where a person had been and follow them to where they were going. Of course, there were significant limits to this skill. She could 'lose the scent' if they got into a car and drove away.

Besides disease, Franclynne could tell an individual's sexual orientation by their smell. She could identify friends' scents, as well as strangers. Crowds could also sometimes confuse her because they overwhelmed her senses. There were too many inputs, too many things to process. Franclynne tended to shop during late hours when stores were less crowded; hence, the less aromatic environment was less overwhelming.

Because of her sensitivity with smell, Franclynne always carried a small porous pouch with her. In it, she kept coffee beans. When she wanted to divert her ultra-sensitive nose, she held the pouch to the side of her nose and the coffee aroma, blocked other scents. Her preferred smell was from Hawaiian Kona beans. They smelled like sweet herbs, but beneath, she could sense the smell of nuts. Her second favorite was Blue Mountain Jamaican beans. They too smelled of herbs and nuts. It was ironic that Franclynne did not like the taste of the coffee she smelled. She much preferred tea.

Court created many problems for Franclynne. The last time she testified she could read the judge's feelings. The judge was suffering from early onset Alzheimer's disease and this led to her having more problems answering the attorney's questions. It was distracting, sometimes leading to Franclynne's stuttering and losing her train of thought. She felt stupid, as the stimuli interfered to such a large degree with her thoughts. She had considered bringing her coffee pouch to the witness stand, but eventually rejected the idea. She believed it would make her appear strange.

That was another problem with her condition; she could not turn it off or selectively focus it. When she walked into a crowded room, she knew the feelings of everyone in the area. They were fleeting and changing, but she could read them. It was like opening a window and having the air rush in, hitting you in the face. She could read who was attracted to her and who was not. She knew who was tired, and who had enough rest. Nothing much escaped her. She could clearly read fear. However, she could not read intention. She knew a person was frightened, but not necessarily why. There were some subtleties in that feeling, and at times, it would confuse her.

Franclynne was tired, and scared on this day that she had to go to court. She had finally composed herself, pulling herself off the bathroom floor. Well, externally she appeared collected, but inside the chaos ran through her veins like a raging storm. When she pulled her car onto the street in which the court stood, her dread was palpable. For a second, she considered just driving past the building and not going in. But that was only a brief terror. Franclynne rubbed her legs trying to calm herself. She swallowed, and as she was getting out of the car, she wondered whether she could actually walk to the courthouse.

The courthouse was a large, white building. A few grayish steps led to the pillars that guarded the doors. Upon entering the court, she had to go through a metal detector guarded by two ominous police officers. They looked at everyone with suspicion, and Franclynne could sense her insecurity. She immediately smelled the whiff of testosterone from these two guards. But as she emptied her pockets, she noticed she had completely forgotten her coffee pouch. "Damn", she thought, and her anxiety level took another step up the ladder towards panic. One of the officers noticed the uptick in anxiety.

"Are you OK, ma'am?"

Franclynne was staring blankly at the officer. He moved closer. *"Ma'am, are you okay?"* Again, she did not look at him. The officer reached out to her and when he touched her, she jumped and backed away. Now she looked at him with some concern. *"I'm sorry, Ma'am, I didn't mean to startle you." "It's okay. I am just nervous."* Finally, she gave a small half smile and walked through the doors.

After going through the metal detector, she had to walk up a large winding staircase. This place was very intimidating, and her legs landed unsteadily on every step. She held tightly onto the railings as she slowly made her way upward.

The courtroom itself had a musty redolence. The windows had probably not been opened in fifty years. The wood on the walls was stained in a dark walnut color, but here too, she noticed some spider webs in the corners. The judge's seat was higher than everyone else's, indicating his/her superiority over the assemblage.

As the courtroom filled, Franclynne's anxiety rose. People paraded through the doors of the courtroom, unaware that as they passed this unassuming woman, they were silently being evaluated. Police and many observers who were preparing to witness the upcoming trial, passed by her. She cursed herself for forgetting her coffee. She turned her head in an attempt to divert her sensitive nose, but this was not very effective. She usually wore perfume on her wrist that she would put up to her face to cloud her own nostrils.

She put her wrist to her nose and realized that she forgot that as well. How could she be so stupid? However, as the people piled into the court, she had already assessed that two people had infections of a minor variety, one woman was gay, one male was bisexual, but of concern was that one woman who appeared to have some form of bladder cancer. Over the course of her life, she had experienced some women with bladder cancer, so the smell was familiar to her.

She glanced and tried not to look at some of the people who passed her, except the one woman who was very ill seemed to pull her attention. She could read fear, sorrow, and heartbreak. She knew the emotional status of everyone who entered. She kept her head turned, trying desperately to ignore her senses. It was to no avail; her senses were on fire. The only positive of the all-consuming array of scents, was that it took her mind off her fear, at least for a few minutes.

The overload was painful for her, and at times, she became dizzy, with feelings of vertigo. Her head would spin and she would reverse spin to try to stop it. She considered walking out to go into the bathroom to throw up. However, there was nothing in her stomach to regurgitate. She sat, trembling inside, pulling all of her energy into an attempt to steady her mood. Her legs were locked. She knew she might not make it to the ladies' room, if she even decided to try to make the voyage. Luckily, nobody came to talk with her, as she might not have been able to put two words together. How would she testify? She had to get herself together.

Finally, everyone sat in his or her chairs. So even though she still could not distract her nose, it had settled to some degree, for nobody was moving. The judge walked into the courtroom and everyone stood. As they sat, the judge looked at Franclynne directly.

"Because we have Dr. Longaire here today, she will be the first to testify."

Keeping her eyes fixated on a specific spot to dissuade her apprehension, she hoped that nobody noticed how her knees shook as she rose. She stood for a second, hoping to steady herself. She wanted to look erudite. She slowly made her way to the front of the court, trying to appear professional and in total control. She was a magnificent looking woman. In truth, her beauty hid her inner turmoil. Tall, blond, thin, and graceful. Of course, she did not feel so blessed, and she naively wondered why people stared as she passed by. She often felt a little paranoid when she knew other people were looking. She felt as though she was translucent, with others being able to peer into her soul, evaluating the internal terror she felt.

She made it to the chair to the right of the judge without incident. After the clerk swore her in, the first attorney approached her. He was the obnoxious man she spoke with on the phone.

"Ms. Longaire",

"Excuse me".

She cut him off. It was unusual for her to be so abrupt, and she even surprised herself with the impulsive reaction. The attorney lifted his gaze to her, appearing surprised at the rebuff. Franclynne look directly into the attorney's eyes and did not immediately reply. She gracefully shook her head (nobody knew this was a sign of her anxiety), and said, *"The name is Dr. Longaire."*

"I'm sorry, Dr. Longaire". He smiled, but it was evident that the man did not like being reproached by this woman. He turned, walked slowly back to his table, and picked up a piece of paper. He walked back to Franclynne, made eye contact, and continued. *"I am handing you a report. Please look at it."*

She took the report, but before looking at it, she stared for a heartbeat at the attorney. How did she gain this composure? When thinking about it later, she would throw up recalling it. However, at that moment, she was very proud of herself for insisting he call her Dr. She wanted him to know that she was irritated by his irreverence. She had worked hard for her degree, and even though she was no superstar, she had earned the respect. Other people must have thought she was so assertive. They did not see the sweat that was forming under her arms and on her legs. To this day, she still did not know where she found the fortitude. She finally looked down at the report, hoping that nobody noticed her shaking hands.

After a second, the attorney, having regained his composure, asked, *"Is this your stationary?"*

"It is."

"Is this your report?"

After looking at the report for a few minutes, Franclynne said, *"It is not."*

The attorney's eyes widened in shock. *"What!"*

He protested. "Dr. This is not your report?"

"It is not," Franclynne said, mostly assured it was not.

"Wait, I'm confused", the attorney exclaimed. *"Let me understand this. It is a report on your stationary, but you didn't write it?"*

"That is correct."

Confused, the attorney turned to the judge and said, *"Your honor, I need time to discuss this situation with my client."*

Looking irritated, the judge responded, *"Fifteen minutes, I have a very busy schedule"*.

The attorneys met with the judge in his chambers before the court was called back into session. Franclynne was back on the stand when the judge reentered and sat behind his bench. He looked directly at her. *"Dr. Longaire, this court must apologize to you for wasting your valuable time. You may leave."*

Franclynne looked directly at the judge and asked, *"Your honor, am I allowed to know the reason that my stationary was used in this fashion, and how it happened?"*

"I am sorry, Dr. Longaire, but I cannot divulge now what happened, but my clerk will call your office after the proceedings to answer your question."

Franclynne rose, and slowly left her seat. She entered the room anxiously; she was confused as she was leaving. But as she proceeded down the aisle towards the courtroom door, she stopped and bent over to whisper something in a woman's ear. *"Can you please meet me in the hallway; it will only take a minute."*

Looking surprised, the woman rose and followed her out of the courtroom. Standing in the outer hallway, Franclynne confirmed her suspicions by the woman's odor. They stood face to face and Franclynne looked at the ground and said, *"I'm sorry to disturb you. What is your name?"*

"My name is Linda."

Franclynne introduced herself and swallowed hard. Finally, she forced her eyes up from the floor and said, *"I have a sixth sense about things. I believe it would be important if you made an appointment with your gynecologist."*

Look surprised, Linda blurted out, *"What?"*

"I think you might have a problem." Of course, Franclynne could not reveal why she had this suspicion.

Linda's face dropped. She then whispered, *"Thank you. I already know that I have cervical cancer. My treatments start next week. But how did you know?"*

"It is too detailed to explain, but I am glad you are getting help."

Franclynne smiled and left the woman standing with a stunned look on her face.

Prelude

She remembered the moment vividly. He arrived at the register, and she could feel her legs weaken. He was only purchasing a few things, but the scanning of the items seemed to take forever. She tried not to make eye contact but could not help it. He was not an overly handsome man, but there was something about him she could not resist. She swallowed and said, *"Did you find everything you were looking for?"* He didn't immediately answer, but smiled at her for a heartbeat and said *"Yes, thank you for asking."* His eyes were molten blue and his smile was magnetic. She resisted the urge to ask him his name, but the words that came out of her mouth were, *"You must be new in town. I have not seen you here before."* His answer surprised her. *"Actually, I have been here before, and I have seen you."* Really, she thought, impossible, how did I miss him?

With his smile and his tone, there was an emphasis on the word "you". He paid for his items, smiled again and left. She felt the urge to follow him out of the store, and in her impulsive pattern, called her manager and said she had a headache and had to leave. She bolted out of the building and saw him standing by his car and speaking with another man. She ran to him and said, *"I think you forgot something in the store"*. He looked in his bag, and said, *"I have forgotten nothing, but thank you."* He smiled again, patted his friend on the shoulder, and began moving toward the car door. *"Are you sure?"* She heard the words come out of her mouth. She was now babbling now, but she didn't care. He had gotten into his car, and she was standing by the window. He lowered the window and said, *"My name is Bobby, what is your name?"* Gaining a slight amount of composure, she said *"I'm sorry, Bobby, I must have been mistaken."* "But *your name,"* he insisted. *"My name is Jillian"* *"Nice meeting you, Jillian."* Now she smiled and turned to go. However, as she left, she could feel his eyes follow her. Again, she became aroused, but as she walked, she thought, *"Oh my god, he read right through me. Did I make a fool out of myself?"*

Chapter III

La was sulking again. What her life had become was not what she had anticipated. She had moved away from her home under the bridge to another small city west of her home. She had become somewhat of a celebrity after murdering the psychopath who was beating her therapist and best friend to death. La felt that she had to relocate to try to rid her mind of the horror of that day. Nevertheless, the change did not work. In fact, it had backfired horribly. Her destructive memories were like shadows, following her wherever she went. She found that her thoughts were still entangled with her friend, Helen DeJarden. DeJarden was La's therapist, but in truth, La worshiped the woman. She recalled with frightening clarity the exact moment of the slaughter, as she repeatedly stabbed the psychopath. In front of her on the ground lay her friend, and it took many police to convince her to release her to the hospital. Why could she not let go?

La had become friendly with a local priest when she was trying to help her friend. She continued her devotion to her new-found religion after the move. But the church near her new home was different than her previous one. The priest was more aloof and not willing to devote time to her questions. She had mentioned to Father Realto that she had killed a man. The priest, outraged by the admission, contacted the police and La was brought in for questioning. She was released after a few hours, but it left a very bad taste in her mouth. La was also perplexed by her action. Did she sin, or didn't she? Was she destined for hell, or wasn't she? She acted out of passion for her friend and would do the same if a similar situation arose, but she still killed someone.

Since leaving her house and giving it to the homeless man, it took almost two days, with La sleeping under trees for her to get back to her old bridge. She carried the black bag over her shoulder and when she arrived, she just stared at the structure. Her stomach felt settled, even though she really had not eaten for two days. Many memories came flooding back. She remembered her beloved rats and what it was like spending the days and nights with them. Besides the positive thoughts, her mind was flooded with very negative events. The contentment quickly left and she felt her muscles tensing and she began feeling nauseous. As she stood and stared at her old haunt, she began to sense something behind her. She turned to see a young police officer coming towards her. La stood as stiff as a tree as she watched the young man approach. The police had never been her friend, and she had an immediate feeling of anger and rage. It was an instinctual response for her, as she had no rational reason for it. As he drew closer, she could sense his tension, or at least she thought she could. In a gruff voice, he barked, *"Identify yourself!"*

La stood, stoically staring at the young man.

"Can I see some identification?"

Again, La stood frozen, staring the young man down. Because of the strangeness of her dress and her lack of cooperation, the young officer became suspicious.

"Let me see what's in the bag!"

Again, no movement, just a blank stare.

Alarmed now, the officer reached for the bag. La pulled her bag back and instinctively swung it, hitting the officer in the shoulder with it. The altercation did not end pretty, as the officer wrestled La to the ground. But even having been grabbed to the ground, La remained silent. Resistive, but quiet. With handcuffs locked on her wrists, she was dragged into the car. She was being arrested. She thought, maybe her sins had finally caught up to her.

Chapter IV

As she walked, the grass felt pleasant under her feet. The grass was soft and slightly cold and wet. Such feelings always relaxed her and comforted her inner thoughts. She did not used to be able to do this, as she used to be very fearful of snakes, either real or imaginary. Nevertheless, the fear was not present, not today. Today she was comfortable. After a while, in the distance, her destination came into sight. The gazebo was beautiful. It stood with nothing around it, just solitude. It was a timeworn structure but remained sturdy. As she approached it, she began to make out the beautiful artwork and the carved intricacies that completed this primal structure. Once one had experienced its peace, it was impossible not to recognize and desire its serenity. She had intimately gotten to know this place after many visits. Visiting it was her lifeline to security. It was her refuge.

As she approached it, Franclynne stopped to admire the carvings as she did every time she entered. She had found that if she spent time studying the structure, each time she noticed more detail than she had never noticed before. It was new with each visit, small changes. She had once considered naming this place but rejected the idea. She just referred to it in her mind as, 'the place'

Franclynne stepped onto the first board of the steps. There was an almost silent squeak as the board slightly gave way under here weight. It was a very strange feeling, as if returning to the womb. Complete security and wellbeing. Franclynne's life was one of trauma and conflict. The place created a time of peace, a time of refuge. And it was not dissociation, it was not the kitchen. This was a choice This visualization allowed her a vacation for her mind and her emotions. But more so, it allowed her to talk about her fears and her thoughts.

Weather and temperature did not exist in 'the place', and once entering it, the grass, the woods, the field all disappeared. Only the inside of the gazebo existed. She sat for a moment before asking any questions or making any requests. When the time came to inquire, she knew it instinctively. She did not need a watch or an alarm. Sometimes she sat for longer periods than others, but she always recognized when it was time.

Franclynne closed her eyes for a moment of reflection. Now the Gazebo was getting noticeably warmer. She could feel it. Franclynne had come to realize that the more she engaged her senses in the experience, the more of an impact it had on her. She opened her eyes, silently asking to see the image of Helen. Helen DeJarden was her mentor. This was a way she could continue to communicate with her.

The mist immediately engulfed the structure and clear sight became difficult. It was like being in a steam room, with the white mist the only thing that was evident. She could feel the droplets on her body and the sweat slowly rising from her pores. However, it was not uncomfortable; it was as if the mist engulfed her in gentle warmth, as an infant being cuddled and protected by its mother.

After a while, a figure seemed to materialize across from her. The face was vaguely familiar and she quickly made out the features of her friend and mentor, Helen DeJarden. A smile rose through every pore in her body as she studied the face. Time and space all disappeared at this moment. The mist vanished, as the face of her friend was omnipresent.

DeJarden had been dead for over two years, but Franclynne could make out every wrinkle and curve of her face. Helen smiled at her friend. Without words, but with pure thoughts, Franclynne said, *"I am troubled, my friend. Life seems to be overwhelming me. I recently had to go to court and the situation unnerved me."*

Silence met her statement, although Helen did seem concerned, but her face did wrinkle at its forehead.

"The more I understand people, Helen, the more fearful I become. I think becoming a psychologist was a mistake for me. It is too much trying to help others when I cannot really help myself. How can I help put people back together when I am so broken?" She stopped for a moment, and then she said, *"Helen, many nights I end up on the bathroom floor. It happens around 3 a.m. At that time my history comes roaring back into my thoughts and I can't stop the intrusiveness."*

Helen continued to stare at her with an apprehensive face. She then said, *"Quiet child"*.

After a while, Helen continued to speak: *"Do you remember what I have told you in the past?"*

"Yes, Helen, I remember"

"What have I told you?"

"You said, trust yourself."

Hellen smiled and said, *"You still have a way to go. I also told you that I always saw strength within you. You were given a gift. You understand the emotional states of people immediately. You do not have to ask questions; your gift tells you what they are feeling. People need you because they cannot hide from your incredible sense. Visit me again. Remember, I will always be here for you."*

"I love you, Helen."

"I love you too, Lynn. Find La, your future and hers are intertwined. They always have been."

"Please don't leave Helen. Why can't I stay here with you?"

"It is not your time, Lynn. You have more to do. Be prepared, Lynn, the future will be complex."

"Be prepared? Are you the one who visited me?"

"No, Lynn, not me. But someone else who loved you."

"Who?"

"I cannot tell you anything else, Lynn. Stay strong, others will need you."

Franclynne closed her eyes and began to weep. She then felt the urge to sleep and the visualization was immediately broken. Helen had taught her this visualization/meditation, as a way of maintaining contact when they had not spoken. Of all of the series of visualizations she learned, this brought her the most understanding and peace. The gazebo was her favorite.

Chapter V

When Sean awoke from the ablation, a woman sat next to him. He immediately sensed that he was in a hospital room, although he was unsure where he was. He could not tell what had been a dream and what was reality. He was quite confused. A woman sat next to him, but he did not think she was a nurse as she was in street clothes. His head hurt as if he had been hit with a hammer. When the woman noticed him opening his eyes, she almost jumped out of her chair.

"Oh my god! Thank god! Sean, you've come back to us!"

He stared at her, noticing the tears well up in her eyes. The woman stood, but then quickly dropped to him, hugging him. He remained quiet, but he felt uneasy at the closeness of this stranger. The woman lingered with her weight making Sean very uncomfortable. The woman seemed to regain her stability. He kept staring at her. She then asked: *"Sean, what do you remember?"*

Sean? Who the hell is Sean he thought? He had no memory of that name. Again, he remained silent, staring with a blank face at this woman. He really did not understand what she wanted. His head pounded and this mystery was too much for him to digest.

"Sean, I have some bad news to tell you. During your ablation procedure, you had a serious stroke. The doctors had difficulty bringing you back to life. You've been in a coma for the last two weeks. Now you are back. I have been praying every day for you to return to us and my prayers have been answered. Thank god".

Sean just kept staring with a questioning look in his eyes. Finally, in a soft, whispery voice he admitted, *"I'm sorry, but I don't know your name. Who are you?"*

The woman looked shocked at the question. Then after a moment she quietly, and in a gentle fashion, responded, *"The doctors told me that you might have some memory problems. Don't you worry, your memories will return."*

She began crying and he asked again. *"Please tell me your name."*

"My name is Beth; I am your wife."

Confusion covered his face. Sean knew that he had never seen this woman before, and yet there was a familiarity. He tried to understand. She was looking at him with questioning eyes, wanting him to say something, but he really did not know how to respond. Finally, after a few seconds, Sean began feeling tired. His mind seemed to slowly start spinning and he lost the sense of what was happening. Sean closed his eyes and fell into a deep protracted sleep.

Chapter VI

She had to hurry home. She walked through the market, not really paying attention to what she was buying. She was quite anxious, as she had not yet found the most important thing that she needed. It was imperative, she could not return home without it. She finally reached the flower store and their tulips were not up to expectations. That meant a trip across town to her second favorite store. She had to decide whether to be late or to return home with the inferior. Either choice made her disconcerted. As she stood contemplating the dilemma, she decided to buy the tulips where she was in order to return home on time. In her haste, Angelique forgot the Italian bread.

In her short life, Angelique had never had a solid self-image. She always felt that she had to make others happy for her to be content. Unfortunately, this interpersonal approach did not work well. Angelique was now feeling the wrath of this poor adaptive behavior.

On the way home, Angelique realized her miscue, lost concentration, and ran a stop sign. How could she forget the Italian bread? It was his favorite and he ate it every night. A young aggressive police officer pulled her over. She sat in the car waiting on the side of the road. She could feel her right leg shake as she began to realize that she would not return home before the chosen time.

To make matters worse, Angelique was involved in a very volatile relationship. Her boyfriend did not work. He spent his time playing an on-line game called, "The Cult of the Souls". He also had a tattoo on his hand to identify that he was a player in this game. His name was Manuel and he was a nasty soul. Angelique was physically attracted to him, which for her, influenced the beginning of the relationship. He moved in almost immediately, and for the first few weeks, Angelique was very happy. For the first few weeks. After that, it became apparent that Manuel was avoiding finding a job, and all the pressure in the relationship fell on her shoulders. In addition, Manuel was very demanding and controlling. Everything had to be his way. If not, then there would be hell to pay. In the beginning of the relationship, Manuel said many nice things about Angelique. She was beautiful, she was great in bed, and they were truly soul mates. But after the two-week period, this approach deteriorated into emotional put downs. "Why couldn't she do things correctly?" "Doesn't she love him as much as he loves her?" His comments then deteriorated into outright cursing. "You're a stupid bitch." "You're lucky to have me, you're just dumb."

Angelique felt trapped in this relationship. She knew deep in her heart that she had to extricate herself from it, but she didn't know how. The constant badgering was having a detrimental effect on her already weak self-esteem, and she was breaking down having crying fits at work. Her fellow employees were becoming concerned about her, and a few attempted to help. For some reason, mostly fear, Angelique pushed them away. She was scared and trapped. She began overdrinking and her mother was worried because addictive behavior ran in the family.

The young officer slowly walked toward Angelique's car. He leaned over as she opened the window.

"Young woman, "May I see your license".

"Officer, I'm very late. I know I ran the stop sign."

"Yes, what are you late for?"

"I have to get home; my boyfriend will be angry with me."

The officer looked at her in surprise.

"Your boyfriend will be angry with you?"

"Yes. Please officer, he gets very upset if I'm late."

"Please step out of the car."

"No! I can't wait"

Angelique stepped on the gas and almost rode over the officer's foot in her bid to escape. It was as if she was possessed. She had to leave; she had to get home on time. Nothing else seemed to matter. Her logical thought processes escaped her. Only fear and anxiety were left. She had to leave, she had to flee. The officer ran back to his car and caught her three miles away from their initial encounter. He dragged her out of her car, handcuffed her and took her to the station. Angelique knew that she could not call her boyfriend for help, but even if she could, he probably would not come. This would only irritate him more, so she called a cousin to help.

Her cousin Dave was a sweet young man. He and Angelique had been close growing up. He had heard through the family grapevine about Manuel, and did not like him at all. He could not understand why somebody as nice and attractive as Angelique would involve herself with such a sadistic individual. When he spoke to a co-worker about it, the only conclusion was 'opposites attract.' This did not make much sense to Dave. When they got in the car, he said, *"Are you okay?"* Angelique did not look at him. She appeared in a daze. He continued, *"You appear worried, is everything alright?"* Angelique stared forward and nodded her head. Dave pulled the car over to the side of the road. *"Angie, something is wrong and I want to help. What can I do?"* He could see her leg shaking. *"I'm okay, believe me. I'm just embarrassed that I got arrested." " Come on, Angie. I know there is more going on. What is this guy doing to you?" "Nothing, Dave, everything is fine."*

Dave pulled the car into the lane and continued on their way. Angelique walked into her apartment five hours late, without tulips, and without Italian bread.

Prelude

OKAY, enough hesitation. Jillian decided to knock on the door. She had come all this way; she could not leave without attempting to see him. She raised her arm and used the knocker, but as she let go, she could feel her legs begin to tremor. She now didn't know if she was prepared for him to answer. What would she say? She stood silently, waiting. She needed all of her strength to resist the urge to run.

As she waited, she could feel his fingers, the first time he ran them over her body. Just thinking about the first time he slowly removed her pants gave her goosebumps. She closed her eyes, reliving the experience as she waited by the door. Her eyes began to close and she immersed herself in the recollection. The images calmed and excited her.

It had never happened before. Of all the men she had slept with, this had never happened. After they made love, she was able to relive the experience when she was alone in her room. A couple of times she actually reached orgasm, just thinking about the experience. He was not the greatest lover she had ever had. He did not have the largest organ, but his technique was gentle and subtle. She felt electricity every time he touched her body. She could imagine his hands running up her thighs, reaching her behind. It was like a volcanic wave traveling across her lower body. However, when she thought of his hands, the image of that strange tattoo came to her. She had asked him about it but he dodged the question. Did the tattoo add or detract from the experience? She couldn't answer the question, but it really didn't matter. He had told her that the tattoo was a symbol of a game that he was playing.

But here she waited. She had knocked. Both her anticipation and fear simultaneously welled through her veins. As she stood in this exhilarating state of anticipation, she realized something else. What was this feeling? Was it need or was it love?

Chapter VII

When Beth Whitford spoke to the neurologist who had evaluated her husband Sean, his answers left her despondent. The neurologist reported that he believed her husband's brain had been wiped clean of memories when he awoke from his coma. Actually, the Dr. said, "When *he awoke from his coma,* he wouldn't know who she was, nor any of his friends or children. In truth, although Beth did not know it this at the time, her husband's brain was not washed completely clean. It was only wiped of the memories of the last five years. Sean knew exactly who he was, but it was not Sean Whitford, It was Andrew Keller.

This realization did not arrive occur to him immediately. It took days before it coalesced in his mind. It was a gradual awakening. But what he clearly knew was that Andrew Keller was very different from the man that this woman thought he was.

Sean/Andrew was now in the rehabilitation wing of the hospital. His motor skills were still weak and clumsy, and it took him a while to formulate thoughts and words. It took a short time for him to process incoming information. All of his executive function, problem solving abilities were affected by the stroke. After her visit with the physician in charge of the rehabilitation unit, Beth went to speak with her husband. When she entered the room, she noticed a strange expression on his face.

"Hello, Sean, are you feeling better?"

He stared at her with a side glance. He could tell she was desperate for his attention and probably his approval. He liked this. He realized he felt good when others felt vulnerable. He decided to lie.

"You look wonderful today, Beth. Did you change your hair color? It looks great"

"Thank you, Sean".

She bent down to hug him but she could feel him tense in her grasp.

"Is everything OKAYAY?"

"Yes, Beth, I am just struggling to regain all my senses."

"How is your memory doing?"

"Not great, bits and pieces."

"Do you remember me?"

"Yes"

Another lie, but said with a big convincing smile. Sean/Andrew did not find this woman attractive. Yes, she was physically attractive, but he did not like this physical closeness. It made him uneasy. He evaluated every nurse that helped him. In his mind, he decided which of them would make good bed partners, and which he would reject. During his rehabilitation in this facility, Sean realized he was not the domestic type, he was more of a predator. That word, predator, for some reason made him comfortable. The process of accepting who he really was, in fact, was the purpose of rehab. Others did not know it yet, but everything was about to change.

Chapter VIII

It was 3 a.m. and Franclynne was wide-awake again. She had read somewhere that the time between 3 and 4 a.m. was the death hour. It was that hour when the night was beginning to give rise to the morning, a very dark ominous time, hovering between the two, not night and not morning. It was a time of transition, a time of intense nightmares, a time of quiet, when ghosts of one's past came back to visit.

In Franclynne's case, her traumatic past was a constant visitor during this eerie time. During the day, she was at least able to partially block her traumatic memories, with work or other deflections. However, during this 'death time', her distractions didn't work. She would end up shaking under her blanket, lying in a fetal position, often in the bathroom. She continually relived the events in all of their terror. Repeatedly the horrible tape replayed in her thoughts. She could actually feel the hands on her body, she could feel the hands caressing her thighs, and she would begin to feel nauseous. It was especially bad when her behind began to hurt. She heard the words over and over, *"You will enjoy this bitch, I love a virgin ass."* Franclynne kept a bag by her bed, as there were times that she vomited at the memories. The sexual abuse incidents were bad enough, but eventually they became horrific physical abuse.

This night was different. Yes, the memories did flood her thoughts, but somehow there was a qualitative difference. It was close to a hallucinatory experience. This night she could feel his body on top of her. She was on her stomach, with her head buried into the mattress. The weight of his body was literally taking her breath away. She began gasping for air. Then in a low voice she began saying, *"No, no, please get off me, please"*. The boundary that she had established between past experience and current behavior was beginning to deteriorate. She could hear the laughing and could feel the slapping on her thighs. She heard the words "Give *it to me bitch*". She was only half dreaming, not awake, yet not asleep, not currently real, but very much tangible.

Franclynne could not move, she was pinned to the floor. Her body began shaking as her chest heaved. She cried out again and again, but the death time did not answer. There was nobody to hear her fear and her complaints. Skittles cuddled up next to her, but even this closeness did not alleviate the sense of urgency and vulnerability that overcame her. Franclynne continued to shake and cry. The worst part of the flashback was the smell, the overwhelming stench that she would never forget.

Franclynne had smelled the scent many times in her life. Out of all the smells that she had categorized in her mind, this one always stood out. It was the scent of a psychopath. She recently sat in a restaurant, wanting to eat her lunch in a quiet atmosphere, when the familiar smell hit her. A woman had just walked by her table, and Franclynne began to shake. Paying no regard to the fact that she had already ordered her meal, Franclynne quickly rose from the table and made a beeline to the door. She had to get out of there. She had to leave. Logic had left her and her traumatic emotional past had taken over. When she arrived at her car, Franclynne was completely out of breath. She sat in the car making sure the woman didn't follow her. She locked all of her doors but needed to steady herself before she attempted to drive. The psychopathic odor cut through her logic and undermined her composure. She stayed frozen in the car for at least a half hour. A number of times she heaved. Luckily, Franclynne kept a bag in the car specifically for this purpose.

Five o'clock Lights began to replace the dark, and Franclynne knew she had to get out from under the covers. She needed to get off the floor. The beginning of dawn always helped her to recover from the torment of her flashback. She needed a shower as she was drenched from her own sweat. The hot water running over her body seemed to rejuvenate her body and soul.

That morning, as Franclynne entered her small office, a young woman sat in her waiting room. Although she had never seen her before, she immediately knew many things about her. This young woman was scared. Her system was out of sorts, out of equilibrium. The woman was attractive with short brown hair. Franclynne noticed a strange tattoo on the woman's thin, right arm. It was a name with a sword through it. She also noticed burn marks on her wrist.

The woman met Franclynne halfway across the waiting room. The odor was strong and robust. It was now much clearer; this woman was not scared, she was terrified. She also knew that the woman had an ear infection.

"Excuse me, are you Dr. Longaire?"

Franclynne took step back at the woman's approach.

"Dr. Longaire, I really need to speak to somebody."

"What is your name?"

"Dr. Longaire, my name is Angelique"

Franclynne gained her composure. *"Does your ear hurt?"* The woman reached for her head and stared with a surprised expression. *"Does your ear hurt?"* Franclynne repeated. She then smiled and put her hand on the woman's shoulder. *"Sit for a few minutes. I will be ready to talk soon."*

Chapter IX

Sean Whitford was finally able to leave the rehabilitation center at which he had been in for over a month. His speech and his motoric skills were close to normal. He still stuttered at times when he was anxious. He also still had to think for a moment or so, before speaking. Much of his memory had returned, but he kept his secret from his wife. He certainly did not want to tell her what he had remembered about his life before he met her. He had either forgotten about his previous life, or by some strange psychological phenomena, blocked it from conscious mind. Every day he was remembering more details about his former life, and it was like remembering a favorite blanket or a comforting situation. It was very reassuring to him as the holes in his memory were being filled.

Sean recalled the month he met his wife. He awoke one morning, finding himself in a different town than he had remembered. The room in which he awoke was stale and sterile. He knew it was not a place he had been before, but he was not quite sure why he sensed that. Even the air smelled and tasted unusual. His head hurt, but he did not know why. His memory of the past was blocked and was not available for him to use. He sat for a minute on the side of the bed trying to clear his thoughts. But even as his eyes cleared from sleep, nothing seemed to make sense.

Who was he, and why was he here in this cheap hotel? Why couldn't he remember anything? What was his name? Did he have a job? Who was his family?

Sean left his room, and began walking the streets. No face looked familiar, nor did the streets. He was confused. He did find $10,000 in his room, but he did not know how it got there. He walked into a coffee shop and sat down to have some food. While he waited for his meal his head spun. He had to have a plan. He had to figure out who he was, or start his life from this time forward. What he did learn about himself was that he had a skill with math. He heard others in the coffee shop asking for clarification about their bills and he was quickly able to add the numbers. Math seemed to come easily to him. After a couple of hours of wandering the streets, he found himself in front of a large office building. For some unknown reason, he entered the building.

Sean was a smooth talker. He also had a winning smile, which led him into the mailroom of a brokerage/financial firm. He applied for an entry level job, and to his surprise, was offered a position. It was not long before Sean's mathematical and evaluative skills became known in the office and he was able to quickly move up the corporate ladder. With no remembered history, he made up his memories on the fly when the situation arose.

Sean easily settled into his new life. After a few months, it was noticed that his mathematical skills were exceptional and he secured a position in the accounting arm of the company. He did not know whether or not he had any higher educational degree, but what he did know was that he was more proficient then any of the accountants working in this area. There were 10 accountants in the office of the large firm in which he worked. Quickly, Sean began correcting their errors, to the point that the accountants began to admire and dislike him in the same breath. He was like a mathematical savant. Any task that was given to him was completed in record time. In fact, in Sean's mind it was not if he could complete a task successfully, it was how quickly could he do it. He would actually set time restrictions and race himself to the finish.

Then one day, while walking through the secretarial pool, he glanced at a young woman and was immediately entranced by her. Her name was Beth Holmes. Sean had already gained an almost mystical reputation in the company for his ability to manipulate numbers. When he went over to Beth's desk, her smile sealed the deal for him. It was a whirlwind romance, and the two were married in record fashion. Sean's skills continued to impress, and eventually he became the head of the entire financial arm of the company. He made few if any mistakes, and he completed tasks in record time. Their life was perfect. He had a wonderful wife, great children, was financially secure, and then the palpitations started and threw everything into chaos. Because of the neurological event during his ablation, his wonderful life was now left to only partial memories, and his former life had returned in full clarity.

It was a rude awakening for Sean when he realized that his former life was not only less than perfect, but criminal. Besides his memories, his old feelings and urges were also returning. These had been blocked as well. But as with the memories, these feeling were very comforting to him, even though they were quite manipulative and negative. Actually, defining them as negative was an underestimation of his urges; sadistic was closer to his desires. But Sean knew they were his own and fit him like a glove.

Many of the emotions that he felt with his wife Beth were uncomfortable, but he could never put his finger on the reasons. Now things were becoming clearer. With Beth, he always felt a need that he could not explain, but now he realized it was these true feelings from his previous life that were trying to surface from the darkness. It was very strange with Beth. During intimate times he would be gently caressing her and get a sudden urge to dominate. He successfully blocked this urge every time it emerged. It was an intense feeling but did not last very long and he was able to easily deflect it into more kindly responses. Now, as his true self was reemerging, these negative emotions were intensifying and invigorating his body and soul. It was like shedding a false armor and feeling your correct skin once again. It fit, it was comfortable, and he knew it was his true nature. He felt like a snake shedding his tight skin for a more comfortable one.

But now his desires were different. At times he felt the need to inflict pain, both on himself and on others. It was now harder to restrain these urges. He had to find an outlet, without exposing his true nature to his wife Beth and his children. He silently began cutting himself to relieve the tension. Beth noticed some of the wounds, and he successfully deflected her concerns. She was such a trusting soul.

At one point, his daughter said something that bothered him, and his rage exploded through his body and his mouth. As he stood over her, he began shaking and eventually he turned and just left the house. Sean found himself taking pleasure in running over squirrels and other animals while driving his car. He would even pull over and stare at the dead carcass whenever possible. A woman once stopped her car after he had hit a stray cat. She came over to him while he stood gazing at the dead animal.

"Oh my god. I cannot believe you killed that animal. If I didn't know better it appeared as if you were trying to hit it!"

Sean's first thought was:

"That was fun"

But what he said was, *"I tried to avoid hitting the animal. I have never killed anything before. This is horrible,"* all the while smiling to himself. That was another trait he recalled and was able to utilize all the time. He could feel one thing and portray another, usually the direct opposite of what he was feeling.

He drove away from the scene, shaking his head.

Sean's most difficult task was living with Beth. She was attractive, to a degree, and he enjoyed having sex with her. Well, enjoyed only to a point. He wanted to tie her up and make her beg, but he had not yet approached her with this new ritual. However, one thing for sure, he knew he did not love her. He needed her for her body, but he did not love her. He pondered how to extricate himself from this relationship/situation. The urge to hurt her physically was building within him. The problem with just lashing out at her, which he so desired to do, was that he would have to answer to someone for his violence. However, he did begin to take more advantage of his urges during sex. He would force her to assume certain positions and satisfy him in different ways. It was not the sexual aspect of their copulation that made him reach orgasm, it was the control issue. He would put his hand around her neck and press until her desire turned to fear. Then he would stop and apologize, claiming that her beauty just pushed him out of control. He would spend time considering other sexual adventures, and he enjoyed springing them on Beth when she couldn't resist it. He would demand a certain position and then make the change. He enjoyed her complaints and her fearful facial expressions. When she felt pain, it pushed his sexual desires to new heights.

For her part, Beth was becoming more and more concerned about her husband's change in behavior. Actually, her fears were beyond concern. After every sexual encounter, she was in pain. She had welts, and a few times she almost lost consciousness. Of course, he always apologized for his behavior, promising not to do anything like that again. But that never stopped the next event.

Before his stroke, Sean was a gentle and kind man, now he was increasingly becoming hostile and aggressive. She had heard that brain injury could change a person's personality, but a complete reversal? She noticed it with the children, with neighbors, and many times when they went out as a couple. That past week, during dinner at a fancy local restaurant, he reached out and grabbed the waitress's ass as she stood at another table. It created a big stir as the server dropped her pad and let out a scream. Sean did apologize for the incident, but when they got back in the car, his attitude shifted from remorseful to belligerent.

"That whole incident was the waitress's fault. She had been eyeing me most of the night, and then, when she almost shoved her ass in my face, I couldn't help myself but to touch it. Besides, she wanted me to, I could read it on her face. I think I just startled her."

Sean's new urges did not stop in his personal relationships. At work, his thoughts began shifting toward embezzlement. He wanted more than he had and had to figure out a way to obtain it. Having risen to such a high level in the company, he had access to the company's banking interests and financial records. He decided to set up a "dummy company" to receive kickbacks. He created false agreements, and created the automatic payments from the banking to the dummy companies. He realized that this was a similar scheme that he had used in his 'previous life'.

Chapter X

Missy McCarron was one of the sweetest women that Franclynne had ever encountered. She had lived a very difficult life. Two of her husbands had passed away from serious health problems. She now found herself in a hospital bed, with the doctors telling her that her life would not last much longer. Even within her troubled life, Missy continued to be a positive force in the world. She shrugged off all of the adversity that passed her way, focusing instead about how she helped others. And help others she did, winning Volunteer of the Year award numerous times in her long life.

Franclynne started as her therapist, but quickly became one of her closest friends. Before her current hospitalization, Missy met Franclynne for lunch on a regular basis. Her hospitalization came as a surprise, both to Missy and to Franclynne. One day she seemed fine, and the next, she was in the hospital having been told that her life was draining away. She was having a heart failure incident, and was losing the battle. The doctors had recommended putting her into a self-induced coma, but Missy refused the treatment.

Franclynne had lost track of how long she had been sitting by this bedside. Missy was always thin-boned but strong. However, now she appeared quite frail. She had almost stopped eating. Finally, she opened her eyes and they twinkled a bit when they noticed Franclynne sitting next to her.

"You've been crying, Franclynne."

Franclynne raised her head and her eyes were red and dripping with tears.

"I love you, Missy."

"I know you do, my dear, and I love you."

Franclynne squeezed Missy's hand in reply.

"My time is arriving quickly, my friend."

That comment brought more tears from Franclynne.

"No, Missy, no—I will miss you too much!"

"I know, my dear, and I will miss you. Death doesn't scare me as I thought it would. The worst part will be missing our lunches."

Again Franclynne squeezed her hand.

"Can I tell you a secret?"

Franclynne imperceptivity nodded.

"I have been visited. It has happened since I have been in this room. My first husband has come to visit me. He told me you will help me on this side and he will help me on the other side."

"I don't know how to help you, Missy. What should I do?"

"You already have, Franclynne. Tell me, what does your sensitive nose tell you?"

Missy was one of the few people that Franclynne had actually told about her exceptional sense of smell.

"It tells me that you are at peace."

"I am, Franclynne. Now, please do me a favor. Go downstairs to the hospital restaurant and have a nice meal. Come back afterwards"

"No, I want to stay here Missy. I cannot eat"

"Please, Franclynne, have an ice cream sundae for me."

Franclynne let go of her hand, kissed her on the forehead, and reluctantly rose to leave. She knew in her heart that she had seen her friend for the last time in this life. Missy had once told her that when you die, it is better to die alone. Franclynne did return after having an ice cream sundae, but she cried all the way through it. When she returned, Missy was gone.

Franclynne stayed until the staff demanded her to leave. She knew that her past had created a giant hole in her heart, and this death would only deepen that hole even more. Few people had actually loved her in her life, but Missy was one of them. She had lost her other true friend, Helen DeJarden, at the hands of a brutal psychopath. She would now go home and cancel the following week of her schedule. It would be spent in her bed, under the covers, filled with suffering. Time would also likely be spent on the bathroom floor. As she rose from her chair in the hospital, she knew this to be true.

However, before she left the hospital, something was troubling her. When Missy had passed, Franclynne could smell the death. For hours after she passed, she could smell it. It was like a mist that followed her, circling her body. Yes, it lessened over that time but she could still smell it at times when she was tense. Yet there was something else, something different about the odor when Missy passed. It was different from other deaths that she had witnessed. She had smelled it when her mentor, Dr. DeJarden passed, but this smell had a qualitative difference. It was slight, almost imperceptible, but it was different. She could not shake it. Why was there a difference? Was it because she loved Missy? But she also loved Helen. Franclynne even went into another room and sat with a dying man. He had been in a coma, so she did not need to explain herself. But when he passed, the scent was the same as with Helen. It did not have the subtle variation that she sensed with Missy.

When Franclynne returned to her apartment, she was perplexed. She was desperately sad that Missy was gone but the dilemma of the scent troubled her greatly. Could it only be that this was her minds way of diverting her from her sadness? On the other hand, was she just losing her mind? She was tired. She put her head down, and it wasn't long before sleep overcame her.

Prelude

As she stood, waiting for a response from her knock, many thoughts vibrated through her mind. A man from a previous relationship had accused her of what he called 'emotional destruction'. What he meant by this was that she had a history of building up closeness, then ripping the rug out of from under the relationship. Men would fall for her and then she would indiscriminately terminate the love. He believed that she set men up for an emotional implosion. She never considered this as truth, but now, the words he said resounded in her mind, vibrating with a sense of truth. Was this true? Her attitude towards Bobby seemed to fit the profile of which her ex-lover accused her. It had never bothered her before, this type of accusation. However, now, it stuck in her mind. Was she doing it again? Was it some kind of strange, sadistic ritual that she played out with every man with whom she slept? She even pictured herself as a black widow spider, killing its lover after mating.

Maybe this was a mistake. She was the one who broke off the relationship, and now here she stood with a red rose. Did she mean to hurt him again? He did not react with pain when she ended the relationship. Maybe she was starting again to hurt him further, make him feel the loss of her affection. However, surprisingly, she was the one who felt the loss. She was emotionally confused.

No response to her knock. Should she knock again, or just leave? No. I am here. She decided to knock again.

Chapter XI

Andrew/Sean stood on the threshold. His internal cravings were driving him. He was having difficulty restraining his urge to take a random woman. This thought was haunting him. He felt the urge so strongly, that he believed he had no choice. He took long walks in the park and followed certain women who were also taking walks. Up until this time, he was discrete, but a few times, he did retreat into the woods to masturbate and relieve his tensions. Luckily, he found a spot where other walkers could not see him.

But today was different. As he walked, a woman appeared in front of him with short shorts, and by his evaluation, a perfect pair of hips. She swayed as a willow tree in a breeze as she walked. He wanted to be strong and just admire with his eyes, but the urges were too great. He had considered how he would stage such a rape and had planned the exact place he could most successfully accomplish the act.

He followed the woman for about a half mile and they were approaching the specific spot in which he had envisioned such an event. It was perfect. There was nobody else around. The sky was overcast, and he had his mask with him to cover his face. The urges were beginning to overtake him and he could feel his penis stiffen at the thought. He sped up his walk, trying slowly to overtake her. This chase was also enjoyable. The perfect spot was quickly arriving, and he took the mask out of his pocket. Quickly, he put it over his face. He was now only a step behind her. It was now or never.

Sean grabbed the unsuspecting woman, and with his free hand covered her mouth. He dragged her into the bushes that were next to the path. She initially attempted escape but he quickly overcame her. Then her struggling seemed to stop and she looked at him.

"Please don't hurt me. I have a family with three small children," she pleaded.

"I won't hurt you, but you will do as I say. If you scream, I will kill you. Do you understand?'

The woman nodded her head in a submissive fashion, and Sean slowly lowered her to the ground. Now, standing over her, he said in an authoritative fashion,

"Take your shorts and underwear off, right now!"

She hesitated, but eventually began pulling her shorts down. Now she was now crying, understanding her fate. All of this made Sean that much more excited. His eyes widened as he watched her shaking hands pulling off her panties.

"Please don't hurt me, my children need me."

"Quiet, bitch."

And with that comment, Sean fell to his knees and jerked her legs apart.

"I know you want me. Tell me"

"Tell you what?"

The woman responded in a quivering voice, with tears rolling down her face.

"Tell me that you want me to come inside you!"

"What?"

"You heard me, I do not want to hurt you! Please don't make me!"

Stuttering, the woman garbled out statement that Sean had required. He smiled because he knew that her statement was how she truly felt, and without hesitation he entered her. It was not long before the event was consummated, as Sean almost began to come before insertion. After it was over, he looked at her and said,

"I know where you live. I have followed you before."

All of this was a lie.

"If you go to the police, I will hurt your children. Do you understand?"

The woman nodded in agreement, and Sean stood and left her lying on the ground with blood dripping from between her legs. The woman would recall this trauma many times in the future. She ended up keeping her silence, even from her husband. But she was changed, in both obvious and subtle ways. However, one of the things she did remember, with clarity of vision, was the strange tattoo that her attacker had on his hand. It would not leave her thoughts. She looked for it on men for many years to come.

Chapter XII

Sally Rubster loved her cappuccino. She had specific stores, which she frequented to get her many fixes during the day. Whenever she had to drive to an appointment, her route was determined by these cappuccino stops. Sally had dark black eyes and long curly hair. She had an infectious smile and a vivacious personality. She was not petite and some would consider her overweight. But Sally never had trouble finding male relationships. Nevertheless, such relationships created much of the stress in her life.

Partially because of her charismatic nature, Sally had many male callers. The vast majority of her relationships have been dead ends. Actually, the term 'dead end' was a misnomer, as most her relationships ended in some form of disaster. Sally Rubster had been emotionally injured many times. Her problem centered on trust. Sally trusted others much too easily, and then got burned for her trouble. She would fall for a smile, a comment of desire, or the subtle wink of a man's eye. She was desperate and she knew it. Unfortunately, some of these relationships not only ended in breakup, but Sally was physically mistreated. She had recently had a hospital stay after having her eye blackened and her head beat so badly that she had a concussion.

After leaving the hospital, Sally swore she would never, ever begin another relationship. She preferred being alone to heartache and headache. Her body and her spirit were both black and blue. Yet here she was, even as she left the hospital, thinking about a man that she met at a friend's dinner party. She could not believe it but found herself sitting next to him at the party, laughing more than she had in a long while. She was spending a lot of time daydreaming about him.

About six months earlier, Sally met Franclynne Longaire at the gym to which they both belonged. They became friends almost immediately. They both needed new friends. It was a positive relationship, as they gossiped, talked about clothes and makeup, and other subjects of mutual interest. Without thinking, Franclynne had evaluated many of their fellow gym mates to Sally's astonishment. She never let on about her sensitive sense of smell, but Sally always pushed her whenever a person walked by that they both knew. They might be sitting around a small table, just talking, when somebody would walk by. Sally would say, *"OKAYAY, Lynn, what do you think of her?" "Sal, look, I don't even know that person. What do you want me to say?" "Come on Lynn, I know you, everyone is under scrutiny. So, tell me." "She seems nice, Sal, she smiled as she walked by." "Come on Lynn, you're copping out, not good enough. Tell me what you think."* Franclynne would smile and look at the person again. *"She has a sinus infection."*

Sally smiled, jumped out of her chair, and went after the young lady about whom they were both talking. When she caught up with her, she said, *"Excuse me, but I noticed your sniffles."* The woman looked startled, but smiled and said, *"Yes, I have a sinus issue."* Sally gave her that infectious smile of hers and said, *"I always notice fellow sufferers. I use a Neti pot. It might help."* The woman smiled back.

Sally ran back to Franclynne. She waited for a few seconds until the woman was out of earshot, then she turned to Franclynne and said, *"OKAYAY, Lynn, how did you know?"* Franclynne smiled and said, *"Lucky guess, Sal, lucky guess." "I don't believe you, Lynn. There is something that goes on in your beautiful head that other people don't understand. "Just luck, Sal, just luck."* Sally look at her, smiled and pointed her finger at Franclynne. *"Okay, Lynn, I'll let you off the hook, but there is something about you that you're not telling me, Miss Sherlock Holmes."*

One would think that Franclynne would be averse to criminals, considering both her traumatic past and her upbringing. However, in actuality, the reverse was true; Franclynne was drawn to them like a bug to the flame. She believed that contact with the socially uncompassionate would help her get past the demons that lived within her mind. So far, this strategy had not really had the desired effect. This had nothing to do with Franclynne feeling sorry for the criminal element. In fact, it was just the opposite. There was an element of hate in her gut when she came into contact with psychopaths. Her synesthesia was oversensitive to the smell of immorality.

At some point, when she had evaluated a man for the courts, and determined by her overly sensitive olfactory system, that the man had, in fact, committed the crime for which he was being tried. Both the court and the police were duly impressed with the lovely young woman who could seemingly tell the truth from lies. The 'human lie detector' was how one of the officers put it.

She was asked by the police to come in and interview suspects. The court sought her insight into their veracity. On this specific day, Franclynne was called into a local precinct.

Whenever she went to a police interview, she purposely underdressed. She wore no makeup and wore fake glasses and a gray tint in her hair. The police had no idea how she performed the insightful miracles that they had witnessed in the past, and they really did not care. She was almost never wrong and her insights led to numerous arrests. They even compensated her monetarily for her services as a consultant to the force. Her retainer was quite substantial, and it definitely supported her private practice.

On this particular day, Franclynne wore dark red pants and a large sweater that made her look dowdy. She wore her hair up in a bun. Quite unattractive. Her shoes were flats and as she walked through the precinct, she spoke to no one as she made her way past the desks of uniformed officers and the detectives, who were easily recognizable by their lack of similar dress. She rarely moved head movements, staring straight ahead, as she sauntered through the offices. Many of the men had seen her dressed for court and always were amazed at the transformation. She was one of the favorite subjects of office gossip.

Franclynne was led into a small room in which stood a table and four chairs. There were no windows or mirrors in the room, but up in the corner of the ceiling there was a small camera. Unless someone pointed it out, one would not notice such a trifle. But Franclynne knew it existed and it distracted her, so that she always positioned herself with her back facing the camera. Franclynne was always intrigued by this small room. It was sterile, yet quite menacing to the criminals who were led into this dungeon. Its barrenness was imposing. Often Franclynne was taken with the overt anxiety that was exhibited by many of the incoming 'persons of interest.' She did not know it, but many criminals called her the 'witch woman.' Her reputation preceded her.

Franclynne sat alone in the small room awaiting the first inmate. The wait was always the most difficult part for her. Then, without warning the small door would open and a police officer would lead a suspect into the room. The man would be chained to the table with his back to Franclynne who sat stoically against the wall. A hefty officer slowly opened the small door and marched in with a small, disheveled man. Immediately, Franclynne had a strong impression of both men. She tried very hard to block the odors. She did not want to compromise her evaluation until the questioning was over.

The interview lasted over two hours. The man, whose name Franclynne had no interest in knowing, sat quivering and sweating. The police had accused him of robbing a small store and pistol-whipping the manager. He also resisted arrest. The perpetrator wore a hockey mask, so no definitive identification was possible. The police accused the man of the burglary. They indicated that, in the attack, he had left some of his DNA behind. They had asked him and he volunteered to give a sample three days before. The accused criminal asked for coffee and the officer refused the request. The officer told the man that the DNA confirmed his part in the robbery.

When the interview ended, Franclynne was confronted by Captain O'Brian. He pulled her aside into another small office.

"So, Ms. Longaire, what was your impression?"

"Captain, it is Dr. Longaire!"

She smiled, *"Or, you can call me witch woman"*.

Now it was O'Brian's turn to smile.

"Yes, I know what they call me. I sort of like it. Mysterious, I guess."

"So, witch woman, what did you learn?"

"My impression, captain, is that you should let the man go."

"What?"

"The man is innocent. You need to let him go"

"But we have evidence"

Franclynne shrugged her shoulders.

"Do what you want to, captain, but the man is innocent"

Frustrated, the officer replied, *"He is our only suspect!"*

Franclynne turned to the captain and said, *"There is no evidence, the officer lied throughout the interview. There is no DNA evidence, and your officer continually lied throughout the interview"*.

"That's just not true."

She looked him in the eye. Her expression was 'really?' Finally, Franclynne spoke again.

"*Captain, I can only tell you what I believe. Please excuse me. I have to leave; I have a very important appointment.*"

As she walked away, O'Brian said "*He is guilty, I am sure of it.*"

Franclynne stopped, turned her head back to O'Brian and said, "*Tell your officers not to lie. The witch woman has spoken.*"

While she waited, Sally sipped her drink. She was only partially watching the racquetball game that was going on in front of her. She had been going to this gym for many years. Sally actually enjoyed working out. She was very proud of her muscular legs. She worked very hard with squats and weights. But not today. She was excitedly waiting for her friend to tell her the good news about her potentially new relationship.

Sally was watching the match through the glass window that was in front of her, but she was daydreaming, staring with a blank look at the court. Suddenly, she felt a hand on her shoulder and her head jerked backward, but a smile appeared on her face.

"*Hey, Lynn- it's so good to see you. Sit, sit*".

"*You sound excited, Sal, I sense that means that there is a man involved.*"

Sally's face blushed a bright red. For a heartbeat, she did not respond to her friend, then a smile crossed her face.

Franclynne had suffered with Sally through many boyfriends. Sally went through men like water through a sieve. But, it was always interesting and always exciting. Franclynne had figured out that there was a clear pattern to Sally's relationships. The first stage was what she termed the 'Disneyland phase'. Sally saw the man as flawless without even minor imperfections. This was followed by the 'brief return to reality phase', when she began noticing some of his troubling qualities. This was followed by the 'hurricane phase', where Sally complained and complained about conflict, and desperately tried to solve the conflicts. The last phase was the 'resignation' phase. This was the end. The time between these phases varied by man, but the stages were consistent. Sally actually went through the four stages once over a weekend. Franclynne actually kept track of these phases. Franclynne always felt being a friend of Sally was like being on a rollercoaster. One of Sally's friends used to call her 'Coney Island'. It took a while for Franclynne to figure out why.

"Can't wait till you meet him, Lynn. I know you are a psychologist. This man scares me. He's too perfect for me. I desperately need your opinion."

Sally's face became serious.

"Lynn, we've only known each other for a short time. I have failed in many relationships. I can't afford to fall in love with this man only to find he is wrong for me."

"Sally, you are expecting too much from me, I am not an oracle".

"Come on Lynn. I have been watching you. You seem to be able to read people and dissect them only by glancing at them. I don't know how you do it, but I have watched you".

"I told you Sally; it was lucky guesses."

"Do you remember, Lynn, when we went out for dinner? One of my co-workers was leaving the restaurant while we were sitting. He stopped by our table to say hello. He was there for only a minute. After he left you said, "He is really taken with himself, and stay away from him. He has irritable bowel syndrome". Then, it seemed you were in a daze and you said, "He's cheating on his wife".

"Do you remember that Lynn?"

"I didn't say those things, Sally"

"Yes, you did, Lynn."

*"Just guesses, Sally. Sometimes
I get lucky with guesses."*

Sally gave Franclynne a 'yeah right' look, then, after a moment she said, *"Okay, Lynn- just let me know how you feel, guess for me."*

"When will I meet him, Sal?"

"He'll be here in a minute. I told him to meet us for a drink".

At that moment, Sally stood, and another huge smile appeared on her face. Franclynne could feel the slight change in temperature that meant that somebody else had entered the area. Behind her she heard,

"Hi, Sal."

"Hi, Ko."

Franclynne turned and was surprised to see a short, thin, black man standing behind her. Franclynne stood. Sally said, *"Koko, this is my friend, Lynn."*

"Hello, Lynn, I have heard a lot about you from Sally. She says you are some kind of mystic."

Franclynne smiled and blushed, looking at Sally.

Koko excused himself after only a few minutes. He said that he had an important phone call to make. He gave Sally a kiss on the cheek and told her that he would see her later for dinner.

It was unusual that any man, upon meeting Franclynne, did not do a double take. When she entered a room, it was as if the air was sucked out of the windows. One could almost hear the men in the room inhale. It was as if time stood still for a few heartbeats. Of course, Franclynne never noticed this pause, as it was not concerning, nor important to her.

It was a rare event that Koko paid such little attention. Sally instantly noticed this. As Koko walked away, Sally was fixated on him. Franclynne did notice the connection, and as he turned the corner, the trance seemed broken. She turned back to Franclynne and her face was beet red. Before Franclynne could breathe, Sally wanted an opinion.

"So, Lynn, so?"

Franclynne smiled and said, *"Perfect Sal, perfect."* What else could she say? In truth, she did not read anything unusual about Koko. This could be a winner. Instantly Sally jumped off her seat and grabbed her friend.

"I love you, Lynn, I really do."

And with that she jumped out of her chair and ran after Koko.

Prelude

Still no answer. She could hear the music from within the brownstone. Somebody was home. She thought, *"Does he know it's me, waiting, and purposely ignoring my knocks. I really don't blame him. He should avoid me for his own benefit."* She gave one last look the large wooden door and bent down to place the rose on the ground. She promised herself that she would punish herself for losing this man. *"This is all my fault."* As she turned to leave, she looked back and said, *"I'm sorry, Bobby"*.

As she walked away, her thoughts focused on her heart breaking. She thought about how much it hurt. She lost Bobby, but she cannot afford to do this again. She realized that she needed help. She promised herself that she would seek out a therapist. It briefly passed through her mind that this is what all the people she had broken up with felt like. She walked two blocks and threw up in a garbage can.

Chapter XIII

She walked along the beach, heading to her favorite bar. It was a small place with a seafaring décor and she loved the atmosphere. It seemed to make her feel free and brought back images of her youth. Tabitha loved walking through the sand without her shoes. It created a trancelike state for her. Sure, she had a job, and got paid good money, but she really hatred responsibility. Nothing seemed to excite her anymore. Although that was not really true. She liked going to bars and meeting other lonely people. As she watched these people posturing with each other, she could feel herself becoming aroused. But other than that, men were boorish, and the actual act of intercourse was somewhat disgusting to her. She did enjoy oral sex. Having a man's penis in her mouth made her feel in complete control. She sometimes thought about biting down hard. And when she did use her teeth, men seemed to enjoy the experience. She knew one day that she would just chomp down to see what would happen. In her dreams, she could taste the blood and it gave her a rush.

When Tabitha entered the bar, she did not consider it unusual that she had slept with many of the men that were there that night. However, she noticed a newcomer, a well-built young man who she remembered seeing surfing on the beach earlier a few weeks earlier. He was alone, sitting in a chair in the corner, slowly drinking whiskey.

Tabitha walked over and made eye contact.

"Do you mind if I sit?"

The man barely moved, but he also did not object, so Tabitha sat in the open seat.

"I am lonely tonight and by your bearing, I believe you share these feelings. My friends call me Tabby. What is your name?"

The young man slowly raised his head, and in an almost inaudible voice said, *"Lurrie"*.

"A beautiful name, Lurrie. Is it a family name?"

The man obviously had been drinking for a while and said, *"No my mother loved the blues and named me after her favorite singer, a man named Lurrie Bell."*

"Sorry, Lurrie. I've never heard of him."

"It's okay, neither did I."

"That's an interesting tattoo on your hand. What does it mean?"

Lurrie looked deep within her eyes. "It is a symbol for, *'The Cult of the Souls' "*.

"Sounds scary."

"Not scary for me. Are you adventurous?"

"I guess."

"Good, I will explain later."

The couple was seen leaving together when the bar closed. Other customers observed the woman to be almost carrying him out, as he was quite inebriated.

Tabby was not seen again. She did not show up for work the next day. It took three or four days before the police began look for her. Tabby showed up on a beach about 20 miles from the bar. It appeared at first that she had been strangled. She had also been raped. When Lurrie was found, he was immediately arrested. Others in the bar had noticed the two leaving together. As the investigation proceeded, it was discovered that Lurrie was found asleep on the beach the next morning by an angler. The DNA found in Tabby did not match Lurrie. Eventually he was released. This was added to the list of unsolved crimes.

Chapter XIV

It was 3:30 am and Franclynne was slumped over a chair in her bedroom. She threw up on the floor twice and couldn't regain her composure enough to go back to bed. She did make it back from the bathroom to the recliner in the bedroom. It was dark and quiet, but the silence was shattered by her moaning and crying. She was feeling completely out of control. It was happening again. Her half-awake/asleep nightmare. She held a pillow tightly to her chest as if her life depended on it. It seemed to give her some sense of comfort, as her crying became quiet whimpering. She stayed in that position until the sun finally began peeking its face above the horizon. This was another one of the times that Franclynne wondered if life was worth living. She had been to that dark place before, and always eventually ascended back into the light. The other place her mind always went to at this time was whether she should stay in the psychology field. What was she doing helping others when she couldn't help herself? Maybe some of her professors were correct when they questioned her emotional adaptability to become a psychologist. Nonetheless, she always went back to what Helen DeJarden had said to her, "*Your only limits are those that you impose upon yourself. Do not dwell in the skepticism of others. Many people will want you to fail. Somehow it makes them more secure.*"

During this time, which to her seemed like a lifetime, Franclynne's mind continually pulled her back to the rape. She recalled it with such intensity that she could feel her body spasm with fear and anger. She recalled that she sat in a shower for almost two days afterwards, trying desperately to rinse the shame off of her skin. It didn't work then and had never worked since. She was still drawn to the water, hoping the heat would cool her desperation. Maybe that was why she retreated to the bathroom during the wee hours of the night.

Franclynne still had a few hours until she needed to dress. She willed herself to get off the chair and wearily made it back into the bathroom. She stared into the bathroom mirror trying to find herself. She saw a face, but it was almost unrecognizable to her. She was scared and her bones quivered. She put on a good front, but she felt as if her life was overwhelming her. Thoughts of ending her life quickly flitted through her mind, but she let them pass. The only truth she knew she found in her synesthesia. She couldn't depend on anything else - not her eyes, not her ears, not her mind, nor other people, just her nose.

Even though Franclynne was a licensed psychologist, she never felt like a therapist. She was a freak, a freak of nature. She gained local notoriety, not because of deduction or from insight. People thought she understood emotions and was able to discern the subtleties of the psyche. But as she stared at herself in the mirror, she knew she truly was not good at that. She tried even blocking her nose with cotton at times, taking away her weapon of perception. Cotton never worked, only the coffee pouch did. All of this made her feel as if she were drowning. She felt like a psychological fraud, and yet she could accurately ascertain things that no other human she knew could. As she continued to stare into the mirror, she wondered what her life would be like if she never had this gift.

In the end, none of it made any difference. This was her gift and she had to accept it. Good or bad, it was hers and it made her unique. There was a fine line between being uniquely gifted and being a freak. She often wondered if suffering always accompanied exceptional gifts, and she never knew which side of that tenuous line she was on.

During these times, Franclynne never remembered how long she stared into the mirror. Today it seemed longer than usual. Her legs weakening from the standing broke her mesmerized focus. She sat on the floor regaining her strength. She glanced at the clock and realized that if she wanted breakfast, she needed to start dressing and making herself presentable. Time was running short and the day was not starting well. She felt the tiredness in her bones. She wanted to cry because of this drained feeling.

Angelique was a shy woman. She was bright but very passive and rarely said no to anybody, for fear of angering them. Relationships created conflict for her because she would give into requests and demands that were generally unreasonable. She could not understand why she people took advantage of her and why the men she dated were so bossy and controlling. Didn't kindness matter in this world?

She became increasingly anxious as she sat waiting to see the psychologist. Looking at yourself is a troubling procedure. Maybe she already knew the problem, but did she really want somebody else telling her what was wrong with her? When this beautiful woman appeared at the door and announced herself as Dr. Longaire, Angelique almost smiled and turned to leave. In front of her stood this beautiful person, obviously bright and having all these wonderful gifts. In comparison to that, Angelique felt stupid and ugly. She slowly rose from her chair, and with a tiny voice said: *"Hello, Doctor, I am Angelique."* She followed Franclynne into the office as if she were going to her execution.

Angelique sat in Franclynne's office as quiet as a church mouse. Franclynne had difficulty engaging the young woman, as she seemed to disappear into the arm of the chair. Her nose told her that this woman was feeling blind fear. Franclynne sat quietly, not wanting to make her more anxious.

It took a while, but Angelique finally said,

"I am a quiet person. I don't mean to waste your time".

"You are not wasting my time. It is important to feel comfortable before you speak. But may I ask you a question?"

Do you enjoy flowers?"

"I don't understand".

"Flowers, do you like flowers?"

"I guess."

"Wait, I have something to show you".

Franclynne rose and exited her office. She returned with a planter with beautiful stargazer lilies.

"Aren't they beautiful, Angelique? Notice how their red and white leaves turn downward. The woman in California who invented called them stargazer because their leaves faced downward. Here, smell them, Angelique."

She handed the pot to Angelique. The girl stared at the flowers, as if not knowing how to respond.

"Smell them, Angelique, clear your mind and just allow yourself to enjoy the aroma and the beauty of these creations."

Angelique stared at the pot as if not knowing what to do. It was as if she had never experienced the fragrance. She seemed in a daze. Inside she thought, *"I am in distress and this woman is showing me lilies!"* But Franclynne persisted, again asking,

"Do you enjoy the aroma?"

Angelique seemed to snap out of her daze and smelled the lilies. Franclynne smiled to herself reaching out taking the pot.

"Tell me, Angelique, what brings you here today?"

Angelique began to tear up. Her hands went up to her face and she bent over her knees.

"My life is in a shamble, and I don't know how to fix the problems."

"Well start from the beginning so I will understand what the problems are"

Angelique blushed, lifted her head slightly, and then immediately put her head down, sinking it almost into her chest.

"I was arrested."

"For what?"

"I ran a stop sign and then resisted arrest"

"Arrested- you don't seem like the criminal type."

Now Angelique stared at Franclynne.

"I never even cut school. It's so embarrassing, I will never be able to show myself to others when they hear about this."

"So what was so important that you resisted arrest?"

"I needed to get home."

"What was so urgent? Was somebody injured?"

Again, Angelique sunk her head into her chest. Then she raised her head and stared with teary eyes at Franclynne. Franclynne reached out and put her hand on Angelique's hand.

"No, don't tell me. I can tell it bothers you too much. But don't worry, we will figure it out together."

The odor had changed so dramatically that it bothered Franclynne. She knew this woman lived in trauma. Angelique looked into her eyes. This time, without warning, Angelique pulled her sleeve up revealing a series of black and blue marks. She then pointed to what looked like needle marks by her elbow. Angelique began to cry and Franclynne stood and hugged her.

"It's okay, Angelique. We will figure it out. You have taken a very important step today. It shows courage, Angelique."

She raised her eyes to meet Franclynne's gaze. "I've *never had courage before"*.

Franclynne shook her head in disagreement. *"You've always had it Angelique. It has just been hiding. But now you have found it and it will lead us on a new journey. We will find the real Angelique."*

Angelique jumped up as if shot out of a cannon. She walked over to Franclynne and put her arms out. Franclynne rose and the two embraced. It made Angelique feel more secure that she made the correct decision to come for this help. Unbeknownst to her, it helped Franclynne as well.

The two stood in an embrace for a few seconds. The last thing Angelique said before she left the office was, *"He hurts me."*

Prelude

The streets were generally deserted, as she walked to the bus stop. She felt alone, very alone. She had lived alone for many years, but this was the first time she really felt isolated, cut off. She had always had a game in play. Now she just felt bewildered. Bringing out many deeply repressed demons was extremely upsetting. She never really missed her mother or father. Yes, they tried as parents, but they were overmatched. She was a defiant adolescent who knew how to deflect blame and manipulate emotions. She rarely thought about her upbringing, but today, for some reason, the past came streaming back into her consciousness. Of all of the things she thought she did not care about, now she felt regret at her behavior and the pain it must have caused those who loved her, and in an instant realized she also loved them.

She had not spoken to her parents or her siblings in over five years. They sent cards and presents, but over the last year or so, dates and holidays had been forgotten. She was always too self-engrossed to respond. She smirked to herself that this showed that they really did not care, but now she was starting to realize that the blame had been laid squarely on her shoulders. Maybe she should contact them, apologize for her nastiness, and start again if they would let her.

She got to the bus stop and sat on the bench. The tears began flowing as she continued this emotional dialysis. What had she done? She was only twenty-six, yet she had sabotaged every relationship that meant something to her.

She was alone, and feeling very guilty. He was truly better off without her. Maybe everyone was. Twenty-six and at the end of her emotional rope.

Chapter XV

Sean's wife had finally reached the end of her patience. Since his stroke, he had changed so dramatically that she could no longer afford to minimize or deny his reactions. He had forced her into sadomasochistic sexual rituals, which made her question her own values. She was embarrassed and ashamed at what she was allowing to occur. She had tried talking to her friends about it, but could not bring herself to say the words, or admit to herself the true extent of what was happening. She found herself returning to the church. She prayed regularly for Sean to return to his old self, but she knew that was a pipe dream. She even tried speaking with her priest, but even with him, she could not admit what was going on. She was too humiliated.

Finally, the straw that broke the camel's back, was when Sean began taking his angry disposition out on the children. Somehow, she felt obliged to accept some of his nastiness, but the children, they were innocent victims and needed to be protected.

One day Sean came home in an obviously irritated mood. His clothes were disheveled and he looked terrible. Beth had already learned some of the warning signs that indicated he needed to be alone because he was on the precipice of a volcanic explosion. One of the telltale signs was his clothes. Sean was always a meticulous dresser. He could be somewhat compulsive with his dressing rituals. When he liked a product, he went overboard with that merchandise. Rather than buy one roll-on deodorant, he would buy five. Their bedroom had begun looking like a warehouse with extra supplies that Sean would purchase.

However, this day was different. He appeared extra angry, almost fuming. Something had happened. Of course, Sean would never talk to Beth about any of his problems, such as if something bothered him at work. She recalled that he used to do that, but since the stroke, he would just grunt and walk the other way. Their communication had disappeared, vanished into the misery of the stroke.

The children had always been happy to see their father when he returned home. But over the past few months, Beth had noticed them pulling away, almost hiding when it was close to time for him to return home. Besides the sexual issues, Sean had also become increasingly verbally aggressive at home. He treated them all like prisoners or slaves. The oldest child, Ellie, who was eight, asked Beth what dad was always angry about. Of course, Beth had no clear answer to give her, other than he had a bad day at work. Ellie followed that up with the comment, *"When will he have a good day, Mom?"*

There was another sign of the increasing trouble at home. The children were beginning to go downhill at school. In fact, both of their teachers had called, asking Beth if there was a problem that was bothering the children. Beth's responses were always something to the effect of, *"Our family is under a lot of stress."*

Today, Beth, for some reasons, did not follow her unwritten rules and asked Sean when he returned home what he would like for dinner. Without warning, Sean exploded, rushed at Beth and pushed her up against the wall. His eyes were ablaze with anger, and she immediately felt her life was in jeopardy. This happened in the living room, in front of both children. Beth was now firmly locked against the wall with Sean's hand around her neck. His face was within an inch of hers and he was having some difficulty saying words clearly.

"You know, bitch, that I don't like to be disturbed when I am upset".

Beth tried to nod her head in affirmation. He pushed against her harder, and squeezed her throat. *"So why did you do it?"* Spittle was coming from his mouth, slapping her face. She tried to speak. *"I'm sorry Sean, but you're hurting me."* *"Shut up, bitch. I have a mind to punish you for your insolence".* He raised his other hand as if going to hit her, but he yelled and looked down, before his arm could swing. Biting his leg was Theodore, the couple's youngest child.

"Get off me!" Sean yelled and shook his leg. Theodore let go with his mouth and yelled, *"Let go of Mommy, you're hurting her!"* Sean let go of Beth's throat, and with his right-hand, swatted Theodore. The young child was sent almost halfway across the room by the impact of the blow. Instantly, Sean yelled again, as Ellie was hitting him on the back with one of her toys. He let go of Beth and turned to face Ellie. His face was still in a rage, and he lifted his fisted hand to hit the child. Immediately, Beth began yelling, *"Stop, Sean,"* and she grabbed his arm so he couldn't hit Ellie. Theodore had now gotten back up and rushed his father in an attempt to protect both his mother and sister. But before he

could arrive, the family dog, Chuck, attacked Sean barring his teeth. Sean grabbed the small dog by the neck and began strangling him. Ellie, Theodore, and Beth tried in vain to get Sean off Chuck, but in what seemed like an instant, the dog went lifeless, and Sean dropped him. The children were stunned and immediately ran to Chuck, but he was gone. Sean stood over them, breathing hard. He gave out a loud yell and said, "*I always hatred that useless mutt*". Then he turned and left the house.

It was not easy getting over this incident. The children and Beth all huddled together crying. None of them really understood why this had happened. Ellie asked, "*Did we do something wrong, Mommy. Is that why daddy is angry at us?*" The only answer that Beth had was "*No, sweetheart, we did nothing wrong.*" Ellie was holding onto Beth for dear life, and Theodore was standing and crying, looking at Chuck. Finally, Ellie said, "*I hate him, Mommy. I hate Daddy.*" Beth held her tighter. "*Mommy, I hear you cry every night. Is daddy hurting you?*" Beth looked at Ellie and said, "*Don't worry, we will be airight*". Theodore began walking slowly back to Chuck. "*Is he dead, Mommy?*" "*Yes, Theodore, he is dead.*" "*But I don't want him to be dead!*" "*Neither do I, Theodore, neither do I.*"

So, two nights later, after Sean had tied her to the bed and slapped her during intercourse, Beth waited until he fell asleep. Fortunately, Sean slept very deeply, and nothing seemed to wake him until he was ready. She dressed, woke the children, had them pack small bags of clothes, and packed them in the car. The children quickly fell asleep, but Beth cried her way to her parent's house. It was a five-hour drive. She left no note, for what could she say? "I'm leaving you, Sean. Go to hell!" She knew leaving was her only option. The children had to be protected.

When she arrived at her parent's house, Beth finally broke down. Her mom carried the children upstairs to their spare bedrooms, and Beth and her Dad sat in the kitchen. Beth emptied everything, every lurid detail. She held nothing back, she had to get it out, to somebody. She and her father cried and hugged many times. Her father's emotions varied between anger and compassion for his daughter and grandchildren. After Beth's mother came down, Beth retold the story. Another round of crying and hugs followed. At one point, her father left the room and, in a few minutes, returned with his hunting rifle. "*No, John, no, that's not the solution*". "*So help me god, I'll kill that son of a bitch.*" "*John, we must protect the children and our daughter. Now is not the time for revenge".* Beth's father broke down, sobbing into his hands.

The next day, John took Beth down to the courthouse and she filed for full custody of the two children. Beth's mother had convinced her that she needed to find a therapist to help her with her transition back to who she really was. Her return to normalcy had finally begun. John also contacted a local attorney with whom who he had some previous contact. The attorney, in hearing John's trembling voice, asked that both Beth and her father come in to see him that day. After telling him what had happened, the attorney returned to court and filed for a restraining order to deny Sean access to either Beth or the children.

That action led to a court battle. Fortunately, before Beth had left the house, she had taken a picture of Chuck's dead body lying on the floor. In the first court appearance, Sean had to be escorted out of the courtroom by the police because he lost his temper when he heard the allegations against him. He stood up in court pointing at Beth yelling, "Bitch, *bitch, I will kill you!"* Numerous times the judge had to remind Sean's attorney to control his client. Eventually, the judge called the bailiff and the police assigned to his court had Sean removed.

This judge had a reputation for not taking parental rights away from either parent. Beth's attorney felt that they were operating at a disadvantage because of the Judge's reputation. He recalled a case in which a father held mother hostage, tied the children up, and pointed a loaded rifle at the mother. The standoff lasted for over four hours. Eventually the father backed down. However, this judge still awarded him visitation with his four children.

Eventually, Beth's lawyer convinced him to interview the children to determine what they saw. After the interviews, the ruling was that Sean would be allowed supervised visitation with somebody appointed by the court. It was not what Beth wanted, but her attorney convinced her it was the best they could get. The judge also mandated to attend a local anger management group.

Prelude

Jillian decided to pray for the first time as she was lying in bed, drenched in her own self-pity. She was never sure whether she believed in a god, but she needed someone to talk with, and believed that he was always on call. She lay on her bed staring at the light above her. She kept seeing Bobby's gentle face telling her how wonderful she was. If he only knew, he would have run for the hills. It took until 4 a.m. but she finally drifted off to sleep. She already knew she could not go into work, but it didn't worry her much, as she sensed the manager had a thing for her. There would be no ramifications. At 2 am she accepted the fact that she did have to go back to work. She could not run away again. She concluded she had left a few jobs because of not wanting to face something, and she had to stop that negative behavior. She was twenty-six and she had to act like a woman, not a bitchy, spoiled child. She had to pay for her emotional crimes and face the music, the consequences of her own behavior. She had run away from education, she had run away from her parent's love, she had run away from numerous men, and she had run away from Bobby. But she had to stop running from herself before she could rectify the other areas.

By midnight, she had been desperate. She wondered if Bobby would cry if he knew she was dead. No, she knew she would never kill herself, but her misery and self-pity were overwhelming her.

Her dreams that early morning were of drifting, unstable, changing with the flow of the wind. When she awoke, she felt the pillow next to her body. She had been clinging to it throughout the night. She laid her head on it and opened her eyes. The sun peaked through her blinds, and she could hear the birds singing their morning melodies. She stared at the window. A young robin had landed on the outside windowsill. It seemed to stare at her, and then it fluttered its wings and took off; maybe a sign, a foreshadowing of her new direction in life.

Then the horrible realization came back. She was alone. The thought was frightening. One thing she had always counted on was that she could easily pick up another relationship. She knew though that she could not jump back into another emotional swamp. She had to learn to live with herself, something she had always avoided.

Jillian hatred mirrors. Yes, she was vain, and had to use them for makeup and such, but to use them as a way to peer into you own psyche – she could just not do that. She had to learn to turn inward, evaluate herself and her motives, and not look outward. But diagnosing her emotions made her exhausted and discouraged. It was a daunting task. She decided that before she could face the world, and herself, she needed more rest. She returned to her bed.

Chapter XVI

"Are you Dr. Longaire?"

"Can I help you, officer?"

"There is a woman downstairs. She had been arrested for resisting arrest. She has been bailed out by an old man. She is an odd woman, Dr., but she keeps asking for a psychologist; specifically, one whom she said is young, blond woman with an exceptional insight into others. She was unable to recall a name, but... I thought the description fit you. Would you like to go downstairs with me and meet her?"

"This is a strange request, officer, but let's go see what her problem is."

"Oh, my god, it's you!" and she began running toward the woman. La also seemed transformed by the realization and ran to meet her friend, as well. The two women, very much an odd couple, hugged each other with what seemed like desperation. They both were crying with joy. The officer stood in surprise as he watched the interaction. It was truly an odd scene, a tall statuesque, blond woman, hugging a frumpy, smaller, dark-haired lady. One dressed to the nines, the other looking like a street person.

"I thought I would never see you again,"

Franclynne said, with her face wet with her tears. La seemed unable to speak. Seeing Franclynne again brought back memories of Helen DeJarden. But, she had found another person she could trust. Without a word, she jumped forward again, grabbing Franclynne. Again, the two again hugged, as if they were long lost lovers. Finally, Franclynne said, *"What are you doing here? Why were you arrested?"* La shrugged her shoulders and said, *"I did nothing, I was just standing and looking at my bridge"*. Now, with anger, Franclynne turned to the officer and said: *"Do you know who this is, do you know what you've done?"* The officer looked stunned, not knowing how to respond.

La looked at Franclynne. With a questioning glance, she said, *"Did you bail me out?"* Again, Franclynne appeared surprised. *"I didn't even know you were here."* Franclynne turned to the officer and asked, *"Officer, can you find out for us who posted bail for La?"* The officer returned and said, *"She was bailed out by a man named Aaron." "I never heard of this man, La. Do you know him?"* La nodded her head in affirmation. *"Who is he?"* Franclynne inquired. *"I gave my house to him." "What? You did what?"*

Prelude

It was nearly noon when Jillian was finally fully awake. It was not a bad dream as reality rushed back into her consciousness. She slowly walked into her bathroom to pee and brush her teeth. Standing by the sink, she looked at her swollen eyes in the mirror. They were bloodshot and puffy. However, that was not the real issue. As she stared at herself, she felt embarrassed.

Tears began flowing again, but she quickly gained control, trying to force herself out of the pity party. She put on black shorts and made her way into the kitchen. Today would be the start of her new life. She had to learn how to be human. She already knew how to be an asshole. The coffee smelled wonderful. It was the most pleasant sensation she felt, as it distracted her, for a brief instant, from what she considered her sorry life.

She had to call her parents. It would be difficult to apologize, but it had to be done. The only way she could absolve herself and her actions, was if she were first forgiven. She pictured a ladder reaching to the clouds. It would be a long climb, but standing still was no longer an option. Her demons had caught up with her and it was time to pay her dues. Life sucks when you open your eyes. In many ways, it's better to stay asleep.

She had decided that today she would spend the day in the park feeding the ducks. She felt lost and they were solid companions. She always admired ducks; they always seemed to know where they were going, and they did it with flare and beauty.

The coffee was finished, and so was the half-stale bagel. It was time to face the day. Jillian opened her door, and was shocked by what she saw. There it was, on her stoop. A red rose! *"Son of a bitch,"* she thought.

Chapter XVII

Captain O'Brian had been waiting for quite some time. He was a little confused because it was unlike Franclynne to be late. He had more than a passing interest in her - from the moment he saw her he was immediately attracted to her. That was not that unusual, as many men were immediately attracted to this woman. O'Brian was still a very young man. His rise in the police force was dramatic. No person had ever risen as fast and as high as he had. He had quickly become a detective, but unlike other detectives, he was not assigned to a division. His exceptional instincts had forced the higher ups to make him a "free agent". He took on difficult cases from all over the city, and often solved them. He was the 'wonder boy' of the department. It was not long before he was promoted to captain.

However, with all his success, O'Brian longed for a relationship. He had had a few in the past, but they had all left quite a bitter taste in his mouth. He seemed to be attracted to woman who did not want to love him, but only wanted to control and misuse him. His longest relationship had lasted for six months. Her name was Patty, and although very attractive, she was a fruitcake. Patty flaunted her good looks. A young, attractive man couldn't pass without her either making a comment to him, or to O'Brian. O'Brian himself was an attractive man, well built, and exercised on a regular basis. But when he was with Patty, he felt less than acceptable.

O'Brian had considered himself a better than average sex partner, but Patty was rarely satisfied. The breakup began when she began trying to alienate him from his friends and family. With all her female bravado, Patty was quite insecure, a trait O'Brian only realized months after the breakup.

When he told her he was leaving, Patty dropped to knees and began crying. This behavior seemed more of a rehearsed play, designed for a specific purpose, rather than displaying true emotions. Surprisingly, O'Brian almost began laughing at the make-believe outburst.

It was funny, but whenever his thoughts returned to his loneliness, they also returned to Patty. He really did not understand the connection, for in many ways, he was lonelier with her than without her. Nonetheless, he was daydreaming when he noticed a figure standing in front of his desk. It took a second for him to escape from his daze. His eyes focused on this beautiful image in front of him. Her face was strangely distorted in emotion.

"You seem as if there is a problem. I hope everything is okay."

Appearing distracted, Franclynne looked at O'Brian and said, *"Do you know a man named Aaron."*

"Aaron, Aaron? Do you mean, JJ Aaron?

Still appearing to be distracted, Franclynne nodded her head in affirmation.

"Of course, I know of JJ Aaron. The question is, why do you not know who he is?"

"So, who is he?"

"He is a billionaire. He was a programmer who developed many computer games, probably many of those you know, but don't realize that he developed them. He is also a philanthropist, giving large sums of money to many charities."

"A billionaire?"

"Why do you ask?"

"My friend was arrested for nothing, and he bailed her out."

"Really?"

"Your friend must be connected."

Franclynne smiled. "Actually, she's disconnected. "

"What do you mean?"

Franclynne laughed, "I'll *explain another time".*

"So, Captain, why did you call me to come in? Have I broken any laws?"

"Well, Doc, we have a problem with which we need your help."

"I'm listening."

"We seem to have a serial rapist in our area. There has also been a murder that we are not sure is connected".

"How can I help Captain?"

"Doc, I've asked you before, please call me John."

Franclynne gave that funny look of hers, and responded,

"I am more comfortable with Captain."

"Franclynne, have you ever heard of the Cult of the Souls? Have any of your clients mentioned this?"

"No, Captain, what is the Cult of the Souls?"

O'Brian looked very frustrated. He leaned back in his chair. *"The Cult of the Souls is a computer game. I believe it is on the 'dark web'. It's a strange game. You get points for the game by things that you do. Getting drunk gets you points, as do getting stoned, cutting yourself, and strangling your sexual partner. You get points for all of those actions, including much more bizarre actions. We believe that hurting others will get you numerous points. We also believe that the murder might be connected to this game."*

"So how would I get these points?"

O'Brian gave a disgusted frown. *"You send pictures to a site and receive your points."*

"Can't those things be traced?"

"Well, they seem to have figured out a way to block such an investigation."

"All right, Captain, if I hear anything I will call."

Franclynne began walking out of the office. O'Brian called after her.

"By the way, Doc, I believe JJ Aaron, invented the game."

This last comment stopped Franclynne in her tracks. She turned back to him.

"How did you find out about this game, Captain?"

"One of the officers put 2 and 2 together and figured it out."

Franclynne gave him a strange look. O'Brian shook his head and said, "He *had a friend who played it."*

"Oh, one other thing," Still standing with her back to O'Brian, Franclynne said, *"Yes?"*

"A tattoo." "A tattoo?"

"Yes, most of the gamers have one."

"What does it look like?"

"I'm not sure" said O'Brian. And with that, she left the room.

Prelude

There it was, a red rose. Her eyes were not deceiving her. She stood transfixed on the flower, blinking her eyes, but each time she opened them, the rose did not vanish. Jillian was stunned, frozen in time. She took a deep breath and slowly went down on her knees. She gently picked the blossom off the ground. It was no longer a flower for her; it was a symbol, a harbinger of change in her life. She cuddled it, almost as a mother would hold a crying infant. She began slowly rocking, and found that she was humming a song as she sat outside of her apartment door. But how could she love this man when she could not love herself? The change in herself had begun. Could she really go backwards and renew this relationship?

An older woman, one of Jillian's neighbors, opened her door, preparing for a shopping trip. She saw Jillian and stopped in her tracks. *"Are you alright, child?"* Still rocking and humming, Jillian smiled and turned her head to the woman. A big smile crossed her face, and she nodded her head. The woman smiled in return and went on her way.

But as she sat, another thought interrupted her sense of bliss. *"Why was the rose here?"* Did it mean Bobby wanted her back, or was he just returning the rose that she left on his door, indicating that he had had enough of her? The rocking stopped. He would not answer the door, and he brought back the rose. Maybe this was not positive at all. She wanted Bobby to want her, but she had mixed feelings. She was finding her emerging self and did not want to move backwards into the life she was trying so hard to change. But what if Bobby actually wanted her back, how could she refuse?

Jillian had not expected this bump in the road. She had made up her mind to change, to grow into a person she could admire, and now a flower stood in her way. The flower was pulling her back into her former world. Pulling her back onto a path she had promised herself to end. She was at a crossroads.

Chapter XVIII

Today Franclynne had two clients, one was Angelique, and the other was a woman who called because she had left her husband who had suffered a dramatic personality change after a stroke. Her name was Beth.

Angelique showed up on time. When she entered the office, Franclynne noticed the fear in her aroma again.

"I'm glad you decided to return. Before you left last time, you indicted that your boyfriend was very controlling and he hurt you. Can we talk about this?"

"I'm glad you brought this up. I can't talk to anybody about my fear. If my boyfriend knew I was here, he would punish me."

"Punish you how?"

"Sometimes he hits me, sometimes he takes away my phone or my wallet, and sometimes he forces me into uncompromising sexual acts that I have rejected in the past. It's the only way, he says, that I can show forgiveness."

"How do you feel about that?"

"I used to resent it, but over time, he has convinced me that he is always right and I am always wrong."

Angelique stopped and tears began to appear on her cheeks.

"May I tell you some other things, Franclynne?"

"That's why I am here, Angelique. Everything you say here stays between us."

"He wears a camera during sex. He has a number of videos of me that he threatens to put online if I don't do what he says."

Franclynne cringed inside. She remembered some of the abuse she had experienced. Her rapist had also made videos of her. *"Keep talking, Angelique."*

"He also has an app on my phone where he can hear my conversations."

"Did you bring your phone in with you?"

"I left it in the car"

"Smart, Angelique."
"Why did you decide to come for therapy?"
The woman bent her head, staring at her knees.
"I can't live like this anymore. I feel like a slave."
"What stops you from leaving?"
"I'm scared."

She hesitated, and then said, "Do you know what scares me the most?"

She stopped again, swallowed hard and said, *"He plays this crazy game. It's called the, 'Cult of the Souls'. He gets points for hurting me. So sometimes, for no reason, he will cut me to get to a new level in his game. I feel like I live in terror of this game. When he plays I get scared. I am afraid it will lead to more pain for me."*

"We have a lot of work to do, Angelique. Let's get started. But first, let me tell you about my own traumatic history."

Franclynne was happy that Angelique had opened up about her fears with the boyfriend. However, she felt she was only touching the surface of the pain that this young woman was feeling. To get past the surface, she believed that opening up about her own traumatic past would bond the two. However, doing so was a challenge for Franclynne. It meant dealing with the memories that continually plague her throughout the night. At some level, she knew that it would help Angelique to talk about her trauma, but she also felt it would help her to open up about the pain that was gnarring at her. They would both benefit.

As she prepared to begin telling this young woman about herself, she knew, by staring at her face, that there was more, much more to her story. It was not just the way she held her eyes; it was her aroma as well.

Prelude

Jillian picked up the phone. This would be the most difficult call she had ever made. She had started to call many times. She even dialed the number a few times only to hang up before somebody answered. She knew this was an important turning point in her life and she had to have courage. She had almost decided not to let the rose deter her from the course that she had chosen. Jillian knew that her resolve was not hard cast, and she knew it could dissolve with little encouragement.

Her hands shook as she dialed the number. One ring and Jillian could feel the sweat building on her forehead. It rang a second time, and she began hoping no one was home. Would she leave a message, or just call back later?

Then the phone was picked up and she heard hesitation.

"Hello".

"Hello", Jillian responded. Her voice shaky. The other person did not respond, answering her with silence.

"I know I needed to call you".

Again silence, but she thought she heard her mother softly crying on the other end. Jillian swallowed and somehow retrieved her voice to continue speaking.

"I am calling to apologize to you. I know I've hurt you by my actions, and it has been weighing on my mind." She could hear the other person breathing, and it came to thought that her mother did not know how to respond to her apology.

"I want you to know that these are not just word. I have been reviewing my life, and I know I have to change my ways."

The other person seemed to sigh on the other end. Jillian now had tears rolling down her cheek. *"You know I love you".*

"I love you too, Jillian. I always have. From the first time I saw you I was in love with you. I had been praying for this day for what seemed like forever."

Jillian put down the phone and started sobbing. It took almost a minute for her to get her emotions under control, her voice still choppy and the words not really coming clear.

"I miss you so much. I have been dreaming about you."

"I have had many of the same dreams, Jillian."

Again, Jillian broke down. The other person said, *"Are you Okay?"*

Jillian swallowed and wiped her face. She picked up the phone again.

"I have to go. I don't think I can talk anymore right now."

"It's OKAYAY, Jillian."

"I love you, Mom!"

"I love you too, Jillian. Don't ever forget it."

"Will you please tell Dad I love and miss him as well? I don't think I can talk anymore."

"It's OKAYAY, Jillian. We both love and miss you. Will we see you soon?"

"I hope so. Mom, I hope so."

"I love you, Jillian. But before you hang up, I have to tell you that your call has made this one of the best days of my life. I know now that my prayers have been heard and listened to. Oh my god, I have waited so very long to hear your voice."

"I love you, Mom."

Chapter XIX

La was torn. She hated living indoors, yet she desired closeness to Franclynne. When she hugged her, she realized that Franclynne was the only remnant she had of Dr. DeJarden. Right after she had murdered the kidnapper and held her friend in her arms as life drained out of her, La had thought why couldn't Helen live and Franclynne die? But that feeling was only brief and faded quickly from her psyche. Now, seeing Franclynne again, she realized how much she actually cared about her.

When Franclynne realized that La had no place to live, she demanded that she move in with her. This opportunity for La was important in that she wanted to take care of Franclynne whom she saw as a scared young woman. La was no psychologist, but she could feel that Franclynne needed her. Other than her rats, La had never really felt needed. It was a new and wonderful feeling for her. After thinking about it for an hour, La decided that she would move in with Franclynne, at least for the time being.

Franclynne, as well, had some mixed feelings about this new arrangement. She knew La, and yet she really did not know her. She knew she was brave, and when she wanted something, she could be daunting. Even though La hadn't showered in days, her aroma was fine as well.

The first night that La was with Franclynne she heard a strange noise at 4 o'clock in the morning. When she investigated, she found Franclynne on the floor of the bathroom, huddled in the corner, shaking like a leaf. La went in and sat down next to her. Franclynne's face was red with tears, and her eyes looked terrified. La said nothing, but instinctively put her arms around her friend and began rocking her. She did not know what else to do. The two sat together for 45 minutes. Eventually, Franclynne fell asleep in her friend's arms. La dozed as well.

When the sun arose, Franclynne was back in her bed, and La was back on the couch. Franclynne entered her small living room area and went over to La who was still sleeping. She kissed the woman on the head, left her a note, and went to her office.

The note read:

Good morning La,

Let me first thank you for last night. I had not been comforted like that in a long time. But now you know my secret. I am terrorized by the night and my past. It is not something I talk about because the words hurt too much.

Thank you again for your compassion, but if you find me in the bathroom again tomorrow, please just let me be. I will recover on my own.

Franclynne.

Beth was anxious as she entered Franclynne's office. Franclynne could smell the anxiety, but there was something else. Beth was wearing a perfume that was confusing Franclynne's sensitive nose. She sat down in the big comfortable chair and was very frigidity. She did not give Franclynne eye contact, but was staring off into space. Franclynne remained silent as she sat next to her. The two sat silently until Beth, with her face already wet with tears, turned to Franclynne and said: *"I have no parents."*

Now, on the floor, Franclynne knew this was not just an emotional issue. She said nothing, but continued rubbing Beth's back. Finally, when Franclynne realized this deluge was not stopping, she said, *"Beth, don't worry, whatever the problem is, we'll figure it out. Together Beth, we'll figure it out together."*

Still on the floor, Beth lowered her hands from her face, looking at Franclynne directly, and shook her head *"no"*. Then she said, *"There is no solution"*. Finally, Beth began settling down, and started pulling herself up off the floor. The two women returned to their chairs. Beth smiled and said, *"My husband had a stroke."*

She stopped and took a few breaths to control herself. *"He was the nicest man, but then the stroke did something to him. He became aggressive and nasty. He started forcing me to do things of which I am still ashamed. But then his anger and aggression was turned on our two young children. I even believed that he touched our youngest child while giving her a bath. My daughter, Ellie, became fearful of him, and did not want to leave my side. Then one day he hit Ellie, and I took the children in the middle of the night and left. I went to my adoptive parent's house. You see, I was adopted when I was six. My birth mother died in a car accident when she was killed by a drunk driver."*

"I'm sorry, Beth."

"Thanks. But that's not my problem."

"My problem, Dr. Longaire, is that I am dying."

Franclynne stiffened, and began to speak, but Beth held up her hand and said, *"Wait, Dr. there's more to this tragedy."* She took a deep breath and straightened here posture. *"I'm sorry for my emotionality, but my life is overwhelming me."*

"It's okay, Beth, continue with your story."

"I filed for custody of the children in the court. I didn't want my husband even visiting them. Court was a horrible experience. The judge sent an attorney to talk with and represent the children. I was not in their meetings, but the attorney's report indicated that he believed that the children should have contact with their father." She swallowed deeply, and wiped her face. *"The court said, that even though I could have a restraining order to keep Sean away from me, he needed to have visitation with the children. The court also said that unless I can prove either sexual abuse or that Sean was a danger to their wellbeing, he needed to have visitation. Luckily, the court stipulated that the visits be supervised, and they appointed a woman to be present at the visitations to ensure the children's safety. After a few visits, the woman also submitted a summary of the sessions to the court indicating that the children were afraid of Sean. She said they would not sit next to him and they flinched when he touched them. But, she continued, there was nothing in Sean's behavior that was unusual for a parent".* Beth stopped again to wipe tears. *"So, my children are terrified to be with Sean, and their weekly supervised visits scare them. And I have no say in any of this! The court has made it clear that its intent in to increase the meetings over time, eventually giving father unsupervised time. And when I die, Doctor, the court will probably give him custody of the children."* Again, the tears began coming. Finally, she looked at Franclynne and said: *"I can't let that monster get my children!"* Franclynne realized that it wasn't death that scared her, it was this!

The café she chose was very sweet and European looking. Obviously, Angelique did not know any of the other patrons that sat around her. She had chosen a table outside so she could watch people as she thought. It was not out of fear, but just something to keep her eyes busy as her brain processed. The only problem with this cute café was that it had too many choices. There were over 10 flavors of coffee. Angelique always had trouble with choice. It seemed like even the simplest of decisions left her frozen with hesitancy. But even after she finally decided on an African Roast Brand, the decision of whether or not to have a muffin with it took over her thought. And then, what kind of muffin? The café had five kinds. At that point, Angelique began to laugh at herself. Here she was thinking about changing her life completely, and she could not make up her mind what kind of muffin to eat. The waiter came back to the table, and she instinctively said, *"Blueberry"*. The waiter smiled and Angelique smiled back. She believed that he understood her muffin dilemma.

Angelique put down the coffee and placed her hands over her eyes. She allowed the images to stream, not wanting to repress or block them anymore. She recalled lying in her bed feeling a hand moving up her thigh towards her behind. She could almost feel it now and her legs began to shiver. She opened her eyes and saw the sitter standing over her, and before she could speak, he was on top of her. She vividly recalled him entering her and the pain that was involved. She remembered screaming and having him cover her mouth with his hand. And then the images became more verbal. The sitter said, "If *you tell anyone about this, I will kill your parents and your sister."* When she woke the next day, Angelique kept quiet. It took a number of days before she really put words together in a sentence, having only been responding with just "Yes" and "No". And then, one day, she woke up and the thoughts had disappeared. She had buried them in her subconscious until now. Until now!

She also realized that words were very powerful for her. She bought into them very easily, even though she came to realize most were just smoke, with nothing behind them. She had to stop being so naïve. She realized how disappointed she was in herself, and how desperate she had been, not only to enter into this type of relationship, but to stay in it for the length of time she did. *"What a fool"* she thought. She was not blaming her boyfriend at all. She fell for the routine and bought into it. She rationalized that you could not blame a snake for biting you, it is what they do, natural for them. However, she also realized that you can't change a snake into a puppy. They are what they are, and they follow their destined path. But she was determined to change her path. Angelique banged the table, getting everyone in the café to turn their heads toward her. She raised her hand, smiled and everyone went back to his or her own business.

Angelique stared at the half drunk cup of coffee in her hand. She had an urge. She lifted her hand and smashed the cup on the floor. Other people screamed at the sound and the waiter came running over. "*I'm sorry, I'm very clumsy."* Angelique took out a twenty-dollar bill, handed it to the waiter, and walked out.

Chapter XX

Chemotherapy was not a pleasant process Beth had already begun losing her hair, and there were days when she could not eat. *"Things taste like metal"* she would say. She had started to develop sores in her mouth, and she thought that two of her teeth were loose. Franclynne had gone with her to her last doctor's appointment. The physician was gentle but explained the truth for Beth. This was an aggressive cancer. The treatments were not having the desired effect. He was sorry. The doctor left the office and the two-woman sat crying in each other's arms. It was what some people would call a 'dead man's hand'. Franclynne had grown close to Beth in a very brief period of time, and she felt the pain as well. She had also grown close to the children and was extremely worried about their fate. Her sensitive nose had told her that Beth was not lying about her husband. What she related was truth.

After the hearing, Beth and Franclynne left together, but in the hallway leading to the door, the social worker that ran the anger group was talking with one of the officers on duty. The two were smiling and laughing about something that Franclynne could not hear. She walked up to the pair, and their demeanor immediately changed. Franclynne smiled at the two to lighten the moment, but the two appeared fear struck. Franclynne said, *"Ms. Johnson, may I speak with you for a moment?"* Johnson nodded and bid the officer farewell, promising to speak with him again, soon. "How *can I help you, Dr. Longaire?"* *"Well you said some very nice things about Mr. Whitford in the courtroom, and I was wondering if you actually believed them?"* Johnson looked amazed by the comment, and immediately became defensive. She straightened her stance, and folded her arms on her chest. *"What do you take me for, Dr.? Do you think I would lie to the judge?"* *" No, now that I've met you, I can sense that you were saying things you actually believe to be truth. Unfortunate though."* *"Unfortunate?"* *"Yes, unfortunate that you misread the situation so poorly."* Johnson was enraged, huffed, and turned to walk away. As she left, Franclynne called after her. *"I have time to supervise you if you need it!"*

Arriving back at the car, Franclynne immediately noticed a qualitative shift in Beth. She had clearly taken a step backwards. The court experience had hurt her on a basic cellular level. The disease was tightening its grip, like an Anaconda squeezing the air out of her body. Beth's voice was quite low and gruff. She was also having attentional issues, as she was having difficulty completing complex thoughts.

"His therapists have been saying this glowing stuff about Sean. I don't believe a word of it." "Nor do I, Beth. Nor do I. It is very difficult to read psychopaths. I know this from personal experience. They can fool even the sharpest of therapists. Ms. Johnson is a fool. I sensed her naivety when speaking with her. She can be manipulated by a smile and a nod of the head."

Beth swallowed and began coughing. *"Doc, can I have some water."*

"Of course". Beth took a tissue and continued to cough. Franclynne noticed some red spots in the tissues. "What *time should I pick you up tomorrow for your treatment?"*

"I should be ready to go by 9" *"But remember, you and the children are moving in with us."*

"I will be there. Tell me, Beth, why are you so sure that Sean is not taking his therapy seriously?"

"I have been doing some reading. I also believe Sean is a psychopath. He is fooling them all with his charm. It's like he puts on an emotional costume, making believe he is something he is not."

Beth seemed to fade. Her head rolled back, but she quickly recovered. *"I don't think my attorney is too sharp."*

"What makes you think so?"

"Well, he doesn't seem to listen to me. And, I don't really think he cares about the outcome."

"Beth, let me think on it, but maybe there is something that can be done."

Prelude

She straightened her body, swallowed hard, and knocked with the knocker. This time, she could hear movement and the door began to open. There he stood. Somehow, he looked different. She did not feel the urges she had experienced before when she had seen him in the past. She quickly appraised the situation. There really was nothing different about him. Same clothes she remembered, same posture. Nothing different, really. His face was blank, but she noticed that she felt different. She was less anxious. She had anticipated anxiety to the level of an attack, but here she stood and nothing was happening. He looked down at her. *" If you came to give me the rose, I don't want it. Please, you keep it."* Without really thinking, a lie emerged from her mouth. *"No, I wasn't going to give you the rose."*

"So why are you here?" *"I'm not sure, I think I just wanted to say goodbye."*

He broke the silence: *"Can I help you with anything else?"*

Her mind raced, but she ended up saying, *"I'm sorry I hurt you."*

His face turned sour. *"Yes, well, you should have thought of that before you decided to end our relationship."*

Silence followed, broken when he said, *"If there is nothing else, I have to go. You've wasted enough time in my life!"* And with that, he closed the door in her face.

Chapter XXI

"*Wow, I can't believe you are here. I didn't realize you were waiting.*"

He gave her a hug and escorted her into the office. He looked at his secretary and said, "*Mary I don't want to be disturbed.*"

"*How did you find me?*"

He waved his hand, and said, "*It really doesn't matter, I'm glad you're here.*"

"*I'm assuming La that you need something which is why you spent so much time trying to find me. Tell me, La, what can I do to help you?*"

La was not the best communicator. In fact, she rarely said the correct thing. She had learned that the more she spoke, the more trouble she seemed to get herself into. La sat still and finally said, "*I need money.*"

Aaron's face became serious. "Tell me, La, what you need money for?"

"*Do I have to?*"

"*Yes, La. If you want me to help you, I need to find the best way to do that*".

"*Do you trust me, La?*"

Reluctantly, La continued to avoid eye contact, but she nodded her head in affirmation. Once again, silence followed, but eventually, La spoke, "*The children. I love the children. I can't let them be hurt.*"

Aaron asked, "*Children, La? Do you have children?*"

"*They are not mine, but they are mine.*"

"*Explain, La*"

"*Their mother is dying. She does not have long to live. Franclynne has been taking her to her treatments and I have been watching the children.*"

"*Do you need money to help the mother?*"

"*I need money for a lawyer*"

"*A Lawyer? Why a lawyer?*"

"*Beth's husband is not a nice man. He hurt Beth and he hurt the children. He wants the children when Beth dies.*"

"*I see.*"

Aaron stood and came around his desk. He seemed somber, and was scratching his chin. *"Tell Beth she will get a call in a day or two."*

La stood and her face was wet from silent tears. Aaron went over to her and gave her a hug. *"Don't worry, La, if you love the children, then I also love the children. I will do everything in my power to protect you, Franclynne, and the children. Do you believe me?"*

"Let me tell you something, La. What you did for me when you met me on the street that day was the greatest act of kindness that anyone had ever done for me. I must admit, I continually search for kindness and compassion, but I rarely find it. When I do, I cherish it."

He hesitated for a moment then continued. *"My parents died when I was very young. I have no brothers, no sisters, and no children. You, La, and now Franclynne, and the children, are my family. Do not ever forget that, and do not ever hesitate to come to me with whatever problem you have. Do you understand me?"*

La again nodded her head in affirmation. Then, surprisingly she said, *"I also have no family. I love those two children more than I love life itself. Please, JJ, please help us!"* She began to cry.

"Markus, I was told that you were the most competent attorney in this county. However, as I sit here today, I still do not have unsupervised visitation with the children. What the hell is going on? I went to classes; I went to the bullshit therapist. What the hell do I have to do? Everybody wrote wonderful letters. What is the problem?"

Sean continued, *"Markus, you have not listened to me. I want you to demand certain things."*

"I'm listening, Sean, but watch your tone with me. I might work for you, but I'm too old to take your attitude very long. If it continues, you will find yourself another attorney."

"First, Markus, I want the house. It is as much mine as it is that bitches." Sean stood up. He was clearly angry and anxious. He walked back and forth in front of the attorney's desk like a caged animal. Markus could both see and feel the anxiety as Sean paced. He appeared so angry he almost could not speak. Then suddenly he stopped, and walked closer to the desk. He pounded the desk with his fist, lookd at Markus directly and said, in a spitting, less than coherent fashion: *"I want those children!"*

The attorney abruptly interrupted Sean's rant. *"Sit down, Sean."* *"No, I don't want to sit down!"* *"This discussion will not continue until you sit down."* Sean stared him in the eye and sat in the chair directly opposite the attorney. His face was distorted, as if in a grotesque mask. His eyes were wild, seemingly twice their normal size. Markus waited for a few seconds as he watched Sean's breathing to see if he was calming. Then he stood and walked around his desk to where Sean sat.

"Now you listen to me, young man. I have put up with your obnoxious behavior long enough. If you want me to remain your attorney, you will watch your mouth. Remember this, Sean, I do not like you. You are a dirty, disgusting man. I have been asking myself why I should represent you. But, let's get this straight. I am the attorney. I will do what I think is best. I will not be strong-armed by your demands. Do you understand what I am saying to you?"

Sean responded in an angry tone: *"Listen Markus, you work for me. You will do what I say, not what you want. Do you understand?"*

Markus was irritated. The vain in his forehead was bulging. However, he controlled himself with his breathing. Now made direct eye contact with Sean *"Listen, Sean, I do what I think is best. If you don't like it, fire me and find someone else."*

"I've already paid you a lot of money.

Markus walked slowly back to his chair. He opened his desk draw and pulled out an envelope. He put the envelope on the table and pushed it toward Sean.

"What the hell is this?" Sean asked in a very irritated fashion.

Markus looked at him directly and said, *"Keep your fuckin' money."*

"I'm sorry, Markus. You are correct. You are the expert in this area. I don't mean to step on your toes. But listen, I haven't been allowed to see my children without a spy. Are you a father, Markus? Well if you are, you know how I feel."

Markus adjusted his position in his seat. *"Your wife says you are dangerous. Why would she assert that Sean?"*

"You know what, Markus. I really don't know why she says those things. I think she is losing her mind. She is just making up stuff. She is dying; she is getting what they call 'chemo-brain'."

"Come on Sean, you need to be straight with me. Whatever you tell me is confidential. If I am to help you, I need to know the truth. And let

me tell you why. I do not want to be surprised in court. I need to know what she is asserting so I am able to defend you. Don't give me this 'chemo-brain' shit. What does she mean!?"

"I'm telling you the truth, Markus. There is nothing there. I am hiding nothing. I think she is a narcissist."

"Sean, this is not my first rodeo. You're hiding something. Something you do not want anyone to see. However, if your wife's attorney knows what that is, he will kill us in court. Do you understand me?"

Sean became serious. *"Markus, when she dies, I want those children!"*

"You're not listening to me, Sean. What secret are you protecting?"

The attorney stopped talking and Sean was still staring out the window. *"I think I know what the problem is".* Sean turned to the attorney with a questioning look on his face. *"The problem is your past."*

"Look, Markus, this is not a psychotherapy session. Your job is to get me custody of those children."

"Where are you from, Sean, and how did you get here. I know nothing about your past."

"You don't need to know about my past. Your job is to get me custody!"

"Why, Sean, why do you want those children?"

Sean's anger started to show again. When he had no good answer for questions, anger was his go-to response. He stood stoically by the window, biting his tongue so he wouldn't explode. *"I want those children, they are mine!"*

"The children are not objects to be played with, Sean. Why do you want those children? If I knew the answers to these questions, I could argue more forcibly in court. You just can't say, 'because'."

Sean stopped and began walking back from the window. He was quiet and still. Finally, he said, *"I'm not 100% sure why I want those children. Part of it is revenge against my wife."*

"So, this is a revenge issue, not a love issue."

Reluctantly, Sean said: *"I guess partly."*

"If your wife dies, how is it revenge?"

"She'll know I got the children. She will be in heaven, but she will know. My only wish is that I could see her face when she finds out."

Markus turned his head away. He put his hand on his chin. Finally, he said, *"I'm not sure getting you custody is in the best interests of those children."* *"What are you a social worker?"* Sean blasted back. *"Your job is to deal with the legal issues."* *"Sean, listen to me. Those are two lives we are dealing with, not points of revenge."* Markus continued to have thoughts of his own children. Would he want them raised by this man?

"I want you evaluated, Sean. I will not place those children in harm's way."

"You have a contractual obligation to me!"

"And I have a moral obligation to them."

Sean rose from his seat. His face was beet red. He pointed at Markus. He opened his mouth as if to yell, but no words came out. Finally, he said, *"Do your job, Markus!"* And with that, he left the office. The envelope remained on the desk.

Chapter XXII

The park was beautiful this time of year. There was a big pond in the middle of it, which housed both geese and ducks. The geese could be nasty, but the ducks were worth the bet. There was a willow tree draped over the lake. Underneath the willow was a bench, which was Franclynne's favorite spot. She would sit there and her mind would drift into many distant places. She always brought stale bread to feed the ducks. She often came to this place, especially when she was under stress. Her stress was now hitting toxic limits. Beth was deteriorating. She and the children had finally moved in with her and La. It was close quarters, but it gave Franclynne a sense of control. Beth had decided she would no longer go for treatments. It was a very difficult decision for her, but she was accepting the fact that she could not beat the cancer. The treatments were destroying her body, and she wanted to have some time left when she could enjoy the children. She wanted to spend as much time as she could with the children, without being continually sick and bed ridden.

Beth had joined Franclynne under the tree one afternoon. They tried to resolve the problems of life. The two sat for over four hours and the emotions shifted from crying to depression to crying again. They finally made the decision to stop the treatments. Both knew it was giving up, but the cancer was winning and the treatments were not putting her in remission. It was her time and they both knew it was coming. Beth kept recalling the Queen song, "Hammer to fall." Beth was hearing her name and the hammer was going to fall. At one point, Beth confronted Franclynne with a decision she had made.

"You must promise me, Franclynne."

"Promise what, Beth?"

"Promise me, Franclynne, promise me."

"Tell me what you mean."

"You won't let that monster get the children. Promise me, Franclynne. I cannot die knowing those children aren't safe."

Tears followed this exchange, as Franclynne wanted to promise, but knew in her heart that she might not be able to keep such a pledge.

"I'm not sure I can stop that legally, Beth."

"I don't care how Franclynne, I want you to promise me those children will be safe, and not in that monster's hands."

Beth rose unsteadily from the bench and walked in front of Franclynne. Then she dropped to her knees and placed her head on Franclynne's lap. *"Please, Franclynne, please."* She was now sobbing uncontrollably. *"I am begging you to protect my children. You and La are their only hope."*

"Please get up, Beth. I love your children. You know that. La loves your children. You know that as well."

"Please, Franclynne, please". Finally, after a time, Franclynne said, *"I will do anything I can to protect those children".* The women hugged, but the crying never stopped. Finally, Franclynne wiped her face and straightened herself. *"Beth, once you moved in with me and La, you and the children became family. I promise we will die protecting those children".*

The children loved the park. The two little ones loved to climb on the jungle gym. La took the children to the park every day, same one, same time, every day. To her surprise, La also made some friends. Many of the parents had become used to this odd woman who clearly loved these two young ones. She became close to one of the stay-at-home fathers who brought his two youngsters almost every day, at the same time La was there. His two children happened to be the same ages as Theodore and Ellie. The four children enjoyed each other's company. The man's name was Diego. He explained to La that his family was from a little town in southern Italy. La had no real idea where Italy was, but she always begged him to speak Italian to her. She would relish the words, even though she had no idea of the meaning. Diego would explain the phrases after he said them. She learned that "Buon giorno" meant good morning. She also learned "mi chiamo La", which meant, "My name is La".

However, even though she was enjoying Diego's company, one eye was always on Theodore and Ellie. La was very vigilant in her job. She was like a mother bear protecting her cubs. Gaining La's trust was a job in and of itself.

One day, La arrived at the park and was sitting and talking to Diego when she noticed a strange man sitting on a bench, also watching the children. She had never seen this man before and it raised red flags for her. She could feel her muscles tense and the hairs on the back of her neck rise. Diego noticed La's immediate change in demeanor.

"Is everything okay, La? You appear as though something is bothering you."

La did not say much but just pointed at the man, sitting at the other end of the park.

She continued to watch, and no children ever came over to him. La became more and more suspicious. She pointed it out to Diego again, but he brushed it off, as just somebody resting and enjoying watching the children play. La wasn't convinced. Her internal sense was issuing warning signs.

Finally, La couldn't take the tension any longer. She rose from her chair and walked across the play area to where the man sat. When Diego saw her rise, he put his arm out to try to stop her, but she just kept going.

She wasn't the most effective communicator, but she asked the man if he had any children in the park.

He said, *"Yes, I have two children here"*. Then he pointed to Ellie, who was running in front of them, and said, *"That's my daughter, Ellie."*

La felt a chill run from her head to her toes. She immediately turned and went to fetch the children.

"Ellie and Theodore, it's time to go home. Please come."

Noticing the fear in his friend's face, Diego came over to La. *"Is everything okay, my friend"*.

La was frozen as she stared at Diego. *"No, that man over there claims to be the children's father."*

"Is he, La?"

"I think he is, but he scares me. He is allowed only supervised visitation at certain times. He is not allowed to be here."

After La had called the children to her, Sean had risen from the bench and walked over to La and Diego. Ignoring Diego completely, Sean said to La: *"Those children are mine and I would like to visit with them"*.

In her typical fashion, La ignored his comments and went to gather Theodore and Ellie.

"Didn't you hear me, woman" Sean yelled after her. *"Take your hands off of my children."*

"Excuse me" Diego intervened. Sean pushed him aside and went after La.

La now had both children, one in each hand, when Sean arrived. *"Let go of those children, they are mine,"* Sean demanded. He looked at Ellie and said, *"Come with me, Ellie, I am your father."* Obviously scared, Ellie went behind La. La said, *"Let's go home, children"*. Sean stepped in front of her and said, *"Listen, bitch, I don't want to hurt you. Leave the children and go home."* La didn't flinch. She didn't move, but suddenly, she spit in Sean's face.

Rage emerged on Sean's face, and he swung his right hand hitting La in the left eye, knocking hero down. Standing over her, he looked down at her and yelled, *"I told you, bitch, these are my children."* Seeing La on the ground, Ellie and Theodore both began to cry, putting their hands over their face. At that moment, Diego arrived and stepped between Sean and La. Sean saw him coming and raised his hand as if to stop him.

"This is none of your business, stay out of this."

Diego said, *"It is my business. You assaulted my friend."*

Looking right into Sean's eyes he said, *"Leave, before I get angry."*

"Look, Mister, I don't know who you are or why you are interfering in my business, but I am warning you to stay out of my way."

"Well, I am right in your way, so back off."

A couple of heartbeats went by as the two men stared each other down. Then Sean backed off and gingerly walked away.

La's eye was almost swollen shut. Both children were holding her and crying. Diego helped her up off the ground.

"Do you want me to take you to a hospital?"

"No, thank you, Diego."

"You need to call the police and file charges against that man."

"Thank you, Diego", *and with that, La and the children walked back to the car.*

Chapter XXIII

Everyone was flabbergasted when La returned from the park with the children. Her left eye was almost completely closed. Franclynne was in an uproar when she heard the details. She started walking to the phone to call the police, but La stopped her. *"The children are okay. That is what is important. I am not scared of that man, but if he hurts those children, I will kill him"*. *"Don't say such things La, other people could take that as a threat"*. *"I really don't care, I won't let him hurt Ellie and Theodore."* Their discussion was interrupted by a loud bang on the door. Both La and Franclynne jumped at the sound, and in their minds, they both feared that Sean was coming to try to take the children.

The knock on the door was forceful and definitive. Franclynne was standing with La and made eye contact with her. She slowly and hesitantly made her way to the door. However, before she got there, Ellie called, and Franclynne yelled to La to get the door.

Beth was lying in a large chair. She was asleep in an awkward position, but Franclynne dared not interrupt her rest. She was growing weaker by the day. Franclynne stared at her. She was now only skin and bones. She looked like a Holocaust survivor. Franclynne had grown to love and admire this woman. She was not fighting for herself; she was fighting for the safety of her children. It was a gut-wrenching battle, and Beth was losing, day by day.

Franclynne could tell by the odors that the end was near. Franclynne carried her coffee bag around without putting it down. The smell of death was permeating every pore of her body. She had scaled back her practice to spend more time with Beth and the children. The children were lovely. Although they also sensed that their mother was very sick and would soon die, they really had no idea what that meant. Just the previous night, Franclynne was reading to Ellie before she went to bed. Suddenly, Ellie sat up and with tears in her eyes sand asked, *"Is my mother going to die?"*

Franclynne swallowed hard and answered, *"Yes, my dear, I'm sorry"*.

"Isn't there anything the doctors can do?"

"*They've done all they can, Love.*"

"*Franclynne, what will happen to Theodore and me?*"

"*I'm not 100% sure, but I hope you will be able to stay with La and me.*"

This seemed to brighten the young girl's heart.

"*Do you promise?*'

"*I cannot promise my sweet, because it is up to a court and a judge.*"

"*What does that mean?*"

"*It means that a very smart person will make the decision where you and brother will go.*"

"*Well, if he is very smart, then he will choose you and La. You know Theodore and I both love La.*"

"*I know my sweet, and believe me, she loves you.*"

"*Did she tell you what happened in the park?*"

"*Yes, she did.*"

"*I was scared, Franclynne. I thought that evil man was going to take Theodore and me. He hurt La. Did you see her eye?*"

"*I know you were scared.*"

"*Please, Franclynne, don't let him take us*"

Ellie jumped up and put her arms around Franclynne's neck, "*We want to stay with you and La.*"

"*Things will work out, my sweet. Have trust.*"

As she walked out of Ellie's room, Franclynne knew she had just lied to the child. When she entered the living area, she noticed that La was standing at the front door talking with a man who was on the outside.

"*La, who is at the door.*"

"*A man who claims that he was sent here by JJ Aaron.*"

"*Well, let him in La, he is a friend.*"

The man was short and balding. He had large glasses, and his gait was slow and deliberate. He was wearing a suit, but it was clearly old. Franclynne smelled some unusual scents. He had, she thought, a sinus infection. She sensed a strong tiger-like soul, just the opposite of the physical appearance.

The man entered the room and removed his hat. La followed closely behind, as if she was a guard dog. The man went to the couch, turned, and looked at Beth, still sleeping. He looked at Franclynne and bowed.

"May I sit?"

"Of course."

He asked Franclynne, *"How much longer?"*

The comment clearly made La agitated, as she seemed to bristle. Franclynne was started by the man's directness. She took a breath then said, *"The doctors are not sure. It could be soon, a few days, or a few weeks. She is a tough woman. She will fight to the end."*

"I'm sorry." the man said, *"but first, let me introduce myself."* He stood up and faced the women. *"My name is Hawthorne Holmes. My good friend, JJ Aaron, sent me to you. I am an attorney, and if I may be so bold, I am a very good attorney. Please explain the problem for which I was sent here with which to help you. Mr. Aaron was unclear. He indicated that two women, whom he cared about, were in trouble. His direction was clear. He said, "Solve the problem". So, here I sit. Please explain the dilemma to me, so I can get about solving it. Mr. Aaron is a friend and a colleague. I will clear my schedule to help him. You ladies have become Priority One."*

Prelude

Jillian had returned to work. She was doing well. People seemed to be different. She believed she was noticing more things that were interesting. Others had also commented about her change in attitude. They said she appeared more serious, not as flighty. It made her pleased to hear such comments. For sure, she was moving in the correct direction.

One of Jillian's worries was how she would handle herself if he showed up in her checkout line. What should she say? After a few days though, there was no appearance, and the thoughts seemed to dissolve into the clouds. She had actually practiced the conversation in her mind many times so she would be prepared. She was feeling proud of herself and did not want any negativity to arise in her mind. She was still chatting with the people who came across her aisle, but she was not as loose with her words. She stared at them differently than before. She saw them as people who have regular lives, not just things to impress. She actually began asking about their families and other personal information. It was a transformation for her. Her childhood egocentricity was dissolving into compassion and understanding for others. It was different, very different feel. She really could not explain it in words, but it was different. She was changed.

On this day, a man came down her aisle. He was not overly attractive, but when he came to her checkout, she noticed the strange tattoo on his right hand. The man was in his md to late twenties and appeared distant, almost empty. She couldn't help staring because Bobby, she remembered, had the same tattoo. Was this a coincidence, or did this tattoo mean something more? She knew she was past Bobby, but she had to ask.

"Excuse me, sir. If I may ask, what does that tattoo mean?"

She expected him to say, *"Nothing, just a Tattoo."* However, that was not what he said. He responded with, *"It's a symbol of something very important to me."*

"Do you mind if I ask what is it a symbol of?"

The man looked up and smiled, but it was a funny smile, somewhat sarcastic. His face distorted a bit.

"I would be happy to explain it to you, but you must meet me for coffee."

"Excuse me?"

"Coffee. What time do you get off work?"

"4'o'clock".

"Do you know the Soulful Coffee Station down the road?"

"Yes, I do."

"I will be there at 4, if you wish to know more."

The man put out his hand. *"By the way, my name is Sean."* Jillian stared at him. Finally, she smiled, not touching his extended hand. She really did not want to give the wrong message. He seemed strange, unusual. He smiled, but there was an implicit danger about him.

Chapter XXIV

Lt. O'Brian called both Franclynne and La down to the precinct. He seemed mysterious when Franclynne inquired what the purpose of the request was. When the two-woman arrived at the precinct, they were immediately escorted into O'Brian's office and asked if they would like to sit.

"Well Captain, why are we here? Have we made it to your most wanted list?"

O'Brian ignored the sarcasm.

"Hello, Franclynne, it is nice to see you again."

He stood up and walked over to La. "And *you must be La.*" La did not stand, and she did not speak. She just kept staring at the police officer. La never considered the police to be her friends. They always seemed to cause her pain, so she peered at him as if looking at a coiled snake.

After a heartbeat, O'Brian realized that La was not going to speak, and he moved back to his chair. She was unsettling to him, this strange, silent woman. O'Brian sat down in his chair and looked at Franclynne. Finally, he said, "*As you know, there is a serial rapist terrorizing the city. A man's wife was raped, and La's name came up in the discussion.*"

La jumped up from her seat with an angry, agitated expression on her face. She was breathing hard, but no words came out. Franclynne intervened and got her to sit down again. After La sat down, Franclynne asked, *"How Captain did La's name come up?"*

"Well, for confidentiality reasons, I really can't tell you much more about it."

"So why did you send for us? Is La involved?"

"Probably not, but we are pulling all strings. We are considering anyone and anything to try to get a handle on this man."

La stood and began pacing, from one side of the office to another. Finally, she stopped and said, "If the name of the husband of the woman who was raped is Diego, then I might know the man who is guilty."

"And who would that be?"

She looked at Franclynne who nodded, and La said, *"His name is Sean."*

"Who is this, Sean?"

With continual prompting from Franclynne, La went on to tell her experience in the park and Diego's role in it. After telling her story, O'Brian dismissed the two women. When La left, he held up his hand for Franclynne to stay for a second. He motioned for her to sit.

"I cannot imagine how that park incident could be connected to the rapist. But we will check it out anyway. We have nothing yet on this man. I am sorry to have inconvenienced you both. However, it is coincidental that Diego was the name of the husband of the woman who was raped! I believe the couple is from Italy."

Franclynne rose to leave, and O'Brian said, *"Franclynne would you like to join me for a cup of coffee, either later or tomorrow?"*

Franclynne stopped and smiled back at the detective. *"Thank you for asking Captain, but as I've told you before, I am not into relationships. But I do appreciate the offer."* In truth, Franclynne knew the offer was coming. It was hard to fool her nose. Relationships terrified Franclynne. She felt she could barely understand and accept herself, no less someone else. O'Brian was a nice man. His odors were passable. But a relationship, especially at this time, was not on her menu. Would it ever be? She doubted it.

Unfortunately, Angelique's boyfriend did not accept the fact that their relationship could be over. Angelique was clear enough. She went back to the apartment and put her things together. It was freaky for her, as he stood there angrily, not really saying anything, as he watched her pack, His eyes were menacing, like a raptor watching its pray before it struck. Finally, she was done, and she grabbed her duffle bag and began to walk toward the door. But Mike had blocked the door, standing directly between Angelique and the door, not allowing her a way in which to exit. Angelique was resolute. She took a deep breath. She tried very hard to maintain her calm.

"Mike, let's be adults about this. Please move. Our relationship is over."

Mike was enraged as he blocked the front door. *"No, you're wrong, Angelique You belong to me and you will always. It is up to me when the relationship is over, not you!"*

Mike had never spoken this aggressively to her. His eyes looked deranged. When he spoke, he was almost spitting with anger. Angelique did not expect this type of response. She knew he would be angry, but not unhinged. A chill ran through her. She did not know what she should do in response. Should she become passive or aggressively assertive? She decided to push her way through him and leave. She could not turn back now. She would call his bluff.

Angelique tried to leave but he pushed her away from the door. *"Listen, bitch, I know you love the aggressive stuff. Now I understand. This is just a game for you to get off on. You want me to hurt you."*

"Please, Mike, just let me leave. We can talk at another time. This is not a game."

"No, I said, I decide things, not you."

Angelique walked forward and Mike grabbed her by the neck. His hand was under her chin. His eyes were red with rage. Angelique gasped and tried to say he was hurting her, but only part of the words came through. He almost lifted her off the ground by the neck. Her eyes began to bulge out of their sockets and she gasped for breath.

"I know you love this, itch, so I'm going to give you what you want."

Angelique dropped her case, and with her free right hand grabbed Mike's hand under her chin, trying to free it. But with his other hand, he slapped her hard against the side of her face. Angelique became dizzy from the assault and her eyes began rolling back in her head. She was starting to lose consciousness, becoming terrified that her life was about to end. Suddenly, Mike dropped her and she fell toward the ground, only semi-conscious. As she began falling, Mike grabbed her hair and dragged her into the bedroom.

Chapter XXV

Jillian didn't really understand it, but she found herself inexplicably drawn to this new man who offered to meet her at the coffee shop. She knew it wasn't romantic. She went so far in her reasoning to question whether she was transferring her past feelings for Bob onto this man, only because of the tattoo.

She questioned herself many times. After he made the offer, she immediately dismissed it while at work. But the more she wanted to push it out of her mind, the more it returned. She knew in her heart she was probably going to meet him for coffee, but her consciousness could not rationalize it. *"I shouldn't get into another relationship so quickly."* What was the draw? She was not attracted to this man, so why do this. Remember curiosity and what it did to the cat, she kept telling herself. Yet, here she stood, at the doorway to the Café She finally concluded it was part of her breakup with Bobby. She needed an answer to the tattoo. She hoped, beyond hope, that it was not a self-destructive urge.

Jillian paused again to give it one last thought before entering the Cafe. But she swallowed and decided she was here, so she might as well go inside. Was it just curiosity, or was she drawn to this new man? She did not believe she was attracted to him; he was older than her and not really her type. So why go? It must be inquisitiveness, she concluded again. Another thought entered her mind. How could anything be right if she had to question it so much?

Jillian walked into the Café, and immediately saw Sean sitting in the corner booth. As she walked towards him, she realized that she wasn't repulsed by him, but also clearly not attracted to him. She almost turned and left, but like an automaton, she continued. Halfway to the table she paused and tried to evaluate him from a distance. Nothing special was her conclusion. But there was something about him. Maybe the way that he sat or held himself made her uncomfortable. A thought passed through her mind. He looked like a predator, but she dismissed it for a lack of evidence.

Sean showed an expression of joy as he saw her walking toward his booth. When she arrived, he rose from his seat and pointed for her to sit.

Her initial impression was that he was too slick. More like a con artist. And seeing him again in this setting, she clearly felt uneasy. Maybe she should just excuse herself, beg for forgiveness and leave. Why wasn't she doing that? Instead, she, too, had a smile on her face.

"I am so happy you came. I have never really done this before, but when you asked me about my tattoo, I felt like I wanted to know you better. You have such a sweet voice".

Oh my god, she thought. He's coming on to me. Sweet voice, please. All of the sirens in her mind were going off, telling her to leave. But like a moth drawn to the flame, she sat down.

Finally, Jillian spoke, *"So, Sean, I don't want you to misinterpret why I am here. It is pure curiosity about that tattoo."*

"Have you seen it before?' Sean inquired.

"Actually, yes. A man I was dating had the exact same tattoo and I never got around to ask him the meaning. And when I saw it on your hand, I impetuously asked about it. I hope I didn't offend you by the question. I guess I can be impulsive at times."

"It's okay. I sometimes do things without thinking as well."

"Tell me, Sean, what does it mean?"

"Well, I am almost embarrassed to tell you. It is not some heavy-duty spiritual thing. It is a computer game called, 'The Cult of the Souls.' Everyone who is really into the game, gets this tattoo."

"What type of game is it?"

"Well, it's hard to explain. The game directs you to do things and if you accomplish those tasks, you get points. You actually have to send pictures of what you did to the server before you get the points."

"Like what types of things?"

"Everyone has different tasks, and the games give a point total to achieving the task. Did you ever hear about JJ Aaron?"

"Yes, he's that really rich programmer who made tons of money selling his games."

"That's right, he invented the game."

"I heard he is somewhat of a strange duck."

"I guess. So, you see my tattoo doesn't really have any deep spiritual meaning."

"Do you play the game often?"

"Moreover, recently, because I have been depressed." Sean paused and picked up the napkin as if he was wiping a tear away from his eye. Sean had become an accomplished actor, especially when attractive women were involved. He did not remember how he learned the tear thing, but he would use it when necessary. Again, Jillian felt ill at ease. Here comes the pitch, she thought. It was time to leave. She had learned about the tattoo, so why was she staying? However, to her shock, instead of leaving, she said,

"Why are you sad?"

"Well, my wife left me and I haven't been able to see my children."

She paused, what am I doing? I'm showing compassion to a man I don't know, whose problems might be bullshit, and just using the story as a way to draw me in. She thought to herself she should say, *"I'm sorry to hear that. Thank you for the information about the tattoo."* Then, politely get up and leave. But those were not the words that came out of her mouth. She was being betrayed by herself!

"How horrible! I also recently had a breakup. But luckily for me there were no children involved. You must feel terrible".

Sean wiped his eyes. There were no real tears, but he knew that he had to put on a show. *"I'm sorry for this display of emotion, Jillian. I did not mean for this to happen. I just wanted to meet you. Well, I guess we are somewhat in the same boat. Maybe we can help each other. Don't get me wrong Jillian, I am not looking for a new relationship. But honestly, I don't have many friends and I would like someone to talk to."*

Later, Jillian would realize that this was one clue she missed. Not realizing the emotional trap that she was walking into, Jillian said, *"As long as you understand, Sean, that we will only remain friends, then I, too, could use someone to speak with."*

"No romance, Jillian, I promise. Just talking, maybe meeting for dinner and talking. It always makes me feel better to be in the company of a beautiful woman."

Again, her internal thoughts were issuing a warning. 'Beautiful woman'. This is a trap. Nevertheless, at some level, it was nice to hear.

"So tell me, Sean, why did your wife leave you?"

"It's a long, awful story, Jillian. Are you sure you want to hear the details?"

"I'm a good listener, Sean, tell me what happened."

"Jillian, I'm afraid the tragic story about how I lost my wife and my children is too long a story for coffee and I have to return to my job."

"What do you do, Sean?"

"Well, Jillian if I may be so bold, I am an accounting genius. Can I pick you up for dinner?" Her internal warning system was squawking again, but she was becoming relationship blinded, so, she said,

"I guess."

"Wonderful, Jillian. Give me your address and I will be there at eight."

Sean smiled, held out his hand, and left the café. Jillian sat there, stunned. "What have I done?" she thought. "You must really be stupid." She berated herself. "You were hesitant about the coffee and now you're going to dinner. YOU GAVE A STRANGER YOU'RE ADDRESS! What is wrong with you?" This personal spanking went on for some time, as Jillian sat in the café. She had to figure this out, had to get this straight, so she would not be trapped again in a situation in which she did not to be. Did she just like dancing by the flames? Was that the pull of this man? She knew inside that this was wrong for her, but she could not help herself. Maybe she just gets off on the pain???

Franclynne had decided she needed some time with the ducks. The stress of the court and the decision regarding the children was taking over her thoughts in an intrusive manner and interfering with whatever peace she could fine. Like she needed more stress!

As she sat by the pond, she considered her decision to become a psychologist for the umpteenth time. Her special attribute and her love for her mentor made it somewhat of a logical choice, but was it a good one? She always loved to bake. Would it have been an easier life if she became a baker? Teaching was not her thing, too much internal politics, even though she loved the children. But a baker? The thought seemed to allow her to drift into a reverie. She giggled to herself, "hot cross buns". It seemed to make her comfortable to dream about hot cross buns. "How unusual", she murmured to herself. Some of her friends suggested she should have been a model. But she really believed she was only average in looks. Besides, hearing others comments about herself would have driven her crazy. Yes, she was tall and slender, but her nose would have betrayed what others were thinking. Nope. Wouldn't work. Back to hot cross buns. The funny thing was she had never made hot cross buns, but she liked the name. She pulled out her phone and looked up hot cross buns. What came back was that they were yeasted, sweet buns, filled with spices and various raisons. They had a cross of icing on their top. Yup, sounded good, much more pleasant than what was now happening in her world. She drifted away, hot cross buns!

Her thoughts then made another turn and drifted to Beth. She was dying and the things she loved the most, her two young children would be put in harm's way. She was trusting Franclynne and La to save the day, but the odds were, they couldn't. However, Franclynne knew that the possibility of a good outcome was not likely. She was adjusting to the idea that she would have to turn the children over to Sean. She shivered at the prospect, but she had to prepare for it. A thought drifted through her mind that she should take La and the children and run. Hide in some small country for the rest of her life. She had some money saved, but was sure JJ Aaron would support the idea with capital. This was only a fantasy; she knew that it wouldn't work. She and La would end up in jail, and the children would end up with Sean. She quivered. Hot cross buns seemed the most reliable choice. Of course, for now, that also was only an illusion. It was a wish, an imaginary hope, something to think about to take her mind off the reality of what was happening.

Franclynne thought about her mentor, Dr. DeJarden. She had taught her many life lessons before she died. One of them was of the uselessness of hope. "Hope bleeds the soul", she used to say. Franclynne responded, *"if I shouldn't hope, what should I do?" "Plan. P*lan was the answer"*. DeJarden believed that everything in life had to do with preparation and planning. *"There is no such thing as luck",* she used to say. *"Luck is when preparation and opportunity come together. But without preparation, we are never ready for the opportunity."*

DeJarden also said that every crisis had two parts. They were tragedy and opportunity. *"Always look for the opportunity in the crisis."* But she tried, and for the life of her, she couldn't figure out the opportunity in this dilemma. DeJarden assured her it was there; hiding in the weeds, but it was there. But what the hell was it? She did not think she was smart enough to figure it out. Maybe the ducks knew the answer; she asked them, but they just wagged their tail feathers and looked for more bread. Franclynne looked up in the sky. She silently prayed, *"Please, Helen, tell me the answer to this riddle. I love those children and I fear I will do something crazy if I lose them."*

She felt a hand on her shoulder and almost jumped out of her skin. She turned quickly to see O'Brian standing next to her. *"How did you...."* *"La told me you would probably be here".* O'Brian sat next to her. *"You looked like you were praying, I'm sorry I interrupted you".* Still feeling stunned, Franclynne said, *"Did you ever have hot cross buns?"* *"No, why?"* *"No reason, just a silly question."* She finally gained her wits. "Captain, *why are you here?*

O'Brian's expression became more serious. *"A woman was beaten and is in the hospital. She has been asking for you".* *"Who, what woman?"* *"She is in intensive care; her name is Angelique".* *"Oh my god, what happened?"* *"I don't know the details, but she refuses to talk to anybody except Dr. Longaire."*

Franclynne jumped up. *"I must go".* *"I have a police car waiting. I'll have the officer drive your car to the hospital behind us".* The two ran to the waiting car and both jumped in. The siren was blaring as the two cars pulled out of the park. Franclynne rode in silence, but her legs and her arms were shaking. Finally, O'Brian asked, *"What is this hot cross bun thing?"* *"Excuse me?"* *"Hot cross buns, you asked me at the park."* *"Nothing, just silliness".* As the car pulled up to the hospital emergency entrance, Franclynne flew out and ran into the emergency room.

She burst through the hospital door and almost ran past the admitting nurse into the area where the emergency beds were. The nurse came quickly out of her station and chased Franclynne her the area. *"Excuse me, young woman. Where do you think you're going?"* Franclynne ignored the nurse and just kept moving. After a few more steps, with the nurse on her arm, a young doctor stepped in front of Franclynne. "This *is an emergency room. You are not supposed to be in here."* Her eyes, wider than the full moon, and her face in a panic, Franclynne demanded, *"Where is Angelique?"*

"Are you Dr. Longaire?"

"Yes. Where is she?"

"Your patient, Angelique, is dying. She was beaten up so badly that I'm surprised she is still alive. The paramedics already brought her back a few times when the ambulance brought her here. Whoever did this is a real monster."

"Dr., did she tell you who did this?"

"She has already spoken with the police. I believe she has talked to them about the incident. I do not have to tell you, Dr. Longaire, to be gentle with her. She does not have much time. She is bleeding internally. Her heart is very weak and failing. We are contemplating putting her in a coma in an attempt to help her."

Franclynne looked at the doctor. She knew he was not really telling her the truth, but why would he lie? However, as he was talking, she noticed a tattoo on his hand that looked very familiar. There it was, 'The Cult of the Souls' tattoo!

Franclynne bolted into Angelique's room. She was awake, but looked as though she had been in a brawl. Her face was black and blue and almost swollen to twice its normal size. She walked gently over to the bed and took Angelique's hand. The girl opened her eyes. Franclynne smiled at her, and Angelique attempted a smile back. In a low, whispery voice Angelique said, *"Freedom has a price".*

"I'm here now, Angelique, we will try to fix this."

"I'm scared, Franclynne! I don't want to die."

There was something about the situation that disturbed Franclynne. Seeing the tattoo shook her. She could not get rid of what the feeling meant that she knew that the doctor was lying to her. She could not get it out of her mind. She impulsively said, *"Angelique, there is something about this this hospital that makes me uncomfortable. Would you mind if I ask that you be transferred to the other hospital?"* Angelique shook her head and said, *"Whatever you think is best."*

"I'll be right back."

Franclynne exited the room, and saw Captain O'Brian standing down the hallway. She quickly walked to him.

"Captain".

"Dr. Longaire, how is your patient?"

"I want her transferred to St. Marks Hospital".

"Transferred, why?"

"There is something not right here. I can feel it."

"What do you mean?"

"I don't know for sure, but I want her transferred. She agrees, I just asked her."

"It is an unusual request, especially in her condition."

"That is not the problem, Captain. My senses tell me that she is not severely injured."

"What do you mean?"

"Please, my senses are usually correct."

O'Brian gave her a strange, questioning look. Reluctantly he said.

"I will arrange it".

"Captain, I will not leave here until I am sure that Angelique will get out of here. Do you understand me?"

Franclynne began walking back to Angelique. O'Brian held her by the arm and said *"By the way, the man who beat this girl up is a suspect in our other investigation. I hope he is the guy. He fits all the characteristics."*

"What about the man La told you about?"

"Still checking. Wait, stop Franclynne".

"What, Captain?"

"What's the problem with this hospital? What is this thing about your senses?"

"Captain, look at the doctor's hand."

"His hand?"

"Just look."

And with that, Franclynne was gone, back to Angelique.

Chapter XXVI

Lucas Janicosy was a self-made man. He had started a company and turned it into an industry giant. It was basically a financial company, but its reach was broad, including stocks, bonds, and other investments. He founded the company almost twenty years ago, and in all those years, the company was very prosperous. Janicosy was a fair, but hard boss. He worked harder than any of his employees. He came to work every morning at 7 a.m. and left after 8 p.m. every night.

Janicosy's parents immigrated to the United States from Eastern Europe. Janicosy was multi-lingual, speaking at least five languages. His company had offices in at least five other countries. He understood and had total control over every aspect of the running of the company. Not much escaped his gaze. Even considering the amount of work that Janicosy did, he remained an emotionally evenhanded individual. He was not harsh, nor did he overreact to situations. It was this levelheaded approach to life that, to a large degree, made him so successful.

On this morning, Balazs Janicosy's vice president, was waiting for him as he arrived at the office. This was a highly unusual occurrence, in fact, it had never happened before. When Janicosy opened the door and saw Balazs sitting across his desk, it stopped him in his approach.

Janicosy brought Balazs from Hungary, and out of all of his employees, he was the most loyal. It was not unusual for Janicosy and Balazs to speak Hungarian during meetings, to the consternation of others in the room.

Janicosy recovered his composure, and walked to his desk. Balazs appeared upset.

"What is the problem, my friend?"

"I'm afraid I have some bad news."

"Tell me, what is this news?"

Balazs stood and turned his back on his boss. He took a few steps, and then turned back around. He came back to his chair, sat down, and said

"We have a thief in the company."

"What?"

"I believe somebody is embezzling funds."

"How much?"

"I believe about 100,000, but it could be much more.

Janicosy said, *"Start with upper management and work downward. The people who have most recently been promoted should be your first targets. Also, concentrate on the brightest ones. Do you have any suspects?"*

"Yes".

"Who?"

"Whitford."

"Whitford?"

"Yes, he fits all the criteria. He is new, he is in a position to hide funds, and he's ruthless."

"Ruthless? How do you know that?"

"By talking with others about him. He is not friendly, speaking behind people's backs. Nobody, none of his subordinates trust him."

Switching to Hungarian, Janicosy said, *"It all makes sense." Should I call the police?"*

"Where is Whitford?"

"I don't know. Apparently, he has not shown up for work in two days".

"Call the police!"

Hawthorne Holmes sat motionless, and his gaze shifted between Franclynne and Beth. There was a very uneasy, quiet pause, and then he looked at Beth and said, *"How long?"* Everybody knew what he was asking. By this point, Beth had lost even more weight and looked emaciated. Only one tear came to her eye as she said, *"At best, three weeks."* Franclynne got up from her chair, went over to Beth, and put her arm around her. Beth did not flinch. She looked directly at the attorney and said, *"My problem, Mr. Holmes, is that at the current time, my husband is only allowed limited, supervised visits with the. This is because of his violent temper. I that know that after I die, he will want custody of the children."*

"Tell him everything, Beth."

Beth now swallowed and told the story of the stroke and the subsequent violent acts. *"There are some other things you should know. My ex does not have a history. In all of our years together, he has never talked about his childhood or where he came from. In my heart, I believe he has a very troubled past, maybe even criminal."*

Holmes lifted his hand to stop her. *"Let me understand this. You don't know where your ex-husband was born, or what his life was like before he met you?"*

"Yes." "Oh my!" Holmes stood up and paced a little. He took out his cell phone and dialed a number. *"Jonathan, is that you? We have a problem with which I need your urgent help. I want you to put your best operatives on this. It is urgent, time is of the essence! The man's name is Sean Whitford. We only know the past six years of his life. We need to find out if he had another name and another history before that time. I will forward you a photograph. He works for Lucas Janicosy. Yes, you know, the financial firm. Go to their office and find out what you can. But if you meet Whitford, be careful. He could be dangerous."* Holmes hung up the phone. He looked at Beth.

Now her voice became pleading *"You can't let that monster have my babies!"*

Holmes papered very concerned and thought for a second. *"Are there grandparents?"* Beth shook her head. *"I want Franclynne and La to adopt my children."*

Holmes considered the situation. *"There are a few things we can do, but in all honesty, the judge will lean heavily toward the biological father, unless of course, we can find out about your ex's past."* He stopped for a moment and then continued. *"Beth, I need you to do a few things for me. You must make me a list of everything that your husband has done that makes you believe he cannot parent the children. I want details, not just broad statements, such as, "he sexually abused me." I want to shock the court with our details. I know that writing these things down is emotionally painful, but they are essential. Second, we will videotape you tomorrow. On the video, you will talk about your husband and his violent ways. You will also have to make the case why Franclynne and La would be more appropriate people to raise the children."*

"I will do all of that."

Holmes rose and paced a few steps. He said to Beth, *"this video must be compelling. It will be you speaking from beyond the grave to save your children. Remember that."* Franclynne intervened, and smiling at Beth she said, *"Even after death, you will still have a voice."*

After Holmes left, Beth broke down. She looked at Franclynne and said, *"Please hold me until the fear subsides."* After a few minutes, Franclynne asked, *"Do you know what you will say in the video?"* With tears in her eyes Beth responded, *"I think so."* *"This will hurt, Beth. When you are ready, you and I are going to sit down and you are going to outline what Sean did. We are also going to outline what you will say in the. Do you think you can do this?"* Beth reluctantly nodded her head in agreement.

Chapter XXVII

"Why is your wife such a vindictive person?" Sean looked at her and shrugged his shoulders. *"She is such a nasty person. She has been since I met her, but like a fool, I fell in love with her anyway."*

"You're such a sweet and sensitive person."

"I try." Sean was smooth and he was playing it for all it was worth. He had convinced this young woman of his false sincerity. He had always believed that it was not hard to fool people. Put on a specific face, and others will believe you. It was like taking candy from a baby. Sean believed three things. First, was that he was smarter than everyone else was. Second, people are generally naïve and want to believe what you tell them, and third, that he would never be caught. He stared at Jillian. She had no idea she was with a wolf in sheep's clothing. Sean looked deep into Jillian's eyes and he believed that he saw both sympathy and empathy.

"I know, Jillian that we have not known each other for very long, but I have a favor to ask you."

"What kind of favor, Sean?"

Sean changed his expression to one of gloom. *"The last time I tried to see my children, it worked out terribly. I know they are taken to the park by their sitter, La most days at the same time. Her name is La and she is a homeless woman. Imagine that, Jillian, my wife is leaving my children with a homeless woman who she barely knows."*

Sean started to get agitated. Then he put his hands on the table, closed his eyes and said in a low voice (loud enough for Jillian to hear) *"Keep control Sean, don't get upset."*

Jillian thought, *"Such a sweet man."* At the same time, Sean was thinking, "Boy, am I good!"

"Jillian, I went to the park and this woman wouldn't let me even say hello to the children. I cannot imagine what they have told them, for they seemed afraid of me. To make matters worse, she assaulted me. Spit right in my face when I asked to see the children. I'm sorry. But, when I think about my children, I have to close my eyes and hide."

Again, Sean hesitated, closed his eyes and took a deep breathe. *"This is a big favor, Jillian. Would you mind going to the park and telling the children how much I love them?"*

Although conflicted with the idea, Jillian knew she was getting in too deep in this situation, but she responded, *"Yes, Sean, I will do that for you. Every child needs to know that their father loves them."*

Jonathan sat in the outside office of Lucas Janicosy. He had no appointment, but he sat patiently. The secretary had promised that she would relay the message that he was here to talk about one of the firm's employees, and that it was urgent. He had also dropped the name JJ Aaron to try to secure this meeting.

Jonathan Lock was an excellent investigator. He had an exclusive contract with both Hawthorn Holmes and JJ Aaron. They allowed him to do outside work, but everything had to be dropped when either of those two men called. He actually looked forward to their calls, because their work was more interesting and exciting than the other, sometimes boring work of an investigator. He hated following cheating spouses and taking photos of their affairs. But he couldn't just sit around when he didn't have a case for Holmes or Aaron, so he pursued all of these cases. Lock had three investigators that worked under him. They were also part of the contract with Aaron. They each had a specialty. One was a computer expert, able to break through firewalls with ease. The second was a tracking expert. He could follow anyone, usually unseen. The third man was smooth talking, somewhat of a con artist.

However, the task of talking with Janicosy was his task. He had to get the man to release details of an employee. He knew that employee confidentiality would be a large barrier to such information, and he had been mulling a way around it. Sitting in the waiting room gave him time for such thought.

"Mr. Lock, Mr. Janicosy will see you now."

Jonathan walked into an office that appeared almost twice as big as his own living room. It was exclusively furnished, beautiful art on all the walls. Janicosy was standing behind his desk waiting for Jonathan's arrival. He put his hand out even before Jonathan reached him. A good sign, he thought.

"Mr. Lock, I have heard about you."

"I hope only good things!"

"Yes, good things. You work for JJ Aaron don't you?"

"I do"

"And did he send you here to speak with me?"

"He did. In fact, he sends his regards."

"Did he ever tell you that we met at a conference of financial advisors, oh maybe five years ago?"

"He did not"

"Yes, it quite an interesting story. Your boss is a very unusual man. He is like a ghost, this Aaron. He looks like a slob, does not seem to care what others think, and always appears bored at the events. However, behind that exterior, is a man who understands and assesses everything that is going on. He is very impressive that way - gives you an, 'I don't care exterior, while internally evaluating everything. Quite impressive, I would say."

"He's much smarter than I am."

"Somehow, I doubt that, Jonathan. Mr. Lock, may I call you Jonathan?"

"Please do."

"Would you like some coffee or a drink?"

"Coffee would be nice, thank you"

Janicosy pushed a button and said through his phone, *"Two cups of coffee please"*

He continued, *"You know, Jonathan, I tried to hire your firm a number of years ago"*

"I remember, sir"

"No, sir, please. My friends call me Jaco."

"I remember Jaco." The secretary entered and placed the cups in front of the two men, then she left.

"Good woman, Marilyn, very loyal and honest. Okay, Jonathan. I think I know why you are here. I do not believe in coincidences. We have, here in our company, a man who is embezzling funds. I think I know who it is, but it will take time to prepare a case. I know you have people who can help me in this venture. I want him caught and jailed. If it were possible, I'd kill him myself. I hate thieves, especially ones that I trusted and then turned on me. I believe that is why you are here. For some reason, which I do not know, JJ wants to know about him as well. How close am I?

"On the button."

"So we can help each other."

"What do you need from me?"

Jonathan did not know how much to reveal, but he figured he would chance it.

"This man is a ghost. I am sure you vetted him. I need his history before six or seven years ago."

Jaco swiveled in his chair, a half smile on his face. *"So, if I give you all I have, you will help me to prosecute him?"*

"I see no reason why not"

"Excellent." Jaco stood, put out his hand and the men shook. He then went back to the intercom. *"Marilyn, get all the information we have on Whitford, and give Mr. Lock the small conference room and let him review it."*

Beth was now almost entirely restricted to her bed. She had little strength even to pee in the toilet. Franclynne slept next to her in these final moments. The day had arrived and Beth was fading in and out of consciousness. The children stayed home from school and spent time playing in the bedroom. La stood in the distance, by the bedroom door, trying to blend into the wall. She had experienced so much death in her life, and it hurt her to even imagine it. She tried just watching the children, trying in vain to put Beth out of her mind.

Beth woke for a moment and asked for ice cream. La ran out of the door to the kitchen. Beth was an ice cream fanatic, but in these last months, she had rarely asked for her favorite treat. La brought the bowl, and brought small bowls for the children. Ellie and Theodore jumped up on the bed next to their mother and the three had smiles on their faces. Beth ate a couple of spoonful's, kissed both of the children, told them how much she loved them, and closed her eyes for good.

Ellie seemed to know that her mother was gone, for she dropped her bowl and fell on her mother's chest, crying uncontrollably. Theodore followed suit, and the room was suddenly full of tears and wails. Of course, neither child truly understood that death was forever, but the tears flowed just the same. Ellie was hysterical, kissing her mother and begging her to wake. Franclynne held her, and La stood in the background crying. There was no solace, nothing to be said to ease the pain. Their mother's battle was over.

That night Franclynne read the children the story, "The Fall of Freddie the Leaf." The story is about a leaf who refuses to fall off the tree when winter is arriving. Finally, Freddie cannot hold onto the tree anymore and he lets go. However, surprisingly, as he fell, he saw the world in a different light. He was able to see beyond his place on the tree, and most of his questions about the world seemed almost magically answered.

Franclynne did not know if either of the children understood the implications of the story, but there was a long discussion afterward about Freddie and what happened to him. *"We all must fall from the tree when our time comes"*, said Franclynne. *"Yes but we are not all trees, we are people."* *"Yes my love, but do you remember how scared Freddie was to let go of the tree?"* Both children shook their head in acknowledgement. *"And then what happened?"* *"He was happy"*, yelled Theodore. *"Well"*, said Franclynne," *Freddie realized that he understood things that he had not known before he fell from the tree."* Ellie thought hard about this. *"Do you mean, Lynn that our Mom now sees things she didn't understand?"* *"Yes, my love, she does."* *"I want to be with Mom"*, said Theodore. *"This is the time for you and your sister to grow and become adults. Everything has its time. I know you already miss your mother. So do I, and so does La. But your mother would want you both to grow up and be happy people."*

"How can I be happy?" Ellie questioned Franclynne. *"Just remember, whenever you are sad, think about your mother's smile. Think about how much she loved you both, and remember, when you look in the sky and see the stars, your mother is watching you from above. You can't see or hear her, but she is there, watching over both of you."* The three hugged and Franclynne tucked them in. As she left the room, Franclynne thought, *"Life would not be the same for any of them again. The world had fundamentally shifted, and Franclynne saw dark clouds on the horizon."* One day, she thought, in one day, everything changes. What I knew before is no longer true and the future has been altered."

As she left the room, she noticed La outside of the door. She had obviously been listening to the bedtime conversation. La looked angry and defiant. *"I will not allow it."*

"What are you talking about, La?"

"I will not allow those children to go with that horrible man."

"La, I don't want that either, but this is a court matter."

"The courts don't understand. I will protect those children with my life." La's face turned into a distorted frown. *"If I have to kill him myself, I will not allow it."*

Franclynne grabbed La. *"Look at me La. Do you love those children?"*

La stared questionably at Franclynne. *"Then promise me, La, promise me right here and now you will not hurt Sean."* La began to shake her head and Franclynne said: *"Promise me, La!"* After a few heartbeats, La looked back at Franclynne *"I will not hurt Sean."* But, La knew, if the situation called for it, she would break that promise. She would not have to think, to ponder the circumstances, she would break the promise and kill Sean. He deserved nothing less in her eyes.

Franclynne walked away, knowing that she herself could not make that same promise.

Chapter XXVIII

It took almost a week for the children to return to the park. Franclynne and La both thought it would be a good diversion for them. The children were happy to get out of the house. They had watched the coroner arrive and their mother leave in a black plastic bag. It was not a happy day. The funeral was small, with only a very few people attending. Diego came with his children to be with La, Ellie, and Theodore. Diego told his children about the tragedy, and how they all should go to support their friends. His wife was also very sweet, and she stayed close to her children and to La. Diego arranged to meet La and the children the next day at the park.

Unfortunately, a man who met Franclynne as she was leaving marred the funeral. He handed her court papers, which required her to bring the children to court the following Tuesday. The papers indicated that there would be a custody hearing, as Sean had filed for sole custody of the children. *"Son of a bitch,"* she thought, the bastard didn't even wait for her to be cold. She wanted to rip up the paper and ignore it, but knew she couldn't. She looked away and put the papers in her purse.

The park excursion was a great idea. It allowed everyone a sense of freedom from what had happened within the last week. However, there was another stranger in the park, someone that La had not seen before. Immediately her internal alarms went off. But this was not Sean, this was a woman. Surprisingly the woman walked slowly over to where La sat. Diego could see the tension arising in La as the woman approached. He readied himself for some type of action. He knew the situation and was ready for the unexpected.

The woman seemed very sweet. She came over to La and asked if she could sit with her. La did not respond, but the woman sat anyway. She turned her head to La and said, *My name is Jillian. You must be La."*

La's tension now rose 100%, and like a coiled snake, she was getting ready to strike. Diego interrupted and said, *"Can we help you, Jillian?"*

"I have a friend. His name is Sean. He tells me that he has not been allowed to see his children."

"So, Sean sent you here?" Diego asked.

"Yes, but I didn't want to alarm anyone, which is why I came over to you both."

La began to get up to leave with the children, but Diego said, "Wait *La, let's hear this woman out."* Hesitantly, La sat down again, but she remained vigilant, ready for any unexpected turn.

"Tell me, Jillian, why did Sean want you to come?"

Jillian turned to La and said, *"La, you and the children have nothing to fear from me."* Then she turned to Diego and queried, *"How are you involved in this?"* Diego said, *"I am a friend."* Jillian thought for a moment and boldly said, *"Oh, are you the man who assaulted Sean?"* This immediately got a rise out of La, as she jumped up again. *"Sit, La sit, this woman is obviously confused."*

Diego took a deep breath. *"Young woman, it wasn't La, nor me that assaulted Sean, the children's father. It was he who assaulted La."*

"What! That cannot be. He is such a sweet, nice man."

"Jillian, he is anything but sweet and nice. I was here. He punched La and knocked her to the ground."

"He's a nasty man," La blurted out.

"We can't be talking about the same man." Jillian inquired. Diego went on. *"Do you really want to know the truth, Jillian?"* She acknowledged that she would. *"Do you know where the Overgrown Flower is?"*

"Yes", Jillian answered.

"Give me your cell phone number."

"Why?"

"I will arrange for Franclynne, the child's current guardian, to meet you there tomorrow at 5. But you must promise that you will not tell Sean about this meeting."

"It's a promise."

"I will call your cell phone if she cannot make that time."

"Thank you," said Jillian, and she smiled and rose to leave. She took a step and turned back. *"by the way, the children are beautiful."*

She really did hate hospitals. She disliked the smell, and she must have looked odd walking the halls with her coffee bag held up to her nose. Not that it really bothered Franclynne, she had gotten used to people watching her. Now that Angelique was at St. Marks, Franclynne felt much better. She was not sure why, but in her mind, she could still see the tattoo on the doctor's hand. As she made her way to Angelique's room, she noticed a difference about this place from the other hospital. It seemed more modern, and to her, less depressing. In addition, Angelique was in a room, no longer on death's door.

As she walked into Angelique's room, Franclynne noticed that the breathing tube had been removed. She still looked severely beaten up, black and blue eyes and jaw, but she was alive. There was no talk here about Angelique not making it. The doctors did say she was lucky to be alive, but she was alive, and, she would recover. So why the switch? In truth, Franclynne did not really care. She had other fish to fry. She was just happy that Angelique would pull through.

Angelique smiled as she saw Franclynne approach. A smile, what a wonderful expression, Franclynne thought. She immediately thought about how Ellie and Theodore's smiles brightened her day. Angelique's smile had the same affect. She sat next to the bed and grabbed Angelique's hand. She got another smile because of that action.

"I'm so happy to see you, Angelique. You look much better."

Another small smile and Angelique motioned for Franclynne to come closer. In a whisper she said, *"I look like shit."*

"Yes, you have to heal. But there is definite improvement."

At this point, between the injuries and the pain medications, Angelique slept often. As Franclynne was talking to her, telling her about Ellie and Theodore, Angelique nodded off.

Franclynne stayed with Angelique, holding her hand and looking at her. These last few months had transformed her life, quite dramatically. La moved in, she became emotionally attached to Beth and the children, and Beth passed away. She wanted desperately to put that single fact out of her mind. However, like a window opening to let the cold air in, the fact just kept returning. It could not really be avoided. As she sat there and mused, another thought entered her consciousness. Whenever she felt down, she thought about Ellie and Theodore. Even in Beth's death, these two young souls had brought life back into her. The bathroom floor seemed like a distant memory. Franclynne noticed that since the children arrived, her nighttime routine had improved. Just thinking of the children changed her thoughts and her world. Franclynne was beginning to understand how empty she was before the children arrived. Yes, she had her work, but after that, what was left was her traumatic past. Those traumatic thoughts dominated her consciousness. But now there were Ellie and Theodore to fill the void. Up until the arrival of the children, Franclynne had not even contemplated this emptiness. She knew she was scared; she knew she was in pain from her past. Now, her focus was on them, not on her past. It was like a fresh wind blowing through her. It took another person's death to fill her emotional vacuum. Is that what DeJarden meant about the opportunity that came with crisis? She had the children, but for how long? Tuesday was not far off. She silently prayed for Hawthorne Holmes to create some kind of miracle to save the children from the monster.

When she saw Angelique's smile, it resonated in her. When either Ellie or Theodore smiled, her heart seemed to be reborn. Just a simple smile or a hug filled the void that she had felt for some time. Even in the death of their mother, these little lives had become so important to her, that she could not even imagine them not being around. This realization increased the pressure on her to make sure that Sean never got custody of those children. Sadly, in that area, Franclynne felt completely helpless.

Franclynne was shocked when La mentioned, that if need be, she would kill Sean to save the children. In rethinking that experience she could understand, and even identify with the feeling. She really did not know how she would react if the judge gave the children to that monster. She recalled Beth's pleading face before she died, begging her to promise, and the lie she had to tell her to make her journey less frightful. She might live regret that lie. It burned within her.

Captain O'Brian entered the small room with the two-way mirror. He was quiet and very controlled. He had done this over one thousand times, and he knew every interview was different, but they all followed a general pattern. O'Brian was considered an expert at breaking down potential criminals. He already had Mike sitting in the room for three hours. He was handcuffed to the desk. Anytime Mike put his head down to rest, an officer saw it through the mirror and a second officer went in to ask an irrelevant question, essentially to keep him awake. When O'Brian came in, Mike was tired and scared.

O'Brian sat down and asked, *"Mike, did anyone ask you if you wanted coffee?"*

Mike shook his head and mumbled, *"No."*

O'Brian banged his fist on the table and said, "*I told that rookie to make sure you were comfortable. I can't believe he didn't follow my directions. Would you like coffee, Mike?*"

Mike acknowledged with a nod of his head. "*What do you take in your coffee, Mike? By the way, do you prefer to be called Mike or Michael?*"

"*Michael.*"

"*Okay, Michael, what do you want in your coffee?*"

"*Just black.*"

"*You got it.*" *And with that, O'Brian got up and left the room*"

O'Brian left the room and went into the adjacent room in where the two-way mirror was. Johnson was a rookie and assigned to O'Brian essentially to learn technique. Upon walking into the room, O'Brian said to Johnson, "*So, young man, what do you think so far?*" "*Not much, Captain. He looks tired and washed out.*" O'Brian did not comment on the younger man's observation. It was too obvious and didn't deserve a comment.

"*Johnson, when I have casual conversation with this man, I want you to watch his eyes and listen to the flow of his speech. Watch his eye movements. Where is he looking when he answers the questions? Does he give me direct eye contact, and when he does, to which questions does he give me contact, and to which questions does he look away? Notice the hesitations and the direction of his speech. Is the tone consistent or variable?*"

"*Why is all of this important, Captain?*" O'Brian gave him an, 'are you serious?'

"*Just watch, Johnson, and tell me what you see.*"

"*Yes, sir.*"

As he began to leave the room, O'Brian stopped and turned back to Johnson.

"*When I scratch my head, I will be leaving the informal conversation and becoming more direct. Notice the difference, the eye contact and voice inflections coming from him.*"

He hesitated, and then said, "*Is that understood?*" However, before Johnson could answer, O'Brian said, "*I am very serious about this, Johnson. I will be testing you afterward. It will help me decide whether you stay with the detectives to learn, or you go back to arresting drunks in the allies."* Let me have your gun, Johnson, I will be right back." *"My gun? Why do you need my gun?" "Just give it to me, god damn it."* After a few minutes, O'Brian came back into the room and gave Johnson back his gun. *"Just checking rookie, want to make sure you cleaned it."* As he left the room, O'Brian smiled to himself. He loved intimidation

After about a half hour of general talk centering on Mike's job and his history, O'Brian began scratching the top of his head. He said to Mike, *"Damn dandruff, I can't find a shampoo that will stop the itching. Do you have this kind of problem, Mike?"* Mike shook his head. O'Brian continued: *"Listen, Mike, we have you on assault and battery. You nearly killed your girlfriend. She is still in the hospital. But you know, Mike, the district attorney wants to charge you with attempted murder. That's a nice stretch, Mike. And if she dies, you might never see the light of day again. Attempted murder, Michael, are you paying attention?"*

O'Brian then said, *"Oh, Mike, something I forgot, I'll be right back."*

"Captain, can I go the bathroom?"

"As soon as I get back, Mike."

O'Brian did not come back in the room for an hour. He wanted the charges to simmer. He also wanted Mike to suffer with his bathroom urges. Finally, he went in and told Johnson to go in and take him to the john. Johnson did as he was told, but after about five minutes, there was a loud noise in the bathroom. O'Brian had anticipated this and was waiting outside. He hurriedly walked into the men's room to find Johnson on the ground and Mike pointing his gun at him.

Mike said in a shaky voice, *"Back off Captain, or I will shoot him."*

O'Brian had already drawn his gun and was pointing at Mike's head. *"You know, if you pull that trigger, Mike, you will have a date with the electric chair. I understand that it doesn't work real well, and some men burn to death. It ain't pretty."* Mike looked paralyzed. *"Give me the gun, Mike, before you make this worse."* Again, no movement. O'Brian raised his voice and cocked his gun. *"Give me the gun!"* Realizing the reality of what was happening Mike turned and gave the gun to O'Brian. O'Brian pointed the gun at Michael's head and pulled the trigger. The blanks made a loud noise but no damage. He then grabbed Mike by the collar and dragged him back into the interrogation room.

He locked Mike back to the table. O'Brian said, *"Well Mike, you fucked this up, now you have another charge hanging over your head."*

"You tried to kill me!"

"I did no such thing, the gun had blanks."

Mike started crying. *"It's okay, son."* O'Brian stood and patted him on the back.

"I talked with the District Attorney and I have a deal for you."

Chapter XXIX

Franclynne sat in the coffee shop deep in contemplation. Her mind was wandering, slipping and sliding around many subjects. Her biggest fear was the upcoming court battle for custody of the children. Their position was very tenuous and the probability was that they were not going to win. Hawthorn Holmes was very clear about this. She worried how the children would react to such a decision. What terrified her is what would La do?

The server had brought her a cup of cappuccino and it was already getting cold. Today, time was not an issue for her. Her workday was over, and she needed to see the woman who was Sean's new friend. Maybe she could help their position in court. She doubted it, but maybe. It was like one of those wishes that you desperately want to come true, but you doubt that it will. She had hope. One of her teachers once told her, "Hope is the fuel of desperation." In any case, she had confidence.

Without realizing it, a woman appeared at the table. She was so deep in thought, the coffee bag at her nose, that she did not notice the approach. She immediately put down the coffee bag and let her senses go to work.

"You must be Franclynne", the young woman said with a smile.

"I am, and you must be Jillian. Please sit down."

The two-woman stared at each other for a few seconds, both attempting to glean something from the face. Then Jillian broke the pause, *"I understand you are a psychologist."*

"Yes, I am. How did you know?"

"I have contemplated seeing someone in the past, and I think I remember your name coming up. I checked into you and you have a good reputation."

"Thank you. As a psychologist you do not get much feedback about your work."

"Franclynne, I must ask, why do you and your friend, I think her name is La, have such bad feelings about Sean. He is of course, the children's father."

"Yes, he is. But bear in mind that Beth, when she was alive, had a protective order against him."

"Yes," said Jillian, *"I don't understand that either."*

"Let me tell you a story Jillian." Franclynne's went on to tell the story of Sean, his stroke and the change in his behavior. She became very graphic about the sexual perversions that he forced upon Beth. *"Wait,"* she said. Franclynne reached into her pocket book. *"I have something to show you, Jillian. You can read it but you cannot have it. I need it for court."* *"What is it?"* Jillian asked. *"Before Beth died, our attorney asked her to make a list of the things that Sean did to her. The attorney wanted a graphic account."* Franclynne found the papers, pulled them out of her pocketbook, but then stared at Jillian. Jillian had already reached out her hand to grab the papers, but Franclynne held them back. *"Jillian, before I let you read this, I must warn you of the graphic nature of this. Are you sure you're ready? It will change the way you see Sean."* *"I'm ready, Franclynne, let me see them, please."* *"Okay, but don't say I didn't warn you."* Jillian read the pages and with every story her face distorted even more. Finally, she got up from her chair and ran off to the bathroom. Franclynne waited, distractedly sipping her now cold cappuccino. After about five minutes, Jillian returned to the table. She appeared drained and washed out. *"I'm sorry, Franclynne, I felt the urge to throw up. Do you really believe that Sean actually did those things?"*

"I'm sorry, Jillian, but he did."

Jillian leaned back in her chair. She was quiet for a few heartbeats, and then she said, *"You're a psychologist, Franclynne, what would cause a man to treat a woman like that?"*

"Actually, Jillian, there are many reasons why a person could become so distorted. But in Sean's case, he is something that's called a psychopath."

"Yes, I've heard the term, what does it mean?"

"Well, Jillian, the shortened version is that even though Sean can come across as empathic and feeling, he really doesn't give a shit about others. He has no stable emotions. His goal is to manipulate others to get what he wants. He sees others as objects, not as people."

*"You know, "*she said, *"I have noticed that Sean has some strange inclinations."*

"Like what?"

"Well, first, there is that strange tattoo on his hand. You know the one that means he is involved in that distorted game called, 'The Cult of the Souls'. I did some research, asked around, and found out it is some kind of sadomasochistic game. That worries me. Every time I ask him about it he changes the subject."

"Go on, Jillian."

"I also noticed that sometimes he reacts very strangely when a beautiful or shapely woman walks by. He grabs his cell phone and holds it up saying, "I'm getting a message", when I think he's really taking a picture of her. It gives me the willies."

"Do you mind if I ask you something personal?"

"No, go ahead."

"Are you romantically involved with him, or just friends?"

"No romance- I'm not attracted to him. I feel bad for him, but I'm not attracted to him."

"Why do you feel bad for him?"

"I don't know. He seems lost at times. But at other times he looks predatory."

"Predatory? What do you mean?'

"I can't put my finger on it, but something changes in his eyes, as if he wants to attack something. I used to have cats. They would get a look in their eyes when they were stalking. I have never seen him act differently, just something in his eyes."

Jillian thought for a moment and then said, *"Now it's my turn, Franclynne. Why do you want custody of his children?"*

"Well, first of all Jillian, I love them. They have been part of my life ever since I met Beth. I truly cannot imagine spending my life without them. Does that sound selfish to you?"

"No"

"What will you do if the court gives the children back to Sean?"

"I don't really know, Jillian. I have been trying not to think about it. But I guess I will cry a lot."

Franclynne bent her head and held back some tears. *"You must promise me, Jillian, that if the court gives the children back to Sean, you will stay close to them. They are the two sweetest young souls that I have ever known. I don't want to see them damaged by trauma."*

Jillian's expression changed; *"You're that worried about Sean?"*

"Yes I am. You read the list, would you want your children raised by the man that did those things?"

"Franclynne, tell me again, do you actually believe that Sean is capable of those things?"

"Yes, I do Jillian. You must be careful around him, he can and will turn on you at some point." "You think?"

" No, I don't think, Jillian, I know."

Jillian had a distant look in her eyes. *"Oh my god! Those children cannot be with Sean."*

Jillian put her hand out touching Franclynne's. *"I will do everything I can to help."*

"Thank you, Jillian, thank you."

Jillian got up to leave. Franclynne said: *"Remember, Jillian, court is on Tuesday."*

When Jillian arrived back at her apartment, her head was spinning from the revelations she had just read and her discussion with Franclynne. What should she do? What she wanted to do was just ignore it, ignore Sean, and make believe none of it happened. However, she knew she could not do any of that. She kept seeing the happy children in the park and could not clear her mind of the image. Oh my god, she kept repeating to herself. Franclynne was right. Having read Beth's proclamations completely changed her point of view.

There was a message on her machine. She listened. It was from Sean. He seemed to be begging for her to come to his apartment. He had something very important to show her. Jillian had never been at Sean's apartment, as she saw that move as changing the interpersonal boundaries between them. But, considering what she had just heard, she thought she'd better go. She had to go and tell him in person that she would not help him, nor speak to him again.

O'Brian had Mike back at the police station. This time it was not in the interrogation room, but his office.

"So, what do you have for me, Mike?"

"Before I tell you, Captain, I want to make sure I understand the deal."

O'Brian nodded his head in affirmation.

"Captain, our deal is that if I can help you locate the serial rapist, the District Attorney will lessen my charge."

"That's correct, Mike. Now, what did you find?"

"Well, it's not much, but I do know some of the people who play the 'Cult of the Souls' game. They have a chat site. I asked them for help."

"Go on."

"They seemed to believe there's a guy out there named Sean who has been bragging about the rapes he has committed."

"What's the last name?"

"That's the thing Captain. Nobody knows his last name. We don't deal in last names."

"Keep trying, Mike. I need the name. Somebody must know it!"

Chapter XXX

It was Sunday, and the apartment was filled with tension and anxiety. The children even noticed it and commented to La.

"La is everything okay? You seem angry. Did we do something wrong?"

"No, children, I'm just scared."

La grabbed Ellie and hugged her tightly.

"Are you scared about court?"

"Yes."

"Don't worry, La, we will be alright."

This made La even more concerned. This sweet young child did not really understand the implications of what was happening. She was not sure that she understood the implications either.

La had been spending more and more of her free time out of the apartment. She refused to tell Franclynne where she was going or what she was doing. She would just shrug her shoulders when questioned about her whereabouts. It was increasing Franclynne's anxiety. She knew from her nose that La was lying when she said, "the park." What was she up to? It was ominous and it scared her.

Franclynne herself had barely slept since meeting Jillian. It was not that Jillian said or did anything that worried her, but the reality of the situation was becoming more in focus. She had met with Hawthorne Holmes and he did not present an overly optimistic picture. He indicated that there was nothing in the record that would indicate any current behavior problems with Sean, even though his past was not positive. He hoped the judge would be compassionate, but it would be highly unusual for Sean not to get full custody. Holmes wanted Franclynne to be prepared for the possible outcome.

"Unless we have some clear evidence, not hearsay, not worries, but clear evidence, it would be surprising for the judge not to give a father custody."

These words rang in her ears repeatedly like a misguided song. She thought about it at work, she thought about it during meditation time, she thought about it preparing for bed, and she dreamed about it while asleep. It was haunting her. The negative anticipation was loosening her emotional scotch tape. She had to use more and more energy to maintain control. When she played with the children, she told them she had a cold, so she could intermittently wipe the tears from her eyes. It was going to be ugly, and worse, there was nothing she could do to stop it. She was totally helpless.

The other question that ran through her thoughts was, *"why does Sean want custody? What does he get by gaining custody of the children?"* She knew he hatred Beth, but Beth was gone. *"Why make this fight?"* The more she pondered the question, the fewer answers she got. However, knowing what she knew about Sean there had to be a devious reason, and this terrified her.

Angelique was out of the hospital and continued her therapeutic support with Franclynne. During one of their sessions, she noticed the worried expression on her therapist's face and asked about it. Since her tears were always on the brink, Franclynne broke down and began sobbing. It was a cathartic experience. She told Angelique the entire story, beginning to possible ending. Angelique said,

"Do you realize you saved my life?"

"What?"

"Yes, you, Franclynne, you saved my life."

"I will never forget it."

"I just helped, Angelique"

"No, you didn't just help! You saved my life. I would be dead from the injuries if not for you."

"Thank you for those words, Angelique."

"They are not just words; it is the truth!"

"By the way, Franclynne, when is this trial?"

Franclynne told her the date and Angelique said. *"I will be there!"*

The two-women hugged, and Angelique reluctantly left the office. Franclynne cancelled the rest of her day. She did not go home; she stayed in the office and wept for a good part of the afternoon. Franclynne had been lied to many times in her life, and the lie that she had to tell Beth weighed heavily on her soul. She tried many times to rationalize it, telling herself that it helped Beth to die more peacefully, but the lie was still a lie. Sean would get custody of the children and Franclynne would be scared for the rest of her life. She vowed to herself that if Sean did get custody, she would not let the fight die. She would continue to press with all of her emotional strength to regain custody of the children.

Sean arrived at his attorney's office in preparation for the trial that started the next day. His attorney started the conversation.

"I know I've told you that this is basically a slam dunk. And I do believe it is. But there are still some potholes we need to discuss."

"I'm listening."

"The tape that you wife made is pretty damning and emotional. I was able to view it the other day. People will cry when they see it. It will carry some weight."

"Why?"

"She is speaking from the grave, for god's sake. Her last words on this earth are those of condemning you. This video will carry a lot of weight."

"She was dying, she hated me, and she was a bitch. Of course, she is not going to say anything positive about me."

"Even so, it will not help us."

"What can I do?"

"Well there are some important things for you to do. The number one thing is not to get angry and lose your temper. She says some nasty things in the tape, sexual things. You must remain in control."

"Yes, I understand."

"NO, I do not think you do. If you do anything that the court can interpret as an angry reaction, the judge will know that the tape is truth. We are lucky that this is not a jury trial. That tape, in and of itself would sway many people. It would put you at a disadvantage."

He stopped and took a drink of water on his desk.

"But, it is not a jury trial."

"Sean, I know you've told me that you had a previous life. You went into something called a fugue state. Your memory of your previous life disappeared, and you woke up one day in a different part of the country as Sean. Is there something I should know about that previous life?"

Sean was subdued and quiet.

"Sean, I am your attorney, I am confidential. You can tell me anything."

Still no response.

"Okay, don't tell me, but if they bring it up, I will be unprepared to defend you."

"It's not pretty."

"Let me hear." What the attorney did not explain to Sean was that he was an officer of the court, and if he found out about a felony, he had to submit it to the judge. He had both a professional and a moral obligation to do so. In the back of his mind he almost wished Sean would admit to a felony. This would allow him to get off the case, and would protect those two young children.

She stood staring out of the window. Her mind was numb. She was not thinking anymore, she was too tired and put a lot of effort into just doing regular, mundane things, like dressing, eating, and taking a bath. Her sleep was very irregular. It was Monday; the trial would be the next morning. She had almost stopped worrying, what will happen would happen. Franclynne was in a daze. She wracked her brain for solutions to this problem, but was unsuccessful. One day, she had almost gone to JJ Aaron and asked for money to run with the children, but she couldn't carry that out. She didn't know if that made her weak or strong, but in either case she couldn't do it.

Part II

Chapter XXXI

She thought her anxiety was subsiding; it was not. She had been sleeping better. That ended this night. Franclynne woke up at 2 a.m. to go to the bathroom. She was so tired; she lay down on the bathroom floor and immediately fell asleep. But the sleep only lasted two hours and she awoke with a start. She was not quite sure if she was awake, but as she lay on the floor, she saw a woman standing in the corner of the room. Franclynne tried to clear her eyes, but she was unable to do so. She realized that the woman was not a real person and she almost recognized the vision. It was the same vision that she had seen months ago in her bedroom.

The woman stood with her long brown hair flowing as if standing in a wind storm. Her face was hard to read. It was blank with no expression. The woman stared at Franclynne on the floor. Franc Lynne just stared at the vision. She had no fear, as she was familiar with this apparition. Unlike before, the vision was not ignoring Franclynne, but was staring directly at her.

Finally, the apparition said, *"Why are you on the floor?"* Without thinking, Franclynne said,

"I'm scared."

A hesitancy followed: *"You didn't answer my question."*

Franclynne had no answer. Finally, the vision said, *"There are many people who are depending upon you. Do you understand that?"*

Franclynne nodded her head in affirmation.

"Many people are frightened, Franclynne. That is no reason to hide in this place. Get up off the floor, Franclynne"

She looked up at the vision. The specter pointed at her and repeated, *"I said, get up off the floor!"* Then something happened. The vision put her hands over her face and the room seemed to turn blue. The specter then removed her hands, and her face changed, becoming mentor's face, Helen DeJarden. The specter spoke again. *"I said, get off the floor!"*

Franclynne struggled to her feet. She was shaking.

"What do you smell, Franclynne, what do you smell?"

Franclynne bent her head.

"Again, you don't answer. What do you smell?"

"Disappointment."

"Now, listen to me, Franclynne, you must stand tall. Now is not the time for weakness. There will be plenty of pain. Everyone is afraid. But, other lives depend upon you. The past is just that, the past. It is time to stop looking in the rear-view mirror for answers. Look ahead."

The apparition looked up, put its arms together, and disappeared.

The courtroom building itself was terrifying to Franclynne. She had not had positive experiences in courts. She did not like judges and thought that their decisions were, at times, at best, arbitrary. She could not handle the fact that Ellie and Theodore's lives would be left to a stranger. The time had passed quickly. It was truly Judgement Day, and Franclynne was more afraid of this than almost anything she had experienced. She came to realize that the fear she felt for the children was more intense than the fear she felt for herself. It was easier to experience pain than to watch it. She was unprepared for this. She hoped and prayed that Hawthorne Holmes was ready.

Franclynne put on her most conservative outfit to go to court. Just being there would make her feel uncomfortable. She had taken La shopping so she would presentable at the proceedings. The children wore their 'picture' clothes. They seemed relaxed as they drove to the courthouse. Franclynne had prepared them for all the possibilities, and yet, as children, they fully did not understand the implications of what was happening. They had to park a couple of blocks from the courthouse and walk to the entrance. As they approached, they saw a woman walking up and down the block. She seemed to protesting something. As they got closer, Franclynne realized that the woman was Angelique. She was walking back and forth in front of the court with a sign that read, "Give the children to Dr. Longaire." She did not acknowledge Franclynne as she approached but kept walking and shouting, "Give the children to Dr. Longaire." She was being closely watched by a couple of police officers.

Franclynne had her bag of coffee grinds with her. She had placed it near her car keys so she would not forget it again. As they walked up the steps, Franclynne felt her legs begin to shake. She held Ellie close to her, keeping her hand on her. Theodore was walking with La. Franclynne turned back to look at La and noticed the angry expression on her face. Franclynne had spoken in detail with La about what to expect and how to act. She had to control her reactions. If she got angry and lost her temper, things would not go well.

The four of them walked through security and immediately her anxiety rose exponentially. Franclynne was bothered by seeing all of the police officers. She also did not like answering questions about why she had a small pouch filled with coffee beans. Her usual response was, "It distracts me." Only a very few people knew of her real secret. Once an officer asked for a further explanation and she said, "It's like a security blanket." She became angry when the officer looked skeptical. Finally, she said, with the most authority she could muster, "*Officer, it is really none of your business.*"

They entered the courtroom after officers asked them to wait in a small room. Luckily, it was not a general waiting area, but their attorney arranged for a separate room in which for them to wait. Franclynne was surprised when she entered the courtroom and went to her seat. She would sit up front with attorney Holmes, and the children would sit in the back with La. Besides Holmes, Captain O'Brian was also in the room, sitting in the back row with two other officers. Seated on the other side of the court, directly opposite O'Brian was J. Aaron. He smiled at her when their eyes met. Angelique also entered the courtroom, without her sign, which must have been confiscated by the security police. She also sat toward the back of the court.

Franclynne held the pouch up to the side of her nose. The realities of where she was and the consequences of this day were weighing heavily on her mind. She could feel her blood turning cold as she scanned the area. Then she noticed him. She had seen pictures of Sean, but had never really seen him in person. She became chilled and her hands began to tingle. She felt the urge to throw up. She turned and noticed that La had also seen Sean and Franclynne put her hand up slightly for La to see to divert her obvious annoyance.

Holmes entered the court and gave Franclynne a look. She rose and followed him to the front row. When she rose, she could see all eyes follow her. Again, she felt guilty, although she really had no idea why. As she got to her chair, Franclynne stopped, turned, and looked at the children. She caught their eyes, smiled and winked. Both children smiled back.

The judge entered the room from a door to the left of his desk. He was an older gentleman, who appeared to be very sophisticated. He ascended to his seat and began to look at the papers that were on his desk. He looked up and said, *"The biological father of the two children, has delivered a motion to retain custody. Unfortunately, the birth mother has passed away from a very serious illness. The burden, at this time, is on the defense to make the argument of why father should not be given custody."*

Holmes stood, *"Thank you your honor. I would like to present some information for the court to consider. First, your honor, Sean Whitford's history is a mystery. We only know about Mr. Whitford's life since he married Beth, so that means details of his existence prior to his marriage of six years, are not to be found. Your honor, I have sent investigators out and none of them has found anything about this man's history. It makes me feel, your honor, that Mr. Whitford has something to hide. I have a request, your honor. I would like to meet with Mr. Whitford and find out about his history. I would like him to give the court a DNA sample, and I would like a detailed psychological evaluation to determine whether this man can be an appropriate father for these two children."*

Sean's attorney stood immediately. *"I object your honor. The defense has to show cause for such an investigation into my client."*

Holmes replied, *"Your honor, when Beth was alive, she asked the court for, and received, an order of protection again Mr. Whitford because of past violent behavior during the marriage. In my mind, your honor, this is enough cause to request a detailed history, a DNA sample, and a psychological evaluation."*

Sean's attorney immediately jumped up in protest. Holmes said, *"May I continue, your honor?"*

"Continue, Attorney Holmes."

"Your honor, DNA is used to verify identity. In this case, we have no previous history to compare. Mr. Whitford's recent past behavior leads one to speculate that there might be history that a problem in Mr. Whitford's past regarding legal issues I mean, why should he have hidden his history? I would submit that if there is no problem, let us compare Mr. Whitford's DNA with the Combined DNA Index System, also known as CODIS. "

Attorney Holmes, turned to look directly at Sean. He then turned back to the judge and continued. *"There is another issue, your honor. One in five individuals suffers with a mental illness. I would like to know whether Mr. Whitford's mental health makes him a threat to these two children. That is why your honor, I think a forensic psychological evaluation is warranted. I really question, as their mother questioned, which you will hear in her video deposition, that Mr. Whitford has serious mental health issues. "*

The judge thought for a second and said, *"I am asking both attorneys to present written evidence for me to review. I will expect these briefs in my hands by Friday and I will rule on Monday."*

Sean's attorney again rose in opposition. "Your honor, this is totally unprecedented. There is nothing to suggest that these procedures are necessary."

Holmes countered, *"That is exactly the point your honor. We do not know what Mr. Whitford's history is. There is an implicit opinion in the other attorney's protest that we are violating Mr. Whitford's rights. Your honor, I do not believe that is occurring here. What I believe is that we are conservatively attempting to protect the children's rights to live in an emotionally appropriate setting."*

"Attorneys, I have already ruled. I will read briefs by Friday and rule on Monday. This court is adjourned for today."

Sean Whitford and his attorney gathered together in a private room. The attorney sat at the end of the table and Sean followed him in. However, Sean did not sit, he paced. He was obviously agitated. Finally, he stopped, looked directly at his attorney, and banged his hand on the table.

"That sucked. What kind of bullshit was that? I was planning to leave here today with custody of my children. What the fuck happened in there?"

"I told you Sean that anything could happen. It is hard to predict these things."

"No, that's bullshit!" He pointed at the attorney. *"You fucked up! Why did you let that happen? I'm not paying you to sit on your ass and not defend my rights. I'm blaming this completely on you."* Surprisingly, the attorney sat motionless. Even his facial expression did not change. Sean began his pacing again. Again, he turned to the attorney and said, *"So, what the fuck happened in there?"* Finally, his attorney said, *"If you don't like how I represent you, you have a solution to that problem."* Sean held his hands out, asking, *"What are you talking about?"*

The attorney smiled and said, *"You could fire me."* This really set Sean off. He began pounding on the walls of the room. He made so much noise that an officer opened the door and looked at the attorney. *"Is everything all right in here?"* *"Everything is all right, officer. Don't worry, I'm okay. The man is just pissed off."* The officer closed the door. Finally, the attorney asked, *"You're acting like a scared, guilty man. What is the problem, Sean? I told you, this is a process."*

Sean continued to pace, but he slowed his and turned to talk to his lawyer. *"Look, my past is my past. I do not want it revealed. Do you understand that? I do not want my history splattered all over for everyone to see. Would you want that?"*

"Listen, Sean, do you every wonder why I haven't specifically asked you about your past?"

Sean shook his head.

"Well, the truth is, Sean, I don't want to know about your past. Because, if you tell me and there is a problem, I am under ethical and legal obligation to tell the court about it."

"What about our confidentiality?"

"That's very important, but I am an officer of the court. If you commit perjury and I know about it, I have to reveal it."

"I have nothing to hide. However, Sean, you obviously do. Nonetheless, listen to me. Let's wait until the judge rules on Monday. Maybe you won't have to reveal anything. There is little precedence for revealing DNA without specific evidence of a crime." Sean pointed towards his attorney and said, *"Next time we are in court, I expect you to be more aggressive."*

Chapter XXXII

Monday came very quickly. The joy that Franclynne felt the previous Tuesday hoping to be able to return home with the children for good, seemed very short lived. She decided, on legal advice, not to bring the children to the Monday appearance. She also had a long, detailed discussion with La that if something very bad happened in court she should not even think about running with the children. Throughout the conversation, La did not make eye contact.

"I know what you're thinking, La. Don't do it. If you do it, it almost guarantees we will never get custody of them."

La turned to her with an angry look. *"I won't let him hurt those children."* *"La, promise me you won't run!"* La huffed, and without saying anything else, left the room.

As she glanced over to Sean, she saw such a smug look on his face that she wanted to go and slap him. Actually, she wanted to do more than slap him, she wanted to hurt him. She could not know, especially from this distance, what was in his mind. But what she did know is that it was evil. Of this she had no question. He smiled at her and looked as though he was a cat that just swallowed the canary. She had a very bad feeling in her stomach. Tuesday had felt like a win, but today she was very concerned that the judge was going to rule against them.

Franclynne tried to read the face of the judge as he entered the room. She had wished she were closer so she could catch a whiff of him. She immediately realized how important her sense of smell was to her sense of security.

The judge sat and one could hear a pin drop in the court. Finally, he began to speak, *"I have read the briefs presented by both sides. My rulings are as follows: first, there is not enough evidence to warrant a DNA search of Mr. Whitford."* Holmes stood, and the judge immediately said, *"Sit down, Mr. Holmes."* Holmes reluctantly went to his chair. *"Second, there is enough question for me to ask for a forensic psychological evaluation. I will choose the psychologist for that purpose, and Mr. Whitford will pay for the evaluation."*

Sean's attorney immediately stood and the judge strongly asked him to sit. But he did not immediately respond. *"Your honor, one quick point then I will sit. It is the other attorney who is asking for this useless evaluation. Why should my client bare the total burden?"*

The judge thought for a moment and said *"The burden will be equally shared by both sides."* The judge continued, *"Unfortunately, I cannot allow the video of the children's mother to be presented to the court. It is hearsay and not admissible."*

Immediately, Holmes stood with a forceful objection. *"It is not hearsay, your honor. It is the mother's own words telling the court about the character and nature of the man you are deciding about whether the children should live with him. One of the central questions in this hearing is where would these children thrive. Beth's words and thoughts on this issue are central to this determination."*

"Objection overruled; the tape will not be heard in this courtroom."

"I am appointing a law guardian to represent the children. They will have the same attorney. He will investigate this matter and make a recommendation to the court. If I am not satisfied I may, in the future, order a Lincoln hearing."

"Lastly, today, I am calling Mr. Whitford to the stand and I will ask some questions. There will be no cross examination." *"Mr. Whitford, please take the stand."*

As Sean approached the witness chair, Franclynne began to quiver. She wanted to stand and gouge his eyes out. She believed their best chance of gaining custody came from Beth's video. Now the judge's rule made it not admissible. The judge also would not allow a DNA test. Depending on the ability of the examiner, Sean could fake the psychological exam.

Sean sat in the witness chair and was sworn in by the clerk. The judge looked at him and said, *"Mr. Whitford, now that you are sworn in, it means you understand that you have to tell the truth."* Sean nodded his head in affirmation. *"Mr. Whitford, do you understand the definition of perjury against this court?* Before he could answer the judge said, *"Let me define it for you. Perjury is willingly telling a non-truth in order to influence this court. Therefore, it is an intentional act of swearing a false oath. You have now taken a lawful oath to tell the truth."*

"I understand, your honor."

"Good. Mr. Whitford did you have a name before this one?"

"Yes, your honor."

"Will you tell me what it was?"

"No, your honor."

"Why not, Mr. Whitford?"

"I am a very private person and do not want to reveal my past."

"I am not going to push you further, Mr. Whitford, but let me warn you. I do not trust you. Anyone who is not fully cooperative is usually hiding something. Be careful, Mr. Whitford, for if I find even a hint of criminal activity, I will make sure the District Attorney pursues you with all haste. Do you understand, Mr. Whitford?"

Sean nodded his head in affirmation. He looked directly at Franclynne and smiled before he rose from his seat. It was almost a challenge. He was mocking her, and she knew it. She did not break his gaze. She was terrified. Her legs were shaking and she was sweating. Having, what she considered a psychopath, staring at her and smiling at her, chilled her to the bone, but something in her refused to allow her to divert her eyes. Their eyes must have been locked for at least ten seconds, until Sean rose to leave his seat and leave the courtroom. But that ten seconds. It felt like a lifetime for Franclynne. Nevertheless, she had to do it; she had to stare him down.

Franclynne knew those psychopathic eyes. She had experienced them before having been held and tortured by one. She was not close enough to pick up the scent, but she smelled it, from recall. It rattled through her senses and she felt woozy.

She did not realize it, but it would take months until that stare would fade from her memory. It would plague her at three o'clock in the morning. Past memories of torture had now returned in full force. It was like witnessing the devil incarnate. Evil in the flesh. The only thing that brought her back to her senses was the thought of the children and how much they needed her. If not for them, she would have considered taking flight and hiding out.

Franclynne had taken to become a little paranoid, looking around to make sure she was not being stalked. She went so far as to purchase a switchblade and keep it under her pants by her ankle. She was convinced, at some level that Sean was going to target her and come after her. He did not like being challenged, and her staring at him was definitely a challenge. She almost wanted him to come after her so she could respond.

She was jumpy, even La noticed it, but Franclynne denied the feelings. She went over it repeatedly, in her mind's eye, what she would do or say if Sean confronted her. Then it happened. It was in Wal-Mart. Elle needed socks and under garments, so she decided to go shopping one day when they were in school. She was walking down the aisle looking at clothes for the little ones, when she felt eyes on her. She was used to people staring at her, but this was different. She froze, immediately became rigid, feeling the tension running through her veins. She turned, and there he stood, not five feet from her. All of her practice to decide what to say evaporated like a mist. Her mind was blank, consumed by horror. It must have been evident, for Sean said, *"Is there anything wrong, Dr. Longaire? You look fearful. I hope it's nothing I did."* Her mouth was dry and no words were coming from her lips. Sean began a low but noticeable laugh. *"Dr. Longaire, are you happy with the court rulings. You see, I have nothing to hide."* Then his expression changed. *"But I want, and will get, my children. You have kidnapped them from me and I will not allow it."* He took a few steps closer to her and she could smell the horrible odor of the psychopath. Her face was blank, her legs unstable, and her thighs sweating. *"I must have surprised you, Dr. Longaire. Or, are you turned on? I'll bet you're attracted to me."* He took another step closer and whispered, *"Are you wet?"*

And at that moment, a body pushed between them. La was now standing between Sean and Franclynne, staring directly into Sean's eyes. She was ready to pounce, but surprisingly, Franclynne, moved La aside. *"It's alright La, this psycho doesn't scare me whatsoever. He thinks he's tough but he only prays on the weak."* She took a step towards Sean. *"I am weak no more. You will not scare or threaten me."* She was now within a breath of his face. *"If you come near me again, I will hurt you!"* Now, Sean backed away. He smiled, turned, and left them.

La looked strangely at Franclynne. *"You'll hurt him?"* *"I will hurt him."* But as she was walking away, Franclynne almost collapsed.

Chapter XXXIII

Valerie Lingard was assigned to be the law guardian for the Whitford children. Ms. Lingard never really wanted to be an attorney, but she wanted to advocate for children. She soon realized that the best way to accomplish that was to go to law school and advocate from a position of power. A law guardian is an attorney appointed by the court to represent children and their best interests in the family court. In that regard, Ms. Lingard had the plan to interview the children, then interview both parents, or in this case, the father and Franclynne, before deciding in which atmosphere would the children thrive the most.

Ms. Lingard was an experienced law guardian, having worked in that regard for over 20 years. She had interviewed thousands of children and their parents. She thrived in this role. Sean's attorney had requested a male law guardian, but it was a 'next up' situation, which eliminated any potential bias.

Ms. Lingard asked to interview the children at school, which she considered a neutral environment. The children would not be aware of which day she would choose to do her work, so they couldn't be influenced by the caregiver whatsoever. Ms. Lingard was very sensitive to the concept of parental alienation. That is, when a parent teaches a child how to respond with the direct goal of alienating the other parent. She was also very sensitive not to put the children in a compromising position with her interviewing. This meant never directly asking the children where they would want to live. Deriving that response must be ascertained t from their answers and their body language when certain questions were asked. Even though she did not have children herself, Valerie Lingard studied and observed at a very efficient level. She was rarely fooled.

The day she chose to interview the Whitford children was cloudy and cold. The principal had graciously offered her a comfortable private room for the process. Ellie's teacher brought her to meet Ms. Lingard. As she entered the room, Valerie rose to great her. Her teacher stepped forward and shook Valerie's hand. Valerie said to the teacher, "*I didn't realize that Ellie was such a beautiful young lady.*" The teacher smiled, patted Ellie on the head, and turned to leave the room. Ellie turned her head and watched her leave.

"Hello, Ellie. My name is Valerie. I am here to find out about you. We shouldn't be that long, and I hope we can be friends."

Ellie smiled and sat down. The chair she chose was not close to Valerie, but it was not far away either.

"So, tell me, Ellie do you like school?"

"Yes."

"What do you like about school?"

Ellie thought for a moment and then said, *"I like lunch."* Valerie laughed, but Ellie continued, *"I have a lot of friends. I also like Ms. Halpert. She is very nice. She rarely yells at us."*

"She seemed nice to me as well."

"Besides school Ellie, what else do you like to do?"

"I like to go to the park."

"The park? What do you do in the park?"

"I like to climb."

"On what do you like to climb?"

"I climb up the wall. La doesn't like it when I climb the wall",

"La, who is she?"

"She is my babysitter. She takes me and my brother to the park."

"Really, how often do you go?"

"We go almost every day, unless it rains."

"Sometimes we go swimming."

"Tell me about La, I don't know her. Who is she?"

"She is my best friend."

"Your best friend?"

"She also reads to me and helps me with my homework. But can I tell you a secret?"

"Sure, Ellie, what is the secret?"

"I think I'm better at math than La is."

Valerie chuckles and said, "You are?"

"Yes. Sometimes Franclynne has to help us." Now Ellie laughed.

"Franclynne is a psychologist, right?"

Ellie nodded her head in affirmation.

"What's it like living with a psychologist?"

Ellie thought for a moment, then said, *"Can I tell you another secret?"*

"Sure, Ellie"

"I'm not really sure what she does. I know she helps people."

"Does she help you?"

"Yes, whenever I have a problem, you know like when one of the boys calls me a name, I go to Lynn and she helps me figure out what to do."

"Sounds like you Love Lynn."

"I do. I also love La, and of course Theodore."

"Anyone else?"

"No, I can't think of anyone else."

"Ellie, I would like to change the subject."

There was a pause, and a quiet. Ellie immediately noticed the change in mood. Before Valerie could speak, she asked, *"Are you going to ask me about my mom?"*

"Yes, Ellie"

Immediately the child began to cry. It was not a heavy sobbing, but the tears were quite evident. Valerie rose from her chair and went over to the young girl.

"I'm sorry Ellie, would you rather not talk about it?"

"No, we can talk. I just miss her so much. My body hurts when I think about her. Did you know that before she died, Theodore, Franclynne, La, and I all held her in her bed? She couldn't move or talk. But she did smile. We also ate ice cream together."

"I'm sorry, Ellie. I didn't mean to upset you."

"It's okay, I cry a lot. I have to be strong for Theodore. But La and Franclynne keep us strong."

"How do they do that Ellie?"

"We talk a lot about mom, and how she loved all of us."

"You love Franclynne and La, don't you?"

Ellie nodded her head again. Then, surprisingly she said, *"I don't want them to die."*

"Why do you worry about that Ellie?"

Ellie bowed her head, and the mood changed again.

"I worry that my father will hurt them, like he hurt my mom."

"Did you ever see your father hurt your mom, Ellie?"

Again, she bowed her head, and shifted in her chair.

"Yes I did, but I would rather not talk about it, it makes me upset."

"Does talking about your father make you upset?"

Surprisingly, Ellie did not immediately answer. She was contemplative. Finally, she said, "Not *upset, scared!"*

Jillian knocked on the door, but there was no answer. She knocked again, trying to be patient. She had a key to Sean's apartment. She had reluctantly taken it when he pushed it on her. She had often reminded him that she was not his girlfriend, and therefore, did not require having a key. However, he insisted, stating that he was often out, and she could come to his apartment and wait for him to return.

After the third knock with no answer, Jillian reluctantly took the key out and let herself in. She had not told Sean that she was planning to visit at that time, but she was becoming suspicious about a number of things and decided to go speak with him to relieve her troubled thoughts. She was still very upset about her meeting with Franclynne and did not know how she would broach the subject with Sean.

Jillian had been to Sean's apartment only once before and something was clearly different. She could not quite identify what it was, but it was changed in some way from what she remembered. It bothered her so much that she decided not to stay. She began walking toward the door to leave. As she reached the door to open it, she was shocked to find Sean standing at the entrance, obviously waiting to enter the apartment. He seemed different; his face was strange, distorted. Her first thought was that he looked possessed. He hesitated for a moment, than his face returned to more of a normal stare.

"Jillian, it's nice to see you. I'm glad you came to visit."

There was something in his tone that made Jillian shudder. She realized that, because of the discussion with Franclynne, she could never see Sean in the same light. It frightened her to be standing so close to him. What if everything Franclynne said was truth. She could be in danger.

"I'm sorry, Sean, I have been waiting for you. But I am late now and have to leave."

"No, please stay."

"I'm sorry, Sean, I have to go to work."

"I said, I want you to stay!"

His tone was indignant. She was in trouble and she knew it.

Chapter XXXIV

She needed a day off. Franclynne cancelled all of her patients and decided she would spend the day at the park. The children were in school and she did not feel the need to be responsible. The park had a walking path that surrounded a lake. It was a fairly large, tranquil lake that had many trees leaning over the water, providing photographic spots. There were also many benches surrounding the lake. Franclynne walked for a while and then found a suitable bench in which to sit. She started to drift into her own thoughts. The ducks in the lake were conditioned so that when they saw people on the benches, it could also mean that they would be fed. Before long, there were many beautiful mallard ducks leisurely swimming around near Franclynne's bench. It was truly wonderful, as the time drifted by with nothing for her to do, and no place to go. There were no disturbing sounds to make her jumpy and her mind was able to settle down from the worries and concerns about the children, the court, and Sean.

The other wonderful things about the park were the wonderful scents of nature. She did not need her coffee beans, although she tried to keep them in a pocket no matter where she roamed. But here she could smell the trees, the bushes, the grass, and even the ducks, all wonderful scents, because they were not human. She did not have to protect her nose; she just had to sit and breathe in the aromas of nature.

Her mind eventually drifted to the beach and the ocean. She realized she had not visited a real beach in many years. She promised herself that this had to change. As she relaxed, she actually drifted off to sleep a few times, but almost immediately woke, not with a start, but she just opened her eyes to watch the ducks swimming by. It was wonderful. She thought of a line in a Bob Dylan song, "I haven't known peace and quiet for so long I can't remember what it's like." Again, she promised herself to return more often to this place, to let the tension melt away from her.

It was around noon and there were not many people on the walking path or out fishing in the lake. The sky was blue, with only a few wandering clouds, and the weather was temperate. It could not have been more perfect. She bent her head and drifted off to sleep again.

Captain O'Brian was also having a fairly quiet day when a subordinate came into his office.

"Captain, we just got a phone call from a hospital regarding a woman who had been brutally attacked. She is in The Hospital of the Saints on Morgan St. I have already sent some men over there to determine if this was a random event or part of a pattern. I thought you should know."

O'Brian was miffed, but did not show it to the sergeant. He had informed his squad that he wanted immediate notice whenever a woman was attacked for any reason. O'Brian rose and decided he wanted to interview the woman himself.

Upon arriving at the hospital, O'Brian hurried through the corridors to the emergency area. When he got there, he found it empty. A nurse walked by and he stopped her.

"Hello, young lady, I am Captain O'Brian with the police. Can you tell me what has happened to the young woman who was in this room?"

"My name is Tamron. I am the nurse for this section. She was brought in almost two hours ago. She was unconscious. We had to shock her two times. She is currently in emergency surgery. The doctor said she might have a very serious neck injury that he thought looked like an act of aggression. He is unsure whether they can save her."

"Do we know her name?"

"We do not. She was found in an alley with no identifying information."

"Was she sexually assaulted?"

"I'm not sure, Captain."

"Where was she found?"

"The officers outside can give you the details."

"One more question, nurse. What was the color of her hair?"

"Her hair?"

"Yes, what was the color?"

She continued to drift- she was almost at the point where she did not want to return to the reality of circumstance. Then, her nose sensed something, a familiar smell. For a split second she discounted it, but it too pungent, and almost immediately, Franclynne felt a hand on her shoulder. She jumped in total surprise. She heard a voice and, her blood turned icy cold. Her nose was on fire. Her contentment had been shattered. She bent her head down, and in her peripheral vision, she saw Sean's face. Franclynne's immediate reaction was to reach for her knife. She found it by touch, took it out and opened to the blade. The hand remained on her shoulder. She turned, quickly rose, and slashed. She saw a man fall to the ground, with blood coming from his face. But, as he fell and the sounds of his agony rang through the air, she realized it wasn't Sean. Her eyes grew wide.

"Oh my god." She bent over the man. *"I'm so sorry; I didn't mean to hurt you!"*

Holding his face, the man said, *"You are a crazy woman. I was just coming to ask you if you had a match for my cigarette."*

Franclynne found herself at the police station after she called 911. Captain O'Brian entered the room.

"Well, Ms. Longaire, you are a lucky woman. The cut on Mr. Mancini's face was only a minor scratch. It only required a few stiches. He decided not to press any charges against you. The illegal knife, well, I'm going to bury that information."

Franclynne looked up at him and smiled. O'Brian sat in a chair across the table from her table.

"Are you okay?"

She nodded.

"What was this all about?"

"Nothing, really, I was just spooked."

"And why might you be carrying a knife?"

Franclynne looked up and met his eyes. She said nothing. He swallowed. *"Well, I guess that's really not my business."* He rose. *"You're free to leave, there are no charges. But be careful."*

"Thank you, Captain." She smiled. Franclynne's smile was not an easy thing to ignore. It could melt a man with little effort. O'Brian smiled back, trying to maintain a composed front. He began to leave, but then stopped and looked back at her. *"I almost asked you to go for coffee, but I remembered that you're not into relationships."*

"Thank you again, Captain." Franclynne rose and left the police station.

O'Brian left the room, still seeing the smile in his mind's eye. When he got to his office, another young officer awaited his arrival. *"Sir, I have some bad news. The girl at the hospital has died. We now have another murder on our hands."*

Chapter XXXV

Ms. Lingard wrote a detailed, six-page report to the Family Court judge. She had interviewed both of the children, Franclynne, and she had interviewed the babysitter, La, but the father, Sean, refused. Initially he did not actually refuse; he just never returned her calls. Eventually, she did connect with him. However, he indicated that he did not trust the court and he would not speak with her.

Lingard's report was very specific. In her opening paragraph, she summarized her conclusion:

"It is my conclusion that the children would fare better if they were living with Dr. Longaire than with their father. I reach this conclusion, not out of prejudice because Mr. Whitford would not cooperate with my inquiry, but because of the outstanding relationship that these two young people have with Dr. Longaire and their sitter, La. They trust her implicitly, and the environment she has created would provide these children with a secure and loving place to grow."

In the body of the report, she made these observations: *"The babysitter, La, is an interesting person. Several years ago, she made headlines because she had committed a murder. The murder was committed in the act of trying to save her therapist, and in fact, also saving Dr. Longaire's life. She was also known in our community as 'the rat lady'. Although this is not what you might think of as an ideal babysitter for young children, but after speaking with her a number of things became very obvious. First, she is much brighter than her demeanor would suggest. Second, she loves those two young children. Third, I believe she would sacrifice her life for them. She is a selfless person. I believe she gives loves unconditionally. In conclusion, she is the perfect person to babysit these youngsters."*

Little is known about Mr. Whitford's past. Therefore, I decided to contact his superior to get his impressions about his character. When I spoke with him, I received just the opposite. I found out that Mr. Whitford has been suspended from his position as they are looking into the possibility that he has stolen company funds."

Judge Rinsig was a lifelong Family Court Judge. She loved her clients, even the ones in which she removed custody. She was a lovely woman with sparkling eyes. Judge Rinsig was well respected in the community, both by prosecuting and defense attorneys. It was unusual for her to go to a store and not know someone whom she had worked with in court. People believed in her and often would stop to say hello. Even people whose parental rights she had terminated would stop to chat with her. She never felt threatened or put out. She took her job seriously and her decisions were always guided by what she believed were in the best interests of the children involved.

Police guarded Judge Rinsig's office, and people had to ring in to gain access. But in truth, such security measures were never really been needed. However, in today's world, they were necessary precautions. On this day, Rinsig was shopping at her favorite store. She was an excellent cook, and although thin, she loved to eat. People thought of her also as a gourmet chef. Unlike many others, she loved shopping and experimenting with new foods, spices, and herbs. She almost never used recipes. When she shopped, she was completely engrossed, but something interrupted her focus. She felt something, jerked around, and saw a man standing about ten feet away staring at her. He looked familiar. She had seen him in her court, but she was not quite sure when or where. His face was distant, cold, and when she made eye contact, he didn't flinch. The stare continued for a few heartbeats. He then produced a half smile and was gone. She tried to find him, but to no avail. The judge found herself standing in the middle of the supermarket feeling chilled. For the first time in years, she was scared. Moreover, nothing really happened. Was she just feeling paranoid? Judge Rinsig went home, but she could not sleep at all that night. She just saw that face in her mind's eye. The next day in her chambers, she looked differently at her police guards and the locked office doors.

Rinsig had inherited a very complex, family court case. The judge who had been trying it had had a stroke and she was in line to take it over. She read the briefs and the complaints. She also read the law guardian's report.

It did not take long for Rinsig to call the attorneys. She told them during the call that they had better plan to take the afternoon off. This was such an unusual approach, that when the attorneys called either to inquire about what this was about or to protest, they were told by her law clerk, "*Just be there.*"

Chapter XXXVI

She found herself standing in the morgue. O'Brian had called her and asked her to come down to the morgue to try to identify a body. He really had no reason to think there was a connection to Franclynne, but many things that were happening seemed to be revolving around her. So, he decided to take a long shot. Besides, he always liked having a reason to see her. She was rigid as she stood before him, coffee bag in her hand. O'Brian had seen it before and did not question why she was holding this bag up to her face. But he always thought it was strange. He concluded that it probably was just an idiosyncratic habit.

"I'm sorry to call you down here. I know it's an unpleasant experience, but I'm receiving a lot of pressure to solve these crimes. This is a small city and the rash of crimes we are going through is raising eyebrows and frightening people."

Without looking at him, Franclynne asked, *"Why me?"*

O'Brian blushed, *"No particular reason, just a hunch. I will admit, Franclynne, there has been talk that somehow you are involved with the murders."*

Now it was her turn to stare at the Captain. *"Why would people think that? You guys must really be desperate. Is that what you think?"*

"No, but you have to admit it can appear suspicious to some."

She did not feel the need for sarcasm, so she just turned her head away.

"Let's get on with this, Captain."

He unzipped the bag, revealing the face of the young woman. Franclynne almost jumped out of her skin.

"I know her. Her name was Jillian. She was a friend of Sean Whitford."

"That name again. He is the man who is attempting to regain custody of the children, is he not?"

"Yes, he is, Captain."

"Do you think he was involved in this?"

"What do you think, you're the detective?"

There was quiet for a few seconds, then Franclynne commented,

"He's an evil man, Captain. I sense pure evil!"

O'Brian hesitated as if considering whether he should inquire, then he threw caution to the wind to satisfy his curiosity.

"You know, you've said that before."

"Said what?"

"You're sense, what does that mean?"

"I don't know, just a feeling I guess."

"No, it's more than a feeling Franclynne. How do I know that? Well I know that because of the accuracy of this 'feeling'"

Franclynne shrugged her shoulders. *"Believe what you want Captain. I am no psychic."*

"I'm sorry I didn't mean to offend you, I was just curious."

"Just curious? Remember what it did to the cat, Captain."

Franclynne's left hand was still covering part of her face. Her right hand held the coffee bag. Her eyes began again to water. For a flash, she began having evil, revengeful thoughts. However, they quickly turned to grief.

"She was a nice young woman, Captain. I think she became too involved with a psychopath, and it did her in. I will mourn her. I think she wanted to help. She was walking blindly into something she did not understand. It's such a tragedy."

Franclynne turned to leave. As she began walking away, the Captain yelled after her. *"Do you really think Sean Whitford is a psychopath?"*

She stopped, but she did not turn to look at O'Brian. Instead she said, *"I'm not sure."* Then she turned to look at him. *"What I do know, Captain, is that he is evil." "Mark my words, Captain, he is at the center of all this, not me. I am stained because I am in a custody battle with him."* And with that, she left.

The two attorneys entered the Judge's inner chamber. Judge Rinsig was turned with her back to both men. They sat in the chairs across from the Judge's desk. Finally, she turned her chair around and looked at both men.

"There are things in this case that very much concern me. There is a lot I really don't know." Then, with a very serious, almost accusatory expression, she peered deeply into the eyes of both men. One of the attorneys began to talk and she raised her hand, immediately silencing his question. *"I said there are things I don't know, but two things will*

happen today. Either I will find out what is truly going on in this case, or somebody will be going to jail." She hesitated and her beautiful blue eyes blazed at the two men sitting opposite her. *"Do you both understand me?"* Both men sat transfixed silently processing the threat that the judge just put on the table. When neither answered, she said, *"I asked if you both understood what I just said?"* In low voices both men said: *"Yes, Your Honor."*

"Good. Let me first summarize what I do know." She stood and began pacing behind her desk. *"We have two beautiful children who are doing fine in their current home."* Sean's attorney began to speak, and the judge cut him off. *"Be quiet. I am speaking; I'll tell you when to speak."*

"Yes, Your Honor, I'm sorry."

"These two children have been having supervised visitations with their father, and the reports indicate, that although the visits go well, the children are afraid of this man." She then hesitated, again staring at the attorney's eyes, looking and waiting for even the slightest reaction to what she had said. *"The children are living with a family friend who is a psychologist, who has some strange power that no one can seem to identify. She carries around a bag with coffee grounds. I am no psychiatrist, but it does seem to be a strange habit. Also in the home is a woman who has murdered a priest."* Attorney Holmes raised his hand. Again, the judge raised hers, immediately silencing him. Looking directly at him, she said, *"Yes, I know of the circumstances, but she is a strange woman who lived under a bridge and raised rats."* Sean's attorney had a self-righteous look on his face and the judge pointed at him saying, *"I have yet to get to your side. Don't be so smug."* The judge looked at Holmes and said, *"For god's sake. A strange psychologist and a Rat Lady."* Again, she hesitated and said, *"Yet the children are thriving."* She looked at Sean's attorney and said, *"No objection to that characterization." "Judge, I'm afraid to talk."*

"Good, keep quiet. Now, let us talk about your client. When I look at him I feel like I have to take a shower." Again, she raised her hand and insisted he not talk. She kept looking at him. *"Your client attacked the children's guardian in a park. I have witness testimony." "Your client has no history. That, in and of itself, is a red flag. However, what frightens me more is that I believe he is also stalking me."*

"What, judge?"

"You heard me."

Clearly agitated, Rinsig now sat down again behind her desk. She pressed a button and one of her court attorneys entered the room with a DVD. *"Attorneys, we are all going to watch the video that the children's mother made before she passed away."*

Sean's attorney stood in protest. *"Your Honor, this is hearsay evidence and was already barred from this court by your predecessor."*

Rinsig stared at him and said, *"Sit down attorney. It is also a deathbed proclamation, and as you know, a deathbed declaration is considered credible and trustworthy evidence based upon the general belief that most people who know that they are about to die do not lie. As a result, it is an exception to the hearsay rule, which prohibits the use of a statement made by someone other than the person who repeats it while testifying during a trial because of its inherent untrustworthiness. If the person who made the deathbed declaration had the slightest hope of recovery, no matter how unreasonable, the statement is not admissible into evidence. However, a person who makes a deathbed declaration must be competent at the time he or she makes a statement. Otherwise, it is inadmissible."*

Rinsig pointed to a television monitor that had been set up in her office. *"Before I start this, can I assume that both of you have seen this tape?"* Both attorneys nodded in the affirmative. *"So I am the only one who hasn't witnessed this tape?"*

"Yes, your honor."

"Good, I will be interested into your insights."

The judge dismissed her court attorney before pressing the play button. Immediately, a very ill, emaciated woman was seen lying in a bed. It caught Rinsig by surprise and she gasped. The woman appeared to be a remnant of the concentration camps from Nazi Germany. With intestinal fortitude, the woman began to speak.

"My name is Beth Whitford. As you can see, I am very close to death. The doctors have told my friends and myself that I probably will not last for another day. I have pancreatic cancer and the pain is excruciating, so if I begin moaning, please ignore it as much as possible. It will pass......... I hope." The woman on the tape coughed weakly, got a tissue, and spit up. Her friend brought her a small cup of water and she

continued. "*I assure all who are watching this tape that I am in my right mind while I am making this. I know my name, my birthday, and the month I am going to die. I have two children, or should I say, two beautiful children named Ellie and Theodore. We are currently living with our close friend, Franclynne Longaire, a psychologist, who is helping me through my final hours on this earth. I cannot measure how important Franclynne and her roommate, La, have been to my little family. They have nurtured the children and been their guardians.*"

Again, Beth stopped and began coughing heavily. Saying even a few words was taking enormous amounts of the little energy that she had left. "*Believe me when I tell you that I am not making this tape for you to feel sorry for me. I am making this tape as a last resort, a dying declaration for you to help me save my two children. I will not be around to protect them, and I need your help to make sure they are in an environment that will help them grow into the wonderful people they should be. My children have suffered enough at the hands of their father. They have been traumatized by Sean's behavior, both towards them and towards me. While I still can, let me tell you about my ex-husband. We had, what I would consider, a pretty normal married life. He was a generous and kind man. Then the stroke completely changed his personality. I think it brought back memories of things he had hidden away. He became vicious and degrading. When he wanted sex, he would lock the children in their room, and drag me by the hair into the bedroom. Imagine listening to your children crying, banging on the door, and screaming while your own husband was raping you. In addition, the sex itself was not natural. Sean would tie me up and put tape over my mouth. He would force me to consume alcohol until I was barely conscious. Then he would begin the whipping and the physical cruelty. Many nights, I bled when I cried myself to sleep. My children would see my black and blue and bleeding body and face.*

Tears began rolling down her eyes, as this 80-pound woman attempted to lift herself to her elbows. She got almost half way and then fell back. "*But the most frightening part of this horrific tale is what Sean threatened. He told me that one day he would teach Ellie how to be a 'submissive whore', as every woman should. And he would teach Theodore how to handle a woman properly.*"

Again, the coughing began, but this time she leaned over the bed and vomited. When the spasm stopped, she continued. *"At the end of our routine, Sean would life my head up in his hand and put his other hand around my neck. He would put his face within inches of mine and he would say, "Tell the truth, Beth, you really loved this. I was crying, bruised, and bleeding, and he would make me say that I loved it. He would then jerk my head and say, I will teach Theodore to act like the real man I am, and we will practice on his sister. That is the only way she will learn."*

Judge Rinsig shook at this last comment. The tape ended with this threatening and ominous comment. The judge looked at Sean's attorney. *"This dying woman is speaking about your client, attorney. What do you have to say?"*

"Your honor, I am his attorney, not his conscience. I can no way control his actions as if I could control the rising and the setting of the sun."

"Tell me attorney, what do you know about Mr. Whitford's background. Is this a credible threat, or just the words of a frightened, dying woman?"

"Your honor, I have client confidentiality."

"Excuse, me attorney, but confidentiality doesn't hold when a viable threat is made. So tell me, in your opinion, is the threat viable?"

Sean's attorney thought for a second and swallowed hard. *"Let me say this, your honor, I wouldn't put it past him."*

It did not take much for O'Brian and his team to secure a search warrant to Sean Whitford's apartment. When they arrived, he was not there. However, it did not take a trained eye to find grizzly evidence in the living room. There were bloodstains on the floor, as if somebody had stepped in blood and left tracks. Samples were taken, and O'Brian was pretty certain that they would match those of Jillian.

However, the police also found other things of concern and interest. In a back room, inside a closet, there was a mural of pictures. There were many pictures of his children playing in different venues. There were pictures of Franclynne, and there were pictures of Judge Rinsig. O'Brian found himself staring at the pictures. Everything now was coalescing in his mind. He immediately issued an all-points bulletin to arrest Sean

Whitford. The bulletin was direct, advising that he was a dangerous man and all caution needed to be taken. He could be armed.

Arriving back at his office, O'Brian received some further disturbing information. The company in which Whitford was working had found clear evidence that he had stolen over half a million dollars. O'Brian knew that Whitford's world was unraveling and he had plenty of cash. This, in and of itself, made him much more dangerous. It would also make him more difficult to find. He pondered the next steps.

Chapter XXXVII

She was dozing when the phone rang. Franclynne had not slept well over the past month as she found her fears were beginning to overwhelm her. She was now fighting a two-front war, her past traumatic memories, and the current unfolding trauma. She spent many nights in the fetal position on the bathroom floor. As Franclynne became more unglued, La became more vigilant. She kept telling Franclynne about her fears for the children and the worry she had about Sean. She even wanted Franclynne to go to the children's school and ask if she could sit in on the classes, to make sure the children would remain safe. Of course, that idea was rejected, which led to La having a brief temper outburst.

The ringing phone startled Franclynne. For a moment she didn't know if it really was happening or was a part of a dream. She pushed herself off the couch and went to answer the landline.

"Franclynne?" the voice asked.

"Yes, Hello, Captain."

"Franclynne, I have some disturbing news."

"I'm ready, Captain."

"We searched Sean's apartment and found evidence that he probably had murdered Jillian."

"Why does that not surprise me?"

"Wait, there's more."

"I'm listening."

"In his apartment were many pictures of the children playing in different places. But there were also pictures of you and judge Rinsig hanging on the wall."

"Oh my god!" Franclynne dropped the phone and ran to get La.

Franclynne ran into the living room and found La watching television. La noticed the panic on her friend's face. It startled her and she jumped up out of her chair. Franclynne was shaking as she stood by her. *"The children are in trouble."* La's face turned from surprise to anger. It was beet red and her eyes were almost exploding out of her head. The two-women rushed to the car and drove to the school. Franclynne went to the front door and had to be buzzed in. With La right behind her, the two rushed into the principal's office. The secretary noticed the alarm on both women's faces. Franclynne had one hand on La's arm as she was ready to rush into the hallway and get the children herself. The secretary called the principal who came out with a slight smile. However, upon seeing the two women, her demeanor immediately changed.

"What's wrong?"

"I need Ellie and Theodore right away; they are in danger!"

"What do you mean?"

"They are in danger; their father is out to get them. Please get them."

La broke in; *"Now, we need them now!"*

The principal's face dropped."

"What's wrong?" Franclynne's eyes were now almost bulging out of their sockets. La almost jumped over the counter toward the principal. *"What's wrong, where are the children?"*

The principal could not look at the woman, and then she said, *"The children are gone. Their father showed up with a letter from the court that said he could take them to lunch."*

Franclynne shouted, *"There was no such letter ordered!"*

"Oh my god!" The principal said as she raised her hands over her mouth.

"Why didn't you call me?" Franclynne demanded.

"The letter appeared authentic to me. I'm so sorry"

La was ready to kill this woman. However, Franclynne pushed her toward the door. Then she stopped and looked back at the principal. *"Do you have the letter?"*

"Yes, I'll get it."

"Please make a copy for me." When the principal produced the document, Franclynne studied it. It looked official enough, printed on the court's paper. But, and now it was her turn to cover her mouth.

"What do you see?"

"The letter looks official enough, but the judge's name is spelled incorrectly."

Again, the principal looked forlorn. *"I'm so sorry for the mistake."*

The two women ran back to the car. Franclynne was crying, almost uncontrollably. She looked at La, and with tear-soaked eyes, said, *"What should we do? I don't even know where to start."* The women hugged, and then Franclynne said, *"We have to tell Captain O'Brian."* La looked at her and said, *"I've had enough of this"*, and she began to open the car door. *"What? Where are you going?"*

"I'm going to find the children!" And with that, La exited the car began running toward the road. Franclynne drove after her. When she caught up to her, she yelled out the window, *"La, get back into the car."* La stopped, and in her loudest voice yelled, *"This is my fault; I was supposed to protect them."* She stood there for a moment then said, *"Leave me alone, Franclynne. I will find them."* Then she pointed at Franclynne. *"If he hurts those children, I will kill him."* And with that, she turned her back and began walking away. Franclynne knew she couldn't hear but she said, *"Be careful, La."*

Judge Rinsig was in the courtroom getting ready to hear a custody case when a deranged looking woman burst into the courtroom. As she attempted to run to the bench where the judge sat, an officer stopped her. Franclynne was still crying as she held up a paper toward the judge, still in the arms of the officer. *"I know this woman. It is Dr. Longaire. You can let her go."*

Completely out of breath, Franclynne stumbled to the bench and put the paper in front of Rinsig. Rinsig quickly read the document and then said, *"Oh my god!"* She immediately called the court officer to clear the courtroom and lock the door. She rose off of the bench and came down and put her arms around Franclynne. *"I'm so sorry. We will find them."* The judge called her attorney clerk over and demanded, *"Get Captain O'Brian in here."*

Part III

Chapter XXXVIII

It had been two weeks. Franclynne had not heard from either La or the children. She was past despondent. At night, she was almost exclusively in the bathroom on the floor, and she rarely if ever slept past 2 a.m. Her mind was being overwhelmed by guilt and past traumatic images. At one point, during an extremely difficult period, she even considered cutting herself to attempt to remove tension.

Franclynne's had virtually shut down her psychology practice. She had not seen a patient in over a week. She could not concentrate, nor focus on anything other than images of the children being kidnapped. She also knew that Beth was watching from up above, and she felt miserably high levels of guilt. Why hadn't Captain O'Brian located this man yet? Moreover, where was La? Franclynne had visions of La lying somewhere in a ditch. Her mind raced through the images, the guilt, and the recollection of the past traumas. Franclynne was feeling very sorry for herself. She watched other people with 'normal' lives and couldn't understand why she was cursed. She even wondered, in her delusional state, whether something had happened in a previous lifetime that she was now atoning for.

It was almost noon. She knew this by the amount of light coming into her bathroom window. She dragged herself off the floor and went into the living room. Noon had become an important time for Franclynne because it was when Captain O'Brian would call her with a daily update. That, too, was becoming depressing. He would always apologize saying, *"I'm sorry, Franclynne, nothing yet."* That was the extent of the message *"Nothing yet."* She was sick of those words.

Franclynne was never overweight, but in the past two weeks she had lost at least ten pounds. Having no appetite likely had something to do with that. Her depression had made it such that even getting to the phone was a struggle.

There was the ring. It startled her; O'Brian was early. It was only ten minutes to twelve and the phone was ringing. She ran to the phone, hoping that this change in routine actually had a positive reason. She picked it up: *"Hello."*

There was a hesitation on the other end. *"Franclynne?" "Oh my god, Ellie, where are you?" "Please come and get us Franclynne. My daddy is hurting me." "Tell me where you are, my dear and I will come."* Then, without notice, the phone went dead. *"Ellie, Ellie!"* The phone dropped to the floor. Franclynne stood there for a moment as if in a trance, then she herself went to the floor, sobbing. Then, again, almost immediately, her cell phone range. She fumbled but answered it *"Ellie?" "What, this is Captain O'Brian. Your phone was busy. Did you speak to speak to Ellie." "Yes, Captain. She just called me, that's why the phone was off the hook." "I'll be right there."*

"Oh my god", was the stunned reaction of Captain O'Brian when he walked into Franclynne's apartment. This elegant, statuesque woman looked terrible. He was frightened by the way she looked. *"Have you been awake for two weeks?"* She turned her head away as he walked into her living room. Her comment was *"Just about."*

"Tell me, Franclynne, what happened?"

"She called, just before you did."

"What did she say?"

"She begged me to come get her because her father was hurting her."

"Yes, and then what?"

"Then the phone went dead." She hesitated and looked up at the Captain. *"What's going on here?"*

"Franclynne, would you mind if I put a tap on your phone in case she calls again?"

"Of course not." O'Brian turned to leave, but Franclynne stopped him with her arm. *"You know La is missing as well. Has there been any word about her?"*

"I'm sorry, Franclynne. Nothing yet. I will arrange for the tap. You won't even notice it." And with that, she was alone again.

After Captain O'Brian left, Franclynne fell into a deep, protracted sleep. When she awoke, somebody was banging on her front door. She yelled, *"I'm coming."* To her surprise, she opened the door and there stood Angelique. She was carrying a bag full of food.

"I called your office a number of times and your secretary told me what has been happening. I thought you could use a friend and some food." The women hugged, and Franclynne broke down again, sobbing uncontrollably.

It was a long night, Franclynne drifting in and out of sleep. Angelique was hugging her as they both sat on the couch. When the morning came, Franclynne awoke with a jolt. She stood and immediately fainted. Angelique called 911 and the ambulance took her to the hospital. Luckily, the doctors felt the only problem was that she was dehydrated. They immediately started an intravenous drip, and Franclynne recovered quickly, but only from the dehydration, the emotional scares kept bleeding.

O'Brian came to the hospital not long after Franclynne arrived in her room. He was amazed when he saw her. Even in a hospital bed, in this sleep-deprived condition, not made up, she was still a strikingly, beautiful woman. He stared at her for a few seconds. He thought she was sleeping. As he moved closer, Franclynne opened her eyes. She did not smile, but looked terrified. *"Captain, I'm terrified."* O'Brian sat down in a chair next to the bed. *"I'm not afraid for me, but Beth left the children's care to me. She trusted me. I pledged to protect those children."* She looked down and said, *"I failed."* Franclynne began sobbing. O'Brian reached out and touched her hand.

"I will find the children, but I want them found alive and not emotionally damaged."

Franclynne bent her head, pulled her hand away, and continued to sob. *"This is my entire fault, Captain. All my fault."*

"That's not true, Franclynne. It's Sean Whitford's fault."

"It's my fault. They were my responsibility and now they are gone. We might never find them alive." Franclynne started to became angry and agitated. *"Be straight with me, Captain. The children are gone forever."*

"Not true Franclynne, not true. Trust me."

"You don't understand, Captain, I've only been able to trust one person in my life, and that person is dead."

"Don't you trust La?"

"Yes, I trust her as well." The Captain said, *"Listen, Franclynne, the children will need you when we get them back. They will have gone through a trauma and they will need you to help heal them."*

"Captain, I was supposed to protect the children, not heal them from a trauma."

"Listen to me, Franclynne. I have to leave. However, remember this. We will find the children. You need to get better and get out of this place."

O'Brian rose and started for the door. Franclynne called to him and said, *"Captain, find La alive as well."* O'Brian turned his head and left.

"We will, Franclynne. We will."

Chapter XXXIX

She had been in the park for two days, sleeping in a large drainage ditch for two nights. Nothing had happened. She saw Diego with his children, and she even came out from behind a tree to say hello. He was shocked to see her without the children. He almost ran over to her in distress. La explained what had happened since the two had last spoken. Then Diego said something shocking.

"I saw the children yesterday."

"What?" La grabbed him. *"Where Diego, where?"*

"Do you know that small restaurant on 5th street? It's by the used bookstore and the gas station?" La thought for a moment.

"I think I know it."

Diego called his children over. *"I'll drive you there. But don't you think we should call the police?"*

"No," said La, *"No!"*

They drove to the restaurant. La jumped out of the car. Diego followed her. They both went to the restaurant, and went in to speak to the owner. In Spanish, Diego described Sean Whitford and the children. The owner nodded his head in affirmation when Diego was describing the two. The owner began speaking, describing that the man and the children usually came in every day for breakfast." When La heard this, she left the restaurant. Diego found out that the restaurant opened at 4:30 and Sean and the children usually arrived at 6 a.m.

The next morning was very frustrating. La arrived at 4:30 and Diego arrived at 5, but Whitford and the children didn't show. This had become her only lead. La and Diego went to other restaurants hoping that somebody else recognized their description. By noon, they were both becoming despondent over their lack of success. They stopped into a dollar store, as Diego needed to buy some essentials before he returned home, and by chance, asked the young woman about Whitford and the children. She remembered that they had just been in the store, not more than an hour before. She said they were frequent customers. Now, buoyed by this revelation, La's mood immediately changed. After La left the store, Diego went to the sales clerk and told her that if they entered the store again, she should call the police and ask for Captain O'Brian. He had done the same at the restaurant. Diego was still convinced that the police needed to be more involved with the information that they had.

Angelique was still worried. She had taken Franclynne home from the hospital, and then decided to get her moving again and take her to the beach. After all, she had heard that Franclynne specifically moved here to get close to the water and the beach. The ride there was not too pleasant. Franclynne was curled up in the passenger seat, whimpering every occasionally, *"My fault."* But her mood seemed to change as they drew closer to the water. They were sitting on the beach, when her cell phone rang. *"Franclynne, this is your friend, Sean."* Franclynne's was stunned to hear his voice. Her heart began to bang in her chest *"You and I have unfinished business."*

"Where are the children? If you have hurt them, so help me."

"Please Franclynne, cut the dramatics. I am willing to offer a trade."

"A trade?"

"Yes I think it's fair. I will give the children back to that degenerate woman, La, in exchange for you."

"You are insane?"

"You heard me, I want you. I have dreamt about how to enjoy you since the first time I laid my eyes on you." Again, silence from Franclynne. *"You see, when we met in the store, I could sense how much you wanted me, but were afraid to tell the truth."*

"Where are the children, Sean? Are they okay?"

"They're fine, Franclynne, just fine. But they won't stay fine, unless we can conclude our business together. Do you understand?" Come to Chamber street, on the corner of Chamber and First. You will see a restaurant. Stay in your car when you arrive. I will find you. I know, I know you're anticipating being with me. I don't blame you. We'll have so much fun together. It will be memorable, I promise. Oh, by the way, no police. If they arrive, I will hurt the children.*

Now the anxiety completely and utterly overwhelmed her. She began shaking and crying out loud, *"Why is this happening to me?"* Angelique did her best to try to calm her, but her efforts were met with fear. *"Let's go Angelique. Drive to Chamber Street like he asked."*

"*Are you crazy, Franclynne? Let's call the cops. You can't confront this man by yourself. He will hurt you, and probably the children, as well.*"

A strange look came over the psychologist's face. "*Drive, Angelique, drive. This is all my fault. If I have to exchange myself for the children, I will gladly do it. Please drive!*" Angelique stared at her. She did not know what to do. What terrified her was the look on Franclynne's face. It was crazed and distorted. She did not look like herself.

"*I don't think we should go, Franclynne.*"

"*Angelique, we have to go, the children are in danger.*" "*Well, at least allow me to call the police so they can assist us.*"

"*No, you heard, he will hurt the children. I can't have that.*" Angelique began to drive. She was hoping that she could think of something before they got to Chamber Street.

Then suddenly, Franclynne reached down into her purse and pulled out a handgun. Angelique saw it and swerved the car, almost hitting a pole. She pulled the car over to the side of the road.

"*Where did you get that?*" Franclynne had this strange other-worldly look on her face. She just kept staring into space. "*Franclynne, where did you get the gun?*"

Franclynne turned her head and seemed to be looking through Angelique. "*Why did you stop the car?*" Her voice was monotone, and her affect was flat.

"*I am not driving this car until you answer my question.*" Franclynne held the weapon up and pointed it at Angelique. A chill ran down Angelique's back, and her eye began twitching. She did not know how to respond, and she was terrified.

Franclynne said, "*Drive the car.*"

And without thought, without hesitation, Angelique said, "*No.*" It was not an assertive no, but she repeated it in a quivering voice. "*Why do you have a gun, Franclynne?*"

Again, there was no answer, as Franclynne was just holding the gun pointed at her and staring past her. "*Drive,*" she repeated.

"*No*" retorted Angelique, "*I won't move until you put the gun down and talk to me.*"

"*I will shoot you,*" Franclynne said in the monotone voice.

Again, surprising herself, Angelique said, *"Go ahead, shoot me."* Franclynne's hand began to shake, but then the zombie mood broke, she began crying, lowering her hand and putting the gun down. Angelique reached for the gun, but Franclynne tightened her grip. *"Give me the gun."* Franclynne did not respond and did not let go of the weapon. *"I said, give me the gun, Franclynne!"* After a couple of seconds of silence, Franclynne moved her hand, giving the weapon to Angelique. Still shaking, but now no longer fearful, Angelique said, *"So what was this gun thing about?"*

Franclynne covered her face. *"I want to kill him."*

"I don't blame you, but the children need you. You can't end up in jail." Angelique put the gun to her left side, in the car door pocket. *"Are you all right?"* Franclynne nodded in agreement, and Angelique started the car.

The two drove in relative silence, although Franclynne wanted Angelique to run the red lights and the stop signs. At one point, Angelique said, *"I thought you didn't want the police involved? If we drive through the red lights, eventually we will be pulled over."*

"We must there faster Angelique, the children are in danger."

"Look Lynn, what do you intend to do when you get there?" Franclynne shrugged her shoulders. *"That's the point, Lynn; we need to have a plan!"*

Franclynne looked at Angelique. *"I will do whatever he asks me to do"*

Angelique pulled the car over and turned aggressively toward Franclynne. *"When I came to see you, I was doing whatever he told me to do, and you explained how I can't act that way."*

In a monotone voice, Franclynne said, *"This is different."*

"It is not different, Lynn, it is not. He is going to hurt both you and the children. Look what happened to me! Please, Franclynne, let's call the police!"

Coming out of her trance, Franclynne said, *"Look, Angelique, I have known trauma for many years. It haunts me, especially at night. I do not want the children to live that way. I am already damaged goods. I hope they are not."*

"Put down the cross, Lynn. The goal here is for nobody to experience any trauma, not substitute, or sacrifice you for them!"

"Give me back the gun, Angelique."

"I will not."

"Look, I just want it so I can protect myself and the children. I promise I won't try to shoot unless utterly necessary."

Angelique did not know if she could trust Lynn in the state she was in, but her reasoning made sense. *"Lynn, when we get there, I will decide on the gun, okay."*

"Okay."

It was not long before the women arrived at Chamber Street. It was not in the greatest of neighborhoods, but it also was not a slum. The street seemed deserted, nobody was out walking, and there were only a few parked cars. Angelique pulled the car over to the street and parked by a meter.

"Now what?" she asked.

"Don't know," said Franclynne. *"I guess we just wait."* Her legs were shaking as she sat in the car, and Angelique watched her closely. This was an unpredictable situation and Angelique knew that it could evolve in many ways, many of them bad. *"I can't do this; I can't just sit here. I know the children aren't far away. I have to go search."*

"No, Lynn. Wait until you get a call. You do not even know where to start!

On Chamber Street were a number of small stores with apartments over them. Some had many apartments over them, so choosing where to go would be a wild guess. Franclynne was ready to explode with anticipation and fear. She was already replaying many of her past traumas in her mind, almost in anticipation of what was going to happen with Sean. She already had accepted the fact that she would sacrifice herself for their safety. She owed Beth that much, considering her lies to her.

Then, as if struck by lightning, Franclynne turned to Angelique and said, *"I think I have a plan!"*

"You do? What is it?"

"Let's wait for call." Almost on key, Franclynne's cell phone began to buzz. A fearful look emerged on her face and she fumbled with the cell, almost dropping it to the floor.

"Hello, Franclynne? This is O'Brian. Where are you?"

"No place special, Captain, just taking a drive for something to do."

Realizing what was happening, Angelique tried to grab the phone, but Franclynne held tight. She began yelling. *"It's not true, Captain. We were contacted by Sean and Franclynne is going to"*

At that point, Franclynne turned off the phone and O'Brian didn't hear any more of the message. *"That was stupid Angelique. He said no police. I don't want those children harmed."*

"They might already be harmed, Lynn, can't you see that?"

"But we don't know, so let's just play by the rules." Angelique quieted and the wait continued.

Almost immediately the phone rang again. *"You whore, I told you not to talk to anybody, who were you just on the phone with?"*

"Nobody, Sean, a friend." "She called while we are sitting here waiting for you. Have you become a coward?"

"What?"

"A weakling, Sean, you hurt unsuspecting children, what would you call that?"

"You're trying my patience, bitch. Just do what you're told. But that coward comment will cost you."

"I want to speak to the children, Sean. I will not leave this car until I speak to the children."

"We do things my way, bitch."

"No Sean. If you want me, I want to speak to the children. I want to make sure you haven't hurt them already."

"I haven't hurt them."

"I don't believe you, Sean. Put one of them on the phone or I drive away."

A low small voice came on the line. It was Theodore. He was obviously crying. *"Theodore is that you?"*

"Yes, Lynn, please come and get us!"

"Is Ellie okay?"

"She's tied up. Her face is red but her eyes are open."

"Okay, bitch you heard. Now it's time for the exchange."

"What did you do to Ellie, you disturbed fuck."

"She's okay, just a little dopey. Look across the street, Franclynne. Do you see the drug store? Next to it is a red door that leads upstairs to the apartments. You will take your phone, go to the door, and buzz apartment #3."

"I want to talk with Ellie!" But the phone was already dead.

Franclynne stared at Angelique. *"I have a plan!"*

"What is it?"

"Wait." Franclynne got out of the car and walked around to Angelique's side. She opened the door of the car, and before Angelique could respond, she reached down the side of the car door and took the gun. She looked down at Angelique and said, "The *plan is, I'm going to shoot him in the head!"* Then her expression changed. She put her hand on Angelique's shoulder and said, *"Thank you, Angelique, for everything you've done for us."*

Angelique put her hand on Franclynne's and said, *"Remember Lynn, you saved my life. You never know what's going to happen in the next few hours." Everything will be fine, Lynn, I can feel it."*

"I hope you're right!"

And with that, Franclynne, straightened herself, took a deep breath, and started walking to the red door. When she arrived, she rang bell #3 and the return buzz let her in. The hall was dingy and the steps were thin. Slowly Franclynne began to climb them toward apartment #3. Her phone rang. It startled her and she almost lost her balance.

"I am not in apartment #3, go to apartment #5."

"Are the children with you?"

"Don't worry about them, bitch, just do as you're told." The phone went dead. Franclynne continued to climb. Her mind was almost too scared to think. The only reality she had was that she continued to reach behind her to where she had put the gun in the waistband of her pants.

Finally, after a climb that seemed mountainous, she was standing in front of door #5. A voice came from within. *"It's open, come in."* Franclynne straightened herself, took another breath, and touched the gun to make sure it was still there. The door opened to a hallway, at the end of which was a large living room. With her legs still unsteady, Franclynne continued to walk to the living room. When she reached the opening of the room, she gasped.

Chapter XL

Angelique watched as her friend walked to the red door. She felt mesmerized watching Franclynne. At one point, she realized she was holding her breath. The spell broke when Franclynne disappeared into the building. Angelique reached for her cell phone and called the police.

"I need to talk with Captain O'Brian. It is an emergency."

"I'm sorry, young lady. Captain O'Brian stepped out of the office for a minute. I can help you. What is the problem?"

"Tell Captain O'Brian that Franclynne is in serious danger."

"Who? What? Who is this?"

"Officer, tell him that Franclynne is in trouble. I will hold." It took only a minute or so, but another voice came on the phone.

"Hello, who is this? This is Captain O'Brian."

"Captain, my name is Angelique. I am a friend Franclynne Longaire Prelude."

"I know who you are Angelique, I was in the hospital when Franclynne asked for you to be transferred. Tell me what's going on Angelique."

"Captain, I am sitting in a car on Chamber Street and Franclynne just went into an apartment. She got a call from Sean Whitford that he would exchange the children for her."

"What? Why didn't she call me?"

"She was told not to, Captain. She is scared, and she has a gun."

"A gun. Oh my god! I will be there as soon as I can."

"Quietly though, Captain. Whitford said he would hurt the children if he saw or heard cops."

"I understand."

She was watching from behind a big garbage collector. She was shocked to see Franclynne. Her eyes widened when she saw her get out of the car and begin walking to the red door. She began inching her way out of her hiding place, and as she saw Franclynne, she decided she was going to follow. Franclynne looked in a daze, facing forward, her head not moving. She looked like a zombie, just slowly walking to the door.

Her steps were all measured, and looked like she was being pulled slowly into something.

La began to get closer, but she did not believe Franclynne noticed her. She didn't seem to notice anything. Franclynne entered the door and La followed not far behind. She pressed all the numbers until one let her in. La was quiet, trying not to interfere with whatever Franclynne was doing. She watched her walking up the stairs, and, at a safe distance began to follow her upward. When Franclynne reached door #5, La was on the step watching. Franclynne entered the apartment and La was quick to follow. But when Franclynne began walking to the living room, La walked into one of the bedrooms on the right. In it, she found two small mattresses on the floor and some very old toys. She glanced back into the hallway and went to the next bedroom, closer to the living room.

She saw Franclynne standing at the entryway to the living room with her hand over her mouth.

When Franclynne entered the living room area, the first thing she noticed was both children tied to two chairs. Theodore was sobbing and Ellie looked only half-conscious. She also noticed Sean standing with a gun pointing at Theodore's head. She took a step towards the children, but Sean said, *"Stop, bitch, do not go over there."*

Franclynne turned to Sean and said, *"The children, Sean, what have you done? They are just innocent children."*

Sean looked wild, almost psychotic. *"They wouldn't listen, they deserved punishment."*

Franclynne took a step towards Sean, and said, *"I am going over to Ellie to see if she is alright."* And with that, she aggressively began walking toward Ellie. She bent down to Ellie and held her head in her hands. *"Oh, my sweet. Don't worry, I'm here."* Ellie's face was swollen and she could barely open her eyes. *"Don't worry my sweet."* Now, with an angry expression, she said to Sean, *"Get me water!"*

"What is wrong with you, woman? Don't you fuckin' listen? I am in charge here, not you."

Franclynne stood up, and began to walk out of the living room toward the kitchen. *"Stop, bitch!"* Franclynne completely ignored him and just kept walking. What she did not realize was that when she turned her back on Sean, he noticed the gun in her waistband. He raised his gun, and took a shot through the ceiling. The sound stunned Franclynne and she immediately stopped. Now he was pointing the gun directly at her. She turned her head and he said, "*Slowly, bitch, take the gun out of your waistband and drop it on the floor.*" Franclynne was shaking but she did what she was told. "*Now kick it to me.*" She complied. Keeping the gun trained on Franclynne, Sean began walking toward her. "*Now, you will pay.*" He raised his hand to punch her in the face. Franclynne stood steady knowing the blow was coming. Sean was terrifying with his eyes almost leaving their sockets and spittle coming from his mouth. But as he raised his hand a blur came across the scene and tackled him. The gun shot into the air. La continued to push with her head in his stomach, and as he hit the desk, the gun dropped to the floor.

La was now on top of Sean as the two began to wrestle. Both were yelling. La was screeching and Sean was howling. Franclynne immediately ran to the children and began untying Theodore. When she freed him, she said, "*Run Theodore, run. Go downstairs and go into one of the stores.*"

Franclynne turned to Ellie, who was only semi-conscious. Theodore got off his chair, but rather than run out of the apartment, he ran to where La and Sean were fighting. He grabbed Sean's leg and began biting him as hard as he could. Sean now let out a monstrous shriek and tried swatting the boy off his leg, as he continued to fight La. La was trying to scratch his eyes out. Franclynne had Ellie almost untied.

However, the fight with Sean was not going well. Sean had hit Theodore in the cheek, knocking him across the room. He pushed La off him and began to stand. In her peripheral vision, Franclynne noticed this change and saw where her gun was lying on the floor. But Sean had also found his gun. Franclynne stood pointing her gun at Sean, as he stood pointing his gun at her. He was now standing at the opening of the living room. Franclynne was sweating and breathing hard. The two were only a few feet from each other. Then, surprisingly, Sean began to laugh. "*I like a good fight. This was more fun than I thought.*" Franclynne said nothing. La had gone over to Ellie and was now cradling her. Theodore was crawling over to them. Sean began backing down the hallway toward the front door. Franclynne didn't follow but didn't lower the weapon.

Then, in a quick motion, Sean turned and began to run. A shot rang out, hitting one of the doors in the hallway. Franclynne began to run after him. She was screaming and looked wild. Sean left the apartment and began to run down the stairs. Franclynne followed and got to the railing and began firing her gun after him as he bolted down the stairs. Her aim was terrible and none of the bullets even came close. Finally, Franclynne's gun ran out of bullets, but there she stood, continuing to press the trigger and just hearing the clicks that it made. Sean was gone, down the stairs.

Franclynne was emotionally drained, her hair looking like she had just taken a shower. But then she heard somebody running up the stairs. When the figure got to the fourth floor, Franclynne threw the gun at it. The she heard, "Franclynne, *it's me, Angelique."* Angelique got to the fifth floor and ran to Franclynne throwing her arms around her. *"You're okay, thank god!"*

Franclynne turned and pointed into the apartment. *"The children!"* Angelique let go of her and ran into the apartment. Franclynne turned to follow, but she could not sustain the energy. She dropped to her knees and fainted.

Epilogue

It was not long before O'Brian and his men arrived on the scene. They called for ambulances. Ellie was the first to be put on a gurney, as she seemed to be the most injured. However, the EMT workers did not expect that La would not leave her side. They tried everything, including telling her she needed her own help. La would have none of it. She just grunted in response to their words and they finally allowed her to go with Ellie.

Franclynne was next to get to an ambulance. Angelique picked up Theodore and followed the others down the stairs.

The next day, Franclynne opened her eyes to see O'Brian standing next to the bed. He smiled and put his hand on hers. *"From what I can figure, that was the stupidest thing you could have done."*

Franclynne smiled and said, *"How are the children?"*

"They will both be fine. Ellie was beaten up pretty good, but she'll be all right. You might be the worst shot I have ever seen!" Again, Franclynne smiled. *"There were bullet holes everywhere, except where you probably wanted them to be. From what I hear, that little Theodore is a hero."*

"Brave young one. I am very proud of both of them."

"Yes it was stupid, Franclynne, but you saved their lives. Their mother would be proud."

O'Brian turned to leave, but stopped, and said, *"I forgot, I brought you a present."*

"A present?" A big smile covered his face *"Hot cross buns."*

Franclynne smiled again, closed her eyes, and went back to sleep.

The day was dark and overcast. The first raindrops had just begun to fall. They wet his face as he lay on the park bench. When he felt the moisture, he sat up. He looked around, he was in some kind of park, but nothing looked familiar. He thought for a moment. He did not remember how he got there, but what was worse, he did not remember who he was. He struggled for a few seconds trying to recall some of his immediate past, but nothing came. Although it was an unusual feeling, to not who you are, there was something familiar about it. He rose from the bench

and began to walk. He would have to start a new life, wherever this place
was.

Author's Note

This type of psychological disorder had previously been labeled a 'psychogenic dissociative fugue state'. The fugue state is a real psychological phenomenon. It is assumed that the person's stress level reaches a point where his/her entire personality shuts down. The person loses his identity and memories. The person then finds him/herself somewhere, not knowing who they are or how they got there. Sometimes it involves long travel. A person who goes into the fugue state travels a long distance and takes up a completely new personality. The state can last for a few minutes, a few hours, a few days, or many years. Some people call it 'bewildered wandering'. Fugue states are rare, only .02 percent of the population have been diagnosed with this phenomenon. I should also note that most fugue states (to my knowledge) do not involve violence, just confusion.

I hope you enjoyed this reading.

Other Books by Dr. Donner
(All Available on Amazon)

Descent Into Madness Series
(Now Three Books)

The Great Persian Saga (Historical Fiction—Four Books in Series)

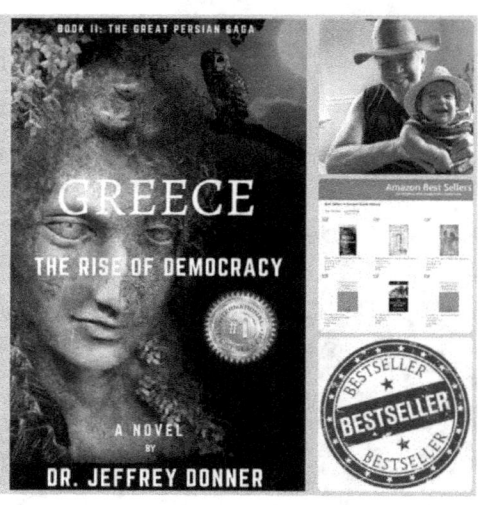

Warrior Women – Fictional Book About Amazon Women of the Southern Ukraine

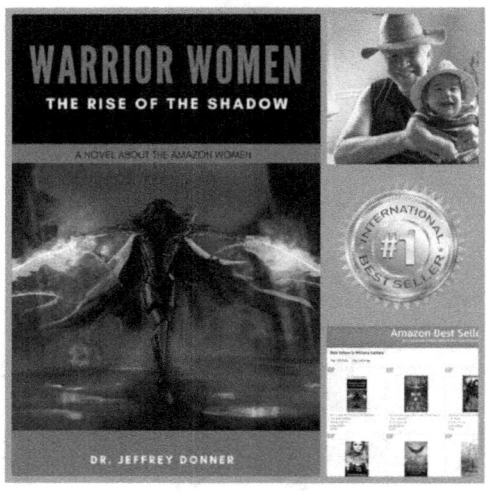

Non-Fictional Book
About Emotional Intelligence.

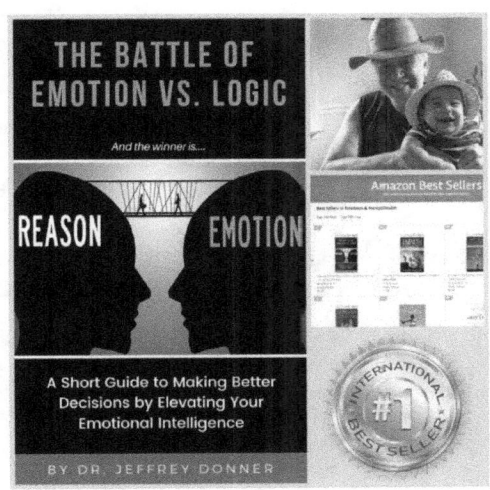

www.ingramcontent.com/pod-product-compliance
Lightning Source LLC
Chambersburg PA
CBHW070449260626
47161CB00004B/1255